THE REUNION
Tracie Podger

The Reunion
By
Tracie Podger

Copyright: TJ Podger 2023
S&P Publishing

CHAPTER 1

Present Day

I logged on to social media to check my accounts, as I tended to do at 3a.m. when I couldn't sleep and noticed a message.

From: Alison Weston

Hi, I'm sorry to reach out like this, and so randomly, but I'm hoping I've found the right person. I think you knew my dad, Sam. I know this is going to be really odd but I'm hoping you were his girlfriend for about ten years, when you were both young?

Anyway, he has an illness, and this is where it gets super weird, he has a list of things to do. One of them is to apologise to you. I don't know what for, but he's managed to tick nearly everything off his list, and he's getting upset about the last two.

Is there any chance you could FaceTime or call him?
He hates social media, but I've shown him your page
(sorry, if that's not okay). You could message me, and I'll
connect you both.

Again, I'm so sorry to reach out so blindly like this.
Many thanks.

I read the message, and then read it again. I clicked on her name, we weren't friends, but I did notice a friend request some months ago. I guess she intended to reach out then. I scanned through her posts. She looked like her dad, for sure! I smiled. More so when I saw a photograph of him.

He still had the buzz cut and he looked pretty fit. There was one of him on holiday, topless. He was toned and I chuckled when I saw one of his tattoos. He'd had my name inked across his chest when we were together. In that image, he'd had a semi-cover-up done. Flowers wove through my letters, partly obscuring them. Of course, I didn't mind that at all. I'd cautioned him against getting my name in the first place.

My first love. The man who took my virginity, who taught me all there was to know about sex, so he said. I'd learned a little more since his days, of course.

I started to reply, and then deleted it. She'd see I had opened her message if she checked, but 3a.m., on just a couple of hours wine-fuelled sleep wasn't the time to reply. I shut down my phone and lay in bed just thinking.

I was fifty years old and smiling away while lying alone.

Recently divorced, although we had been separated for a while, I was used to lying alone. I enjoyed my own company. I had no kids but plenty of foster kids in and out over the years. I'd decided, at fifty, I was going to retire from that.

I picked up my phone again. I reread. I wondered what illness he had, there was nothing on her page and in the photographs. He looked fit and well. Of course, that didn't mean anything, and I wasn't sure on the age of the photographs. I looked for any information on Alison's mother and didn't find it.

I had been fifteen when I met him. I'd lied about my age, and he'd been so cross when he found that out. But I was in love.

I started to remember our time together.

CHAPTER 2
The Past

S am was the local estate bad boy: rode a motorbike, drove a car, a red Ford Capri. He had tattoos and a chipped front tooth from a fight. All the girls were in love with him, and he chose me.

We had been sitting in a field and the boys rode their dirt bikes, tearing up and down the grass hill racing each other. We'd nicknamed the hill the Mad Mile, although we had no idea if it was a mile long. It ran alongside a main road and a railway track. When he'd come over, my friends jutted out their tits and flicked their hair. I just sat, sullen and bored. I would have rather been at the stables. It had been my mum who insisted I should go out more with friends, except, I didn't really have any. I was always that one on the outside looking in.

I had awful brown frizzy hair and no tits. I wasn't quite boy-like but not far off. My 'thing' was, I was thin. Hips jutting out thin. I owned horses at the time and rode every single day, mucked out, and ran around fields catching the bastards when they didn't want to come in. It had kept me fit. I guessed I had a look he liked.

He smiled and, of course, we all melted. He asked me if I wanted to ride on the back of his bike and I received scowls from the girls. I jumped up, having never been on a bike before and nervous as hell. I swung my leg over and gripped his sides. He wore a combat jacket, jeans, and biker boots. He grabbed one of my hands and pulled it around to his stomach. I slid the other voluntarily. I was close, my groin into his backside. It was arousing, more so with the vibration of the engine revving.

He turned his head slightly and called out, asking me if I was ready. I said I was, but I wasn't. I was terrified. I rested my forehead on his back and closed my eyes. We shot off so fast, I was nearly left behind. I gripped tighter and screamed. He laughed. We outran his friends, he had the more powerful bike, and rounded the top of the hill. We slowed down, thankfully, and I was able to look up. My hair blew around my face and I started to loosen my grip. I laughed, looking over his shoulder. He turned his face slightly, and we were cheek to cheek almost.

"All right?" he asked.

I nodded. "I am now you've slowed the fuck down," I replied.

He pulled back the throttle and the front end came up a little. I screamed and laughed at the same time. We circled the top end of the field, first alone, and then with some of his friends.

My stomach was in flutters, my heart was racing, I was in love before he'd even suggested we dated. I laughed to myself.

After about a half hour of just driving around, Sam returned me to my friends. I was bitterly disappointed. They weren't really friends, but they sure all crowded around to ask me about him.

"Where did you go?"

"Did you kiss him?"

"Is he a good kisser?"

"Bet he grabbed a feel, not that you have anything to grab."

These, and more, questions were thrown at me so quick I hadn't the chance to answer any. They then started to gossip among themselves. I decided to leave. I wasn't comfortable in their company, even though we sat together at school often.

I started to walk away, heading towards the dual carriageway and the large pub with a nightclub that doubled up as a youth centre. I'd have to cross but it was at a point where the traffic slowed. Just as I reached the edge, I heard a bike. I turned and he pulled up alongside me.

"You're not crossing on your own," he said, and then looked up the road to ensure it was safe. We crossed the first lane and waited on the grass divide. I then ran across the second lane while he pushed his bike across.

I stood awkwardly, knowing we were then going in different directions. He sat astride his bike, smiling at me.

"Do you want to come to mine for a drink?" he asked.

I nodded, speechless.

Because I didn't have a crash helmet, he climbed off again,

and walked his bike along the road back to his flat. It hadn't occurred to me he might live in his own place and the closer we got, the more nervous I became.

"So your name's Hayley?" he asked, and I was actually pleased he knew.

"Yes."

"Are you Tammy's friend?" he asked.

I nodded. "Sort of. Some days we're friends, some days not," I replied and then laughed.

His laughter with me caused my heart to miss a beat.

"Yeah, she's not a fan of me."

Tammy was dating his best friend, Karl. Because he'd asked about Tammy, I started to panic. Tammy was older than me by a couple of years. She was one year up from me in school.

"How old are you?" he asked.

"Sixteen," I lied. I was a year younger.

"Good." He nodded as we arrived at his flat.

He parked his bike and fished around in his jean pocket for his key. When he'd opened the front door, he held it for me to enter first. He had a ground floor flat in a block of four and in the nicer part of the estate. I stood in his hallway, not sure where to go. It was a small space with a kitchen and living room to one side, a bedroom and bathroom to the other. All the doors were open, and I don't know why, but it pleased me to see his bed made and his kitchen tidy.

He removed his boots and hung up his coat. "Coffee?" he asked.

I nodded, hating coffee but not confident to ask for

anything else. *Surely, all sixteen-year-olds would drink coffee,* I thought.

"Take a seat," he said, gesturing to the living room.

I slipped off my trainers and walked through the door. There was a sofa against one wall, a television on a stand opposite. There was a bookcase loaded with books, some looked well read. On top was a photograph of a woman. An older one and since there was a similarity, I assumed it was his mum.

Other than that, the room was pretty bare.

"Here," he said, handing me the mug and sitting beside me.

He was close and I was wedged into the end. He slid his arm along the back of the sofa and rested it there.

"Have you finished school?" he asked.

"No, I have... Erm, I'll go into sixth form and college, hopefully."

I had one year left to go before sixth form, and had no choice but to stay on since it was highly unlikely I'd pass any exams. I spent most of my time truant. It was only a friend who was super excited to get a Saturday job in a cheap shoe shop in the high street and hoped she'd be able to work there when she left, who gave me the kick up the backside I needed. I had nothing against shoe shops, I just wanted better for myself.

But I hated school and teachers, and most of the pupils. I loved learning, but I detested the lack of respect. I had always been taught respect was earned and not bullied. I wasn't blaming the area, South East London, but most of the teachers didn't seem to care. They were part of radical Labour groups and wanted to pay us to disrupt the local hunt, and protest about stuff we had no idea about, or thought we kids were all growing up to be thugs and the view we'd *enjoy* the most would be one from behind bars. Shouting, caning, and suspension or detention was the norm.

Sam sidled a little closer. I wanted him to kiss me, but I had no real idea how to kiss him back properly. I'd kissed a couple of boys before, but mostly closed lips and gritted teeth.

"I saw you at the field last weekend," he said quietly.

"I was only there for an hour. I have horses so they take up my time."

"Do you ride well?" he said, chuckling.

I blinked, totally getting the inuendo. "Horses, yes. I ride very well." I smiled sweetly in return, and he laughed.

We chatted back and forth. He told me his mum had died earlier that year. She'd had breast cancer. His dad had committed suicide when he was young, and he'd found him. By the time he'd told me that, I wanted to hug him, not the other way round. I turned to face him. Our knees touched.

He leaned forwards and I closed my eyes. His lips didn't meet mine initially. He held himself just millimetres away. I opened my eyes, but he was too close for me to focus on.

"Can I kiss you?" he whispered.

I nodded, of course I wanted him to kiss me. Instead of waiting, I reached up and wrapped my arms around his neck. I pulled his head closer, and he laughed.

It was my first proper kiss.

We spent the next hour on the sofa just kissing. At one point, he'd rested back, and I lay on top of him. I could feel his erection through his jeans and was thrilled I'd produced that, so I thought. I was also terrified he, and I, would want to take it further.

It was with reluctance Sam then drove me home. I was so happy to pull up outside my house in his red car and not seeing my dad's vehicle there. I was happier so when he rushed out and around the front to open the door for me. I stood looking at my front windows and hoping no one could see me. It was Sunday evening, and I should have been home a while ago.

I lifted myself up on tiptoes and kissed him again.

"What are you doing tomorrow?" he asked.

"School, annoyingly."

"After?"

"Sorting my horses straight after, that takes about an hour if I'm not riding," I said, smirking at him.

"I'd like to see you ride," he replied, also smirking. He looked up at my house. "How about I pick you up about six? We can go for a drive for an hour."

"Will you take me out on your bike again?" I asked.

"I'll grab a helmet for you."

He leaned down and kissed me again. I was thankful he'd finished and was heading back to the driver's side of his car when my front door opened. My mum stood in the doorway.

I watched him leave and then skipped up the drive.

"Who was that?"

"His name is Sam," I said.

My mum frowned at me. She was pretty cool and very

open. She'd had me at sixteen, married my dad, and although their relationship was very up and down, they'd stuck it out.

"Sam, huh?" she asked, closing the door behind us.

"I kissed him," I said tentatively.

"How old is he?"

I actually didn't know. "Seventeen, I think." He had to be at least that to be driving a car.

"Mmm, be careful!"

"I know. I'm going to have a shower."

I ran upstairs and to the bathroom. While I stood in the shower, I kept my hand over my lips. I wanted to protect his kiss for as long as I could.

Present Day

When it got to six in the morning, I got up. There was no point lying there anymore thinking about my early days with Sam. Not when I wanted to reply. I took a shower and dressed. I sat with a cup of tea, patting my dog, and scrolling through social media. Only then did I reply.

Hi, Alison. Well, this is a surprise and yes, I think I am the woman you're looking for. I dated your father for about ten years from when I was fifteen – he didn't know I was that young, I lied, so please don't be cross!

I'm sorry to hear he's unwell and I'd love to reconnect. I'm not sure what he has to apologise for, if anything, it is me who owes him the apology. But that's another story. I'll be guided by you as to how we meet or speak.

Although, I would like to see him if that's at all possible. I look forward to hearing back from you.

I read and then pressed send. Yes, I would like to meet him again for old times' sake, and I was curious as to what he thought he had to apologise for.

I went about my day but checked a couple of times for a reply. There wasn't one.

I was a little disappointed, but more worried. She'd said he was ill, and I hoped it hadn't escalated. I went back to her social media. There were a couple of very recent photographs, one showed him in hospital. He was laughing as he stood in a gown with a band around his wrist and a cannula in his hand. Another showed him diving off a boat somewhere exotic. I had to scroll back a while to find him with his wife. I knew he'd married, and I knew her. She had been one of that circle of friends I'd had who were really half friends. She'd also dated my brother at one point. They had two kids, Alison, and a son. Over the years, his name had come up in conversation, and the only time I felt sad about him was when a friend of my brother's and his wife's married. I had been invited to the evening and found out Sam had left once he knew I was attending. That was a shame. I guessed I'd hurt him more than I thought.

The following day, I decided to take my dog for a walk, the predicted heat for that day hadn't kicked in just then. As we walked, I chuckled to myself. I decided to call Pam.

"Hi, do you remember my first boyfriend, Sam?" I asked after saying hello.

"That's a name from the past. Why?"

"His daughter got in touch. Apparently, he's ill, and he wants to apologise to me. He had a list and I'm one of two things he hasn't managed to get done yet. Doesn't that make you think he's dying rather than just ill?"

"Oh, wow. Yes, and what are you going to do?" she asked.

"I've replied and said I'll speak to him or meet up."

"How did she find you?" Pam asked.

"Facebook. She messaged me. I've had a look at her page, and she has photographs of him, so I know she's genuine."

"How strange, though. How long has it been?"

"Years. Twenty-five to be precise. I was twenty-five when we split up."

"It's sort of romantic, isn't it?" she said, chuckling.

"I've no idea on that! I can't remember what romance feels like."

"Send me a link to her page. I want to have a look. Not that I'm doubting you, but you're not exactly social media savvy."

I agreed and promised to let her know what happened next.

Ursa had run off into the bushes and emerged as if he'd camouflaged himself up. I spent ten minutes picking off grass seeds, brambles, and stingy plants. I loved my dog; he was a rescue and the best company. He got me out of the house, and fit. I'd put on weight over the years, I wasn't the *skinny-minnie* Sam used to call me. It bothered me but then I'd think, *I'm too bloody old to worry about it.*

I slipped my phone in my pocket and we walked for another hour through the woods. We stopped to wish a good morning to fellow dog owners and Ursa had a play with his doggy friends. By the time we got back to the car, the temperature was hotting up.

I spent the morning writing. At some point in my life, and I couldn't remember the exact date, I'd decided to write books. I had always wanted to become an author. As a child, I'd pen short stories and read them to my nan. She was a huge letter writer and encouraged me constantly. I remembered when my first book was published, I'd dedicated it to her and given her the first copy off the press. I'd signed it for her, and we'd laughed about how embarrassing that had been. How surreal, as well.

That book sold tons and the film rights had been optioned. Although, it hadn't made it to the big screen, it was still on the cards. I had grand visions of Pam and I walking the red carpet and of me being introduced as the author of the book. I highly doubted it would happen that way, but it was a nice fantasy.

Pam and I had met while I was dating Sam. We'd worked together for a few years and been friends ever since. When my writing had taken off and I knew I needed someone to help me, Pam was the first person I thought of. She was way more organised than I was, and a super admin officer. She kept me focussed and my mind on the job.

Once home, I made a cup of tea and settled in my office. I had editing to do and a deadline to keep.

I didn't pick up my phone for a few hours. When I did, Alison had replied.

From: Alison Weston

Oh, that's super. Sorry for the delay in replying, Dad had a turn, but we're back on track now. I told him I'd contacted you, and he was rather annoyed to start with ha ha ha. He's really pleased now, though. Did you know he has some of your books? I hadn't connected them to you, but then I didn't know your surname. I always knew about you though, we all did. Anyway, he read a couple of your books. He wouldn't let me read them. I had to buy my own copies. I guess, I thought I'd get to know more about you from your writing.

Without it sounding horrid, because it wasn't, you were always with us. I found the writing on the living room wall that you'd done when he redecorated one time. He wouldn't let us paint over it.

Anyway, I'm so glad you've agreed, and to meet up with him would be amazing. If you could give me some dates, I can put them to him. He has quite a few hospital appointments coming up.

Bloody hell, I thought. I wasn't sure I liked the idea he'd kept me 'alive' with his family. I was sure his wife couldn't have been happy; I know I wouldn't have. I screenshotted the reply and sent it over to Pam.

I wondered what had happened to his wife. There was no mention of her on Alison's social media page and the last photo of him and her was from seven years ago. I brought up her page again and scrolled slower, looking for any mention of her mother again. There definitely wasn't any, not even a post in memory of her.

I had to be careful I wouldn't get too consumed. I had to work, but the temptation to google his wife's name was strong. Periodically, I'd googled him, just out of curiosity. Nothing ever came up.

"Afternoon, that's odd, isn't it?" Pam asked when I answered the phone. "And you are meant to be working! That manuscript is due tomorrow," she chastised.

"It will be there on time. And yes. I'm a bit worried now. Seems he never let me go after all. Can't imagine what that would have been like for his wife."

"He married whatsherface, didn't he?"

"Leanne Sands, yes. She left my brother for him! There's no mention of her on Alison's page."

"You're not stalking now, are you?" she asked, laughing.

"I told you, I had a look to make sure she was genuine. Anyway, I've sort of committed myself now. I can't backtrack, but do you think it's a bit creepy? Especially the writing on the wall?"

She sighed. "No, I think it's quite nice. You know he never got over you two. You were his everything."

"So must Leanne have been for him to marry her. He wouldn't have done so, otherwise."

"He was on the rebound, I bet."

"Oh, don't say that. Now I feel worse."

I'd have hated the thought he married someone in that circumstance.

"Well, don't. You can't change what's happened. So, are you still going to meet him?"

"Yes, I think I will, for old times' sake."

"Then make sure you get that bloody manuscript done first!"

"Bossy as ever. I'll get straight back to it now."

We said goodbye and I made a point of turning off my phone and logging out of all social media. I spent the next three hours editing. I only stopped to grab more tea, a sandwich, and let Ursa into my office since it was the coolest place for him. He plonked himself down in front of the aircon unit and started snoring again.

Once I'd finished my work for the day, I made myself something to eat and waited for the heat to die down before I took Ursa out again. I walked and remembered.

CHAPTER 4
The Past

W hen I walked out of school I came to an abrupt halt. Sam sat on his bike outside the gates. He had a spare helmet on the handlebars. His smile when he saw me melted my insides. I was elbowed by a couple of girls and was sure one called me a bitch as I walked over.

"Hi," I said.

"You wanted a ride on the bike, and I finished work early today. So here I am."

"How did you know what school I went to?" I asked.

"You told me you were in the same year as Tammy, so I assumed. I would have looked a right dick sitting here eyeing up the girls waiting for you, if I'd got it wrong. Get on."

I pulled my already rolled over at the waist skirt up a little, tucking part of it in my knickers to keep it up. He glanced down at my legs. I felt childish wearing my white socks and school shoes. I was going to ask my mum for some tights. He handed me the helmet and once I'd slipped it on, he tightened the strap under my chin. He stared at me all the while without blinking. It wasn't my heart that fluttered then. The sensation I'd experienced between my thighs was a throb and I instantly knew it was a want, a need. I stepped closer to him; his knee was between my legs.

"You're ready" he said, and I nodded.

No matter what he meant, I was ready, for sure. Despite being fifteen, I was mature for my age. I'd started my periods when I was ten so felt my body more advanced than others my age.

I climbed onto the back and slid as close to him as I could. He kick-started the engine and with a look over his shoulder, he made his way from the path to the road. I smiled at the group of girls, and some boys, who stood to watch. I had to have been the coolest kid right then.

He drove me home and, again, I prayed my dad wasn't there. Me turning up on a motorbike would have caused a melt-down. Me turning up with a boy probably would have done the same on its own. Thankfully, neither parent's car was there.

"I have to go to the stables," I said, standing awkwardly beside the bike. "You can come if you want."

"Okay, go get changed, I'll wait here."

I rushed up the steps to the front door, frantically twisting the door key to open the damn thing. I dropped my bag on the floor in the hallway, my shoes were kicked off halfway up the stairs and my clothes discarded over my bedroom floor. I pulled a T-shirt over my head and my jodhpurs up my legs. I ran back down stairs and picked up my boots. I was sitting on the front step, sliding my boots on and smiling at him in less than five minutes.

I grabbed the helmet from him and placed it over my head. Again, he secured the chin strap. Then we were off. I had to point the way to the stables and climb off the bike to unpadlock the gate. My dad rented a field and stables for me and my horses. It was a short walk from where we lived, and I knew he was thinking about us moving somewhere where I could keep the horses at home. I had been so enthusiastic about that, but no more. I was in love, even after just the one day. I knew it was love because I thought about him all the time. I dreamt about him. I felt a tingle on my lips where he'd kissed me. I had no idea how he felt, of course.

I walked and he slowly rode beside me until we got to the wooden stable block. He parked up.

"What's first?" he asked.

"I mucked out this morning. So, we get Sovereign in first because I need to exercise him. He's out there," I said, pointing to the paddock.

Sam followed me and at the gate I whistled. Sovereign came trotting over expecting a carrot, which he got. I slipped on his headcollar and gave the lead rein to Sam. He led him back. He wasn't a natural around horses, but I handed him a grooming brush anyway.

"Follow the coat," I said. While I got tack ready, he groomed my pony.

"Have you ever ridden?" I asked. He paused and looked at me.

"Many times."

My stomach ached.

"Have you ever ridden a horse?" I rephrased.

"Never."

"Would you like to try?"

"Sure, why not."

I tacked Sovereign up and led him to a mounting block. Sam took the step up and I showed him how to sit on the pony. While he held the reins, I led him to the exercise arena. We just walked around, and he laughed.

"Jesus, this hurts," he said, tugging at the front of his jeans.

We did one more lap and then he jumped off.

"Do you need help to mount?" he asked as I collected the reins in one hand and held the stirrup towards me.

"I do, yes," I replied, and chuckled.

Sam placed his hands on my arse and on my third bounce, he pushed.

He sat on the fence as I rode. I was entered into a competition and needed to practice the dressage test. Sam was a distraction, but he also made me ride my best. I had wanted to impress him, not that he knew what I was doing. I was *sidestepping* as far as he was concerned.

I'd catch him in my vision. He wore blue jeans, white trainers, a white T-shirt, and a black biker jacket. His cropped hair was a dirty blond, and he had a little stubble around his chin. The more I looked, the more I realised, he wasn't seventeen. He was older. I hoped it wasn't by too much but, in all honesty, I didn't care.

I was going to be sixteen in a couple of months and, in my mind, old enough to make some serious decisions. Of course, I wasn't, but then, I knew best. I knew it all.

I finished my ride, and we walked back to the stables. While I hosed Sovereign down, Sam spread his straw to form a bed. Leaving my pony tied up and eating from his hay net while he dried, I showed Sam how I mixed up the feeds in the small shed that doubled as a feed and tack room.

We then moved to the barn to fill hay nets.

"This is cool," he said, looking up at stacks of bales of hay and straw.

"There's a cat that lives here. She catches the mice. She's usually asleep up there," I said, pointing.

"Show me," he asked. I didn't expect him to be a cat person.

We climbed up the bales, laughing as we fell, and finally making the top. We sat with our legs dangling over the edge, there was no sign of the cat.

"What movies do you like?" I asked him.

"I don't really watch movies, or television. I prefer music."

"And to read?" I asked, remembering his bookcase.

"And to read."

"What music?" I asked and lay back.

He also lay, chewing on a piece of hay. "Pink Floyd at the moment."

My dad had a few of their albums that he played a lot. "Oh, I love them."

He turned on his side to face me. "What's your favourite song?"

"Wish You Were Here," I replied, turning my head towards him.

He shuffled closer. "I am here."

We fell silent and I held my breath. My heart was racing, and my stomach was turning circles. He leaned down and kissed me, gently. I opened my mouth to accept his tongue. He moved his body, so it was half covering mine and I wrapped my arms around him. The throbbing between my thighs started and I wanted to squash my legs together to ease it.

Sam placed one hand on my thigh. His other arm was held over my head. It was the closest he'd been, and I would have liked him to completely cover my body. I inwardly cursed when he broke the kiss.

"I think that's enough for now," he whispered.

"I don't think so," I replied.

He laughed. "Greedy, aren't you?"

I nodded. "Yes, now kiss me again."

He did and it was more passionate than before. He stole my breath, I shook, and was absolutely gutted when he pulled away a second time.

"Are you a virgin?" he asked.

My cheeks flamed and I swallowed hard. I paused, just staring at him.

"Honest answers only," he said, and I nodded.

"Have you kissed anyone like that before?"

That time, I shook my head.

"Good. I want to be your first for everything."

I stilled, hoping that meant like, right then. It didn't. "When you're ready," he added.

I wanted to shout I was bloody ready. My knickers were wet with desire for him. Instead, he sat up, jumped down to the next level, and then held out his hands. He grabbed my waist as I jumped as well. Everywhere he touched me, my skin prickled. The overwhelming desire to be close to him confused and frustrated me.

We stood for a moment. "How will I know I'm ready?" I asked.

"I'll know."

He then helped me back down to the ground. While he made up the rest of the beds, I added buckets of food, topped up clean water, and hung hay nets. We both walked to the field to grab my mother's horse, an elderly boy I loved and a great companion for Sovereign. I also thought he might be suitable for Sam to ride if he wanted to do it again.

Once both horses were put to bed, I swept the yard, and he made up the feeds for the next morning. I had to call out which dustbin contained which food, and then he helped me fill water buckets. We stored the brooms, forks, and wheelbarrows, and then locked up. When I looked at my watch, two hours had passed.

"Now what?" he asked.

"I guess I have to go home and eat."

"You could come to mine?"

I slowly nodded, not knowing what my mum would say. "Can we go to mine first?"

"Sure."

That time I was allowed to fix the chin strap, but he had to check it. I climbed on the bike behind him, and we set off, only stopping for me to lock the gates. Again, I panicked as we got closer to the house and closed my eyes when we pulled up at the same time my mum was emptying the car of shopping.

"I won't be a moment," I told Sam when I took the helmet off.

I walked up the garden path. "What can I get?" I asked.

"Just that last bag. Is that him?" she asked, looking over at Sam. He had removed his helmet and smiled back at her.

"Yes. Please don't make a scene. He's a safe driver, or rider, or whatever it is."

She looked at me. "I'm not the one you should be worried about. If your dad saw you on the back of a motorbike, your friend there better ride fast to outpace him." She laughed and we carried the shopping in.

As we got to the front door, she paused and turned. "Are you coming in?" she asked him. "Don't leave him sitting out here," she said to me.

Sam wheeled his bike onto the drive and joined us. He took

some bags from my mum and carried them through to the kitchen.

"I'm Danielle," she said.

He held out his hand and she smiled. "Sam Weston. I want to say that, although I'm older than your daughter, my intentions are good. I've never had an accident on that bike, but I do own a car if you'd prefer her to be driven in that."

I stared at him open-mouthed. Fuck, maybe he was way older than I'd thought. He sounded like a real grown-up man.

"I'd prefer she was driven in a car, Sam. I've seen you guys over the Mad Mile, and I cringe at how fast you all go."

I hadn't told my mum that was where we'd met, but guessed it was no secret all the kids on the estate went there.

"However, her father might not even like that." She laughed.

"Erm, Mum? Sam invited me to get something to eat with him. Can I do that?" If there was ever a sport for eye-pleading, I would win. I folded my lips inside my mouth and silently prayed.

She looked at me, and then him. "I'd like her back at ten, please, Sam. She has school tomorrow."

I'd never been out until ten on a weekday, not that I had been stopped from it. The occasion had never arisen to have a time. If I was out, it was with my parents, friends from childhood and their parents, or it was school or horse related.

I smiled broadly at her and while my back was turned from Sam, I mouthed a thank you. She winked at me.

"Do not do anything you're not ready for," she whispered

as she leant down to kiss my cheek. "In fact, that's a conversation for tomorrow."

My cheeks flamed again.

Sam and I headed out. While he got the bike ready, I changed from my boots to my trainers. I wasn't going upstairs to change; I didn't want him left alone with my mother for fear of her telling him I wasn't as old as I'd made out to be.

CHAPTER 5

The Past

"We have steak. Do you like steak?" he asked, looking into his fridge.

"Sure. Can I help with something?" I asked.

"You can make up a salad to go with it." He started to hand me things.

"You have a very healthy fridge for a single man," I said, peering over his shoulder.

He had beers, of course, but the rest looked like my fridge at home.

"I didn't know there was a rule. Should I be unhealthy?" he asked, turning to face me.

"No, it's just... I don't know." I laughed.

He placed his hands on my hips and walked me back until I was pinned to the counter. I held a bloody lettuce in one hand, and a cucumber in the other! He lowered his face close to mine.

"I like to be healthy," he said, whispering his words.

I stared up at him and he chuckled. "You're blushing. Why?"

His stare was so intense, I wasn't sure I could answer.

"I don't know."

"Are you embarrassed?" he asked.

"No. Overwhelmed, maybe."

"I overwhelm you?" he asked and frowned at the same time.

"Yes, and these... these feelings inside me."

He raised his eyebrows and chuckled some more. The sound was deep, and it hit me right in the core.

"Good," he said, then kissed my nose and turned away.

I sighed, rolled my eyes, and my shoulders slumped. I had a feeling he was going to be infuriating.

I chopped salad, he fried steak, and we sat on the sofa and ate. After, I washed the plates while he put a record on. We listened to Pink Floyd.

"Do you mind if I smoke?" he asked.

I shook my head. I had friends who smoked, as did my dad. Except, he didn't smoke the same *cigarette* he did. He rolled a joint and moved to stand by the window.

"Can I try?" I asked.

"Have you ever smoked this before?"

"No."

"Then, no. Hayley, I want to corrupt you, but, as I said, when you're ready."

I blinked rapidly. *Corrupt me?*

I stood, not sure if I should run or not. He threw his joint out the window and strode over to me. He placed his hands at either side of my head and his kiss pinned me to the spot. He was demanding, passionate, commanding. He took total control of that kiss, and my body with it. He pulled me close so I could feel his erection. I wrapped my arms around his neck and accepted everything he gave.

I would have to show him just how ready I was.

My body was screaming for him and when we parted, I let my head fall to his chest. I was panting. He wrapped his arms around me and hugged me close.

"Soon," he whispered into my ear.

All I could do was nod.

We listened to a couple of albums and watched the sun set. We talked about all the things we liked and didn't like. When I had to use the bathroom, I opened his cabinet. I looked at his aftershave, wanting to spray my T-shirt with it as a reminder of him when I got home. I didn't think he'd appreciate it though.

"Is this your mum?" I asked.

For a moment, he was silent. "Yes. She died the beginning of the year; did I tell you?"

"You did, I'm so sorry." Tears immediately sprang to my eyes.

"It's okay." He leaned towards me and swiped his thumbs under my eyes to catch my tears.

If it were possible to fall further in love with him, I did just then.

He checked his watch. "We need to leave."

"We have a half hour yet," I said, panicked and not wanting to leave.

He chuckled. "Yep, but by the time I've kissed you goodnight, we won't have."

I frowned. "Come on," he said, standing and holding out his hand.

I wasn't sure whether it was the still open window or him, but I shivered.

"Wait here," he said. He walked into his bedroom and then returned with a sweatshirt. "Put this on."

I couldn't get it on quick enough. Sadly, it had just been washed by the smell.

"What?" he asked, and he must have seen my frown.

"It doesn't smell of you," I whispered.

He stilled, looking at me. All I could do was look at my feet. I wiggled my toes for something to do. Sam reached under my chin and lifted my face.

"I think that's the nicest thing anyone has said to me."

"I want to keep you close," I replied. "Can I?"

It was his turn to frown. I walked to the bathroom and returned with aftershave. I held two up.

"That one is my favourite," he said, pointing.

I sprayed myself with it. He laughed and waved the fumes away. He reached out for it, and I turned to run. He wrapped his arms around my waist, and I bent forwards, laughing and trying to hold the aftershave away from him.

When he kissed the back of my neck, my legs nearly gave way. I'd never been kissed there before.

"Do that again, please?" I whispered. He did. His lips moved from the back of my neck to the side and up to my ear. I moaned and I felt him smile.

"We're going to be late," he said.

"So?"

"So, your mum said ten. Get your arse outside," he said, stepping back and patting my arse.

He held my hand while he drove his car. I was also thankful he pulled up shy of my house. My dad's car was on the drive. He turned the engine off and faced me. He cocked his finger, beckoning me to him. I complied. In fact, I couldn't get there fast enough.

We kissed and I sighed, more so when he moaned and, in front of me, adjusted his cock through his jeans.

"You make me so hard," he said, laughing.

I cocked my head to one side and smiled, coyly. "I have no idea what you mean."

He laughed and left the car. He opened my door for me and held my hand as we walked to my house. The security light tripped on, and my mum opened the front door.

"Bang on time, Sam. Thank you."

"And we came by car, it's just over there," he said, pointing.

She nodded and then stepped back inside. I turned to him. "Will I see you tomorrow?" I asked.

He shook his head. "I'm out tomorrow. Give me your number, though." I rushed in to the telephone stand and wrote it down on the pad.

"Here. Will you call me?"

35

He nodded. "Yeah. I'd like to hear your voice. What time do you go to bed?"

"About half ten," I replied.

"I'll call you just before." He leaned forwards to briefly kiss my lips and then turned. I watched him walk away.

When I closed the door, I leant against it with my eyes closed.

"Hayley," I heard, and I sighed. "Get in here, please," my dad called out.

"Is that the boyfriend?"

"He's not my—"

"He better be, bringing you home this late and kissing you in his car," he replied.

I stared at him, open-mouthed. How had he seen us? I then saw our dog had his collar on. I bet he'd taken him for his last walk. I hadn't noticed anyone walking past and could only be thankful he hadn't banged on the window or dragged me out.

I didn't answer. I didn't know what to say.

"Leave her alone, Chas. What age were you, huh?"

"Different back in my day," he said.

"Which wasn't that long ago, Dad. You're only twenty years older than me."

He threw a cushion at me. "Sassy arse. Now get up to bed."

I laughed as I climbed the stairs. I took a shower and got into bed. I wished he lived closer, next door, or in the one that backed onto our house. We could look at each other through the windows.

I heard a gentle knock on the door. "Can I come in?" Mum asked.

I sat up. "Sure," I replied.

She came and sat on the edge of the bed. "Did you have a good time?"

"I did," I said, smiling and knowing my cheeks were flushed. "He cooked, and we listened to Pink Floyd."

"Anything you want to tell me?" she said gently.

"No. He says I'm not ready." I looked down at my bedding, playing with a cotton strand.

"Good. I'm pleased to hear that. You've only just met him, Hals. Don't rush anything. Tomorrow, we'll get you up the doctor's, though."

She stroked my hair. "I know what it's like, darling. I can see in your face you love him, but I don't want you to get hurt, okay? You're not old enough to have sex with him legally, and I know everyone is at your age, but there are things we need to talk about first."

I was praying I wasn't going to get the birds and bees talk. It had been bad enough walking in on my parents one time, without her talking to me about sex.

"I know what I'm doing."

"So did I, or so I thought," she said, gently. "I don't regret anything, but I want you to have choices."

I didn't answer her. If I had choices, it would be to be with him. When she left, I picked up his sweatshirt and hugged it to me. I breathed in deep.

It had only been a matter of days, I knew that, but I was obsessed with him.

I fell asleep with that sweatshirt in my arms and dreamt of him.

* * *

The following day was agony. Girls I had never spoken to sidled up to me.

"Are you going out with Sam Weston?" one asked.

I nodded, assuming I was. She linked her arm with mine. "Heading to lunch?"

I untangled myself. "Sorry, I'm not," I said. I wanted to tell her to fuck off. I only knew her vaguely.

I shook her off. "Think you're too good now, do you?" she spat back.

I headed off to the common room. I wanted to be on my own and not surrounded by bitches.

"Hey," I heard. I looked up to see Tammy and I wanted to sigh. "Can I sit?"

I didn't really have a choice in the matter, she did so before I'd even answered.

"Piece of advice, take care with Sam. He's got a lot of issues —anger and drugs. You know he found his dad dead? Screwed him up big time." She settled back in the seat.

"I imagine something like that would do it."

"He fights, smokes dope, and he's had a lot of girls before you."

"I'm sure he has," I said, not knowing what to say.

"I just wanted to tell you to be careful." Her voice had changed, and I thought she might be genuine.

"I will and thank you. Remember, Karl is his best friend so maybe you should trust that if he likes him, he isn't all bad." I shrugged my shoulders.

She stared at me, and then nodded. "We're going to be at the crates tonight. Come along."

"Sam's out," I said.

"Yeah, with Karl. They have a job," she said, using her fingers to indicate quotes. "It will just be me and a couple of friends. Same circle as Sam and Karl."

I nodded. "Okay, I'll see."

She smiled and then left me alone. I thought on what she'd said. He was a bad boy; we all knew that. It was his reputation that all the girls loved the most. Then the tattoos and chip tooth, the scar through his eyebrow, the bike and car, and the fact he had his own place and a job. So I'd been told, of course.

I wasn't sure I was brave enough to go to the crates on my own. I'd never been before. I knew where it was, and it really was a pile of wooden crates on some farmland. Kids would just sit and talk, drink vodka or beer, and smoke. I'd always wanted to go there but had never been invited before.

When the bell went to indicate lunch was over, I snuck off home. I changed in my stable gear and walked up the lane to the yard. I mucked out, cleaned the tack, scrubbed the walls where the horses had slobbered while eating, and swept. I rode Sovereign and lunged Alfie. He had been lame and was on light duties. My mum had stopped riding him a couple of years ago. She'd had a serious fall and it had knocked her confidence. I sat on a straw bale and drank a can of Coke. My dad had installed a small kitchenette and we had a fridge for milk and soda. It was a godsend on hot days when I'd spend the whole day at the yard. I thought back to the toe-curling kiss Sam and I had shared at the top of the straw bales and climbed up. I wanted to sit in the same place.

The yard cat was curled up asleep, I gave her a stroke. She purred, totally at ease with me. She wouldn't let anyone else touch her though. My chest hurt as I thought of him. I was missing him and knowing I wasn't going to see him that evening made me want to cry. The rational part of me knew it was infatuation. I was also scared he'd leave me. Especially once he knew my real age. Perhaps, if I gave myself to him, he wouldn't.

I thought I was ready. I wanted to lose my virginity to him, I didn't know how to initiate that. I didn't have any close girl-friends I could talk to. I also needed to think about birth control before I did anything. Annoyingly, I wasn't old enough to make that doctor's appointment and discuss my options myself, and I know my mum had said we should make that appointment, but I wasn't sure I could sit and discuss anything with either of them.

I made a decision. Once I'd settled the horses for the evening, I walked home. My dad was in, which was unusual.

"Hey, baby, how are the horses?" he asked.

"Good, I lunged Alfie, I think he's getting better."

"That's good. Did you practice your test?" he asked.

I nodded, grabbing a drink from the fridge.

"And then what?"

I turned to face him. "I mucked out, the usual."

He nodded. "Right, and you did that all in, what time?"

I stared at him; he knew. Bollocks.

"This time, I'm not going to tell your mum, but Hals, if this happens again, she's the one they will call and you're fucked, young lady."

"How did you know?" I asked.

"The school called. I said I'd forgotten to tell them you had an appointment."

I breathed out a sigh of relief. "Thank you, Dad."

"I get it, Hals, I do. You hate it there. You've changed schools twice now; this is the last one. You'll get kicked out, then what?"

I shrugged my shoulders, there wasn't really anything I could say.

"Are you being bullied again?" he asked, his voice lowered to a gentler tone.

"No. I just... I just hate it there, Dad. I don't have any friends and I'm lonely."

I had been totally honest with him. He stepped forwards and cuddled me, I shed tears.

"It's tough, being your age, isn't it, baby?" he said, and I nodded.

I was struggling with puberty. My periods were awful, painful, so heavy I'd bleed through every pad on the market, even if they were doubled up. I didn't like the way I looked. I was insecure, and my horses and Sam were the only things that made me smile. Aside from my parents, obviously.

"Tell me about this boy," he said.

"Dad! No." My cheeks flamed, and I laughed. He chuckled and let me go to return to the washing up. "He's nice. People think he's horrible, a bad boy, but he isn't. He found his dad dead and his mum died of cancer earlier this year."

"Fuck, that doesn't sound good."

"Yeah. I like him," I said quietly, never for once believing I'd be having this conversation with my dad.

"Will you wait until your sixteen before... You know?" he asked, not looking at me.

"Dad!" I screeched.

"Talk to your mum, have her get you up the doctor's."

I screeched out again and ran from the room.

I sat in my bedroom listening to the same songs we'd listened to at his house. Eventually, my mum came home, and she called me down for dinner. She'd brought home a Chinese takeaway.

We sat at the table, and my brother nattered away about karate. He'd recently joined a local club and was the reason Mum was home late. She'd picked him up from school and headed straight there. Of course, he was the expert already. Dad had wanted him to box, which Dad had done all his youth and into his young adult life, but Dan wasn't that keen. When we'd finished eating, Dan and I cleared the table, and rowed over who was washing and who was drying up.

Once done, I headed up to my bedroom. I showered and then lay on my bed writing in my diary. I loved keeping a diary, I loved letter writing as well. My nan had started me off with it. She loved to send and receive letters and we pretended we were pen pals. I wrote all about Sam, how I felt about him, and what I wanted to do with him. I filled in the whole page and then read it back.

When I lay down, I held the diary to my chest. I smiled and wondered what he was doing. Tammy had said they were at a 'job.' I didn't even know what Sam did for work and if that would take him out in the evening. I didn't care. There was nothing anyone could have told me about him that would have put me off. I was besotted.

I must have dozed off and woke with a jolt when I heard my dad calling me. I rushed from the bedroom and down the stairs.

"It's the boyfriend," Dad said, holding out the phone.

I snatched the handset from him. He lounged against the wall. "Can I get some privacy?" I snapped and he chuckled.

"Hello?" I said quietly.

"Hey. Were you sleeping?" Sam asked.

"No, I was writing about you in my diary," I said, being much braver because I wasn't face-to-face.

"What did you write?"

"It's a secret, which is why it's in my diary. Did you get your job done?" I asked.

"My job?"

"Tammy said you and Karl were on a job. She came and sat with me today."

"Warn you off, did she? Let me guess, I'm a druggy and I have anger issues?"

I laughed. "I won't let my dad hear that; I'll be grounded."

"He said I had to come round to meet him. Should I be scared?" he asked, laughing.

"Yep. He's a tough man."

We fell silent for a little while.

"Will I see you tomorrow?" I asked quietly.

"If you want to."

"I do. I missed you today." I tried hard not to sound needy.

"I'll pick you up after school, how's that?"

I nodded, then remembered he couldn't see me. "I'd like that."

"So tell me what you've done today?"

I did and it did occur to me he hadn't divulged what his evening had been spent doing. I wouldn't push, however.

When I told him I sat on the straw bales and thought of him, his voice changed. "Did you touch yourself?" he asked.

I swallowed hard and thought my face would catch on fire it was that hot.

"No."

"You should."

I had never touched myself in that way. I didn't really know how. Some of the girls in school boasted about having vibrators, having sex, but I didn't believe them.

"I have to go to the stables straight from school," I said, changing the subject.

"I'll help, then drop you back home if you want."

"I don't want," I said, laughing.

"We can decide what to do tomorrow. Now, go to bed, Hayley."

"Yes, sir," I said, and he laughed.

We said goodnight and I sat for a little while. Eventually, I popped my head into the living room. Mum and Dad were watching a movie. They were curled up on the sofa together, he had his arm around her shoulders.

"All right, baby?" Dad said.

"Yes, I'm going up to sleep now," I said. I hesitated.

"Do you need to chat?" Mum said, and I nodded.

She rose and followed me back to my bedroom.

I sat on the bed, crossing my legs in front of me.

"Talk to me, sweetie," she said.

"I want to go on the Pill," I said, not looking up.

"Is this for your periods or because you want to have sex with Sam?"

"Both," I replied, still not looking up at her.

She sighed. "Can we persuade you to wait until you're sixteen?"

I finally looked up. "I will, but I need to be on the Pill for a while first, don't I?"

"Yes, a couple of months, I think. I'll call the doctor in the morning, see if I can get an appointment after school."

"Erm, Sam will be picking me up from school. Then we're going to the stables."

"Okay, but this is important. So, if I can get an appointment, I will, but after you've done the horses. Then you can see Sam after that."

I nodded. "I don't know what to do," I whispered.

Mum stared at me. "About sex?" she asked, and I nodded again.

She scooted up the bed and cuddled me.

"Oh, sweetie. I was a virgin when I met your dad. He wasn't the dirty bugger he'd been. Anyway, he took the lead, he told me what to do, and, well, it sort of comes instinctively. But I need you to promise me one thing. If you don't want to do something, you don't. You say no, do you hear me? It doesn't matter how...heated, things are, you can say no, and he *must* stop. If he doesn't, darling, that's rape."

Her words actually frightened me, and I wasn't sure if that was her intent or not.

"He's your first real boyfriend. Enjoy it, don't take it too seriously," she added.

I leaned into her shoulder. "What if I'm no good?" I asked.

"You're not a sexpert, darling," she said, and I laughed.

"A what?"

"I just made that up. You're not a sexpert. If he can't teach you what you want to know, if he's impatient, or just focusses on himself, he's no good. You need to feel good yourself, darling. You don't just lie back and think of England."

I wanted to cringe, I also wanted to talk more. I'd never had that kind of a conversation with my mum before. As much as my parents were very open, they displayed their affection always, and us kids were loved and hugged and kissed, the *intimate* conversation had never been had, obviously.

"I can't believe we're having this conversation already. I had hoped you'd be way older. I just want to keep reminding you, you haven't known him that long, and I'd rather you wait. But if you won't, then I want you to be knowledgeable and safe."

I nodded. I didn't anticipate jumping into bed in the next few days with him, but I'd like to get to second base. We'd gone way beyond first base already.

"Invite him round for dinner, let us meet him properly," she said, and then kissed my head. "Get some sleep, darling."

As she slid from the bed, I lay down and she tucked me in like she had when I was little.

"Night, Mum," I said. She turned out the light as she left.

I lay for hours just looking at the moon. I wondered what he was doing, if he was thinking about me.

CHAPTER 6
The Past

I went through my day as usual. Avoiding as many people as I could but agreeing to sit with Tammy and her friends for lunch. These girls were different to the others at the Mad Mile. I actually liked them.

"So you're dating Sam?" one asked. I wanted to sigh or add, "If I had a pound for every time I'd been asked that."

I nodded. "It's early days," I said.

"He told Karl he's really into you," Tammy said.

"Did he?" I sounded way more enthusiastic than I wanted to.

She nodded. "Yeah. He doesn't usually date girls your age, and I'm not being horrible." I didn't believe she was.

"How old is he?" I asked, and she stared at me.

"You don't know?"

"I don't think he's ever said."

"Nineteen. He's twenty in July. Same age as my Karl." She beamed, pleased we'd both snagged an older man, I thought.

"How did you meet Karl?" I asked spearing my carton drink with a straw.

"His parents are friends of my parents. Known him for years," she said.

We ate our lunch and gossiped about girls in their year I didn't know, makeup, hair, and clothes. I said I was desperate to do something with my hair and Tammy suggested I let my curls take over. I had been trying to straighten them for years.

My hair, naturally, was like a corkscrew. But I used to brush it out, hence the frizz. My hairdresser, well, Mum's hairdresser, could blow-dry it straight, but it never lasted long.

"Buy some serum, scrunch your hair, and use a diffuser," she said, as if I knew what she was talking about.

She must have known I was in the year below her, but because I was also a July baby, I was a year younger than everyone else in my class.

"Come to mine, I'll do it," she said, and I nodded. It would be the first time a friend invited me to their house who wasn't a family friend.

"Yeah, I'd like that. Maybe you could show me how to do my makeup," I said.

We made a date to meet one night in the week. She said we could do that straight from school and meet the boys after. I'd have to check my mum could do the horses that night. She often covered for me if I had a detention.

I skipped out of school that day and paused at the gates.

Sam sat in the driver's seat of his car with the window down, his arm out, and holding a cigarette. At least I hoped it was a plain cigarette. He wore a T-shirt, and his tattoos were on show.

When he saw me, he climbed out. I walked over and stood in front of him. He placed one hand on the back of my neck and lowered his face for a kiss. Another toe-curling kiss in front of most of the school.

I could hear some name-calling, and when he looked up and stared at them, the group of boys ran off.

"Come on," he said, walking me to the passenger side. He opened the door and then closed it behind me. He dragged on his cigarette before throwing it in the gutter.

"Home first?" he asked, and I nodded.

I told him all about my lunch with Tammy and our date to fix my hair. He nodded along, concentrating on the road.

"Watch that one," he said. "She's not a fan of mine."

"She said the same about you, remember?" I laughed.

As we drove, he reached over and placed his hand on my thigh. I would have loved if he'd slid that hand up a little. He squeezed.

"I bet all the boys stare at your legs," he said.

"They don't. I don't think any boys stare at me. But would it bother you?"

He glanced over. "I do get jealous, Hals. But no, because I'm the only one touching them."

I smiled at him. If it wasn't such a childish thing to do, I would have danced in my seat.

We arrived home and he waited in the car while I changed. I

also grabbed some clean shorts and a T-shirt, my flip-flops for after. I was hoping we'd go back to his house.

I was back in the car in five minutes. "My mum wants to invite you to dinner next week," I said. "You don't have to come, of course."

"Are you ashamed of me? Why would I not come?"

"God, no. I just... Well, I didn't know if you'd want to. They're pretty cool, but my dad will give you the third degree."

"Again?" he asked and laughed. "I want to meet your parents."

We arrived at the gate and left the vehicle to unlock the padlock. Instead of climbing back in the car, I sat on the bonnet, and he drove us to the yard.

As before, he helped me with the horses. Unlike before, I tacked up both horses and he rode Alfie. We walked around the fields, out into the lane, and then back again. We chatted and laughed, and he told me a little about his childhood. I didn't think he'd had a great childhood. Although he knew his dad, it had been just him and his mum. His dad seemed to come and go. He was a drug addict, he told me. He didn't tell me about his suicide, and I didn't mention I knew. He was interested in me, in my family, and I felt he'd missed out on a regular child-hood. I also discovered his father had also dated his aunt. She had two sons by him.

"Talk about keeping it in the family, huh?" he said, and then laughed.

The more I learned about him, the more I loved him.

And, of course, I was going to be the one to fix him.

* * *

"You want to come back to mine?" he asked, as I locked the gates.

"As long as I can have a shower and change my clothes," I said, aware I was hot and sweaty, grubby as well.

"Of course. But it will have to be a bath, nothing as luxurious as a shower at my place."

"A bath would be perfect."

He held my hand as we drove, using both to change gears. "Will you teach me to drive when I'm old enough?" I asked.

He pulled over halfway down the lane and slid his seat back slightly. He patted his lap. "Climb on," he said.

"What?"

He laughed and patted his lap. I scrambled over the seats. I held the steering wheel, and he did the pedals. I remembered doing that as a kid with my dad. I screamed as he put his foot down and drove too fast. He braked with both his arms around my waist and chest, his hand covering one breast. He nuzzled the side of my neck.

"You're going to make me crash," I said, hoping we'd stop before we got to the corner.

He laughed. "I hope so," he whispered, and I didn't know what he meant.

He stopped the car and as I slid back to my seat, my arse was raised, and he slapped it. We continued the journey back to his flat.

While I was getting my boots off, he ran the bath for me.

He poured in something that smelled nice. He said he had no idea what it was, could have been dog shampoo as far as he knew, but it looked nice. While he sat in the living room, I took a quick bath. When I was washed, I panicked. I couldn't see a towel.

"Sam," I called out. "There's no towel."

By then, the bubbles had started to burst, so I wasn't as covered as I would have liked when he casually walked into the room, holding a large bath towel. He stood by the bath and held the towel out. I had covered my crotch with one hand and my arm over my breasts. I had to let go of one to stand, though.

"I won't look," he said, closing his eyes.

I laughed as I stood and held on to his shoulder to climb from the bath. It was when I looked up at him before he wrapped the towel around me that I saw his eyes were open.

"You looked!"

"I did. Can you blame me?"

I grabbed the towel and laughed, more in embarrassment. He pulled me to his chest. "You're beautiful, Hals," he said.

"I'm not," I replied, squirming.

"What will it take for you to believe that?" he asked.

I shrugged my shoulders. He leaned down and kissed one.

He held my hand and led me to his bedroom. He'd laid my clothes out on his bed. I stood totally unsure what to do. He stood looking at me.

"Will you kiss me?" I asked, and he took a step towards me. "There," I said, pointing to the bed. He frowned.

I kept the towel wrapped tightly around me and climbed

onto his bed. I lay on my back and waited for him. He kicked off his shoes, and removed his sweatshirt, leaving him just in jeans, and joined me. At first, he lay on his side, his head propped on his bent arm. He ran his fingers up and down my arms, across the top of my chest. At no time did he attempt to remove the towel.

He slid himself forward a little, his upper body covered mine. He kissed me gently at first. As we became more urgent for each other, he covered my body fully. He held my head, and I wrapped my arms around him. I ran my nails gently over his skin and smiled at the goosebumps that followed my path. Feeling his naked skin above me was arousing, more so when he ground his erect cock into me.

I loved the feel of him on top of me. I felt safe and secure. I liked the feel of his back, the heat of his skin under my fingertips. I felt a scar and as I ran my hand over it, he stilled. He pulled his head back and looked at me. I continued to run my hand over that part of him.

"How did you get that?" I asked.

"Stabbed, in a fight," he said. I should have been shocked, but I wasn't. I was disappointed when he slid to the side of me.

He reached for my thigh and pulled my legs apart a little. I started to shake.

"Is this okay?" he asked, just holding his hand on my thigh.

I nodded. He slid his hand slightly upwards. "You tell me to stop if you want to," he whispered.

I pulled my towel up a little, and he chuckled. When he got to my pussy, I nearly died. A heat rushed over me and all he'd done is just place his fingers over my clitoris. I felt that throbbing return and my stomach was doing somersaults.

I closed my eyes. He kissed my throat, the only part of my chest exposed, as he slid his fingers back and forth.

"So wet," he mumbled, and I wasn't sure if that was a good or bad thing.

He slid one finger inside me, gently and slowly. It was no worse than a tampon, I thought. No pain. He moved his finger in and out and that friction caused my chest to tighten. I found I'd lost my breath. I opened my mouth to pull in air.

He teased me, kissed me, and all the time I just lay there, but I wasn't thinking of England.

"I like that," I whispered.

"I'm glad. Want more?" he asked, raising his head to look at me.

I nodded, again not sure what he meant.

When he inserted a second finger, I breathed in sharply. "Oh God," I said, and then closed my eyes. If I couldn't see him, he couldn't see how embarrassed I was.

He chuckled.

A minute or so later, I felt an overwhelming need to pee. It was a pressure inside me. My skin was aflame and every nerve ending screamed. I grabbed his hand, trying to push him away. I arched my back off the bed, panting.

"It's okay, go with it," he said.

I wasn't sure what was happening, other than I loved it. I loved every tingle that shot though my body. I welcomed the heat to my cheeks and the sweat to my brow. I wanted to part my legs as far as they could go, to discard the towel completely. I moaned, unable to stop the sound that had been bubbling up from my chest. Once I did, his lips crashed down on mine. I exploded around him. I felt the wetness leave my pussy and I didn't care. I grabbed at his head, pulling him closer to me, both of us unable to breathe. He continued to finger me until my orgasm, not that I was aware that's what it was at the time, abated.

When I could hold my breath no more, I pulled his head away. I gasped for air, and tears leaked from my eyes. He gently kissed them away.

"What happened?" I asked, my throat sore and my voice hoarse.

"I made you come," he said. He rolled to the side and raised his fingers to his lips.

I was mortified when he sucked on them. His blue eyes stared at me so intently, I had to empty my mind, otherwise I think I would have pounced on him.

We'd spent more time kissing, and he'd encouraged me to rub his cock through his jeans. I had wanted to wank him, but he'd said no. We still had to take it slow. He groaned also with frustration, and I laughed. He'd rolled to his back, and I'd leaned over him, kissing him, stroking him. *It felt amazing to hold such power over him,* I thought.

I didn't want to leave, but I was aware of the time. I grumbled as I slid from his bed and let the towel fall. It had slipped open anyway. He stared at my naked body, and I didn't feel I needed to hide from him. I dressed and only then did he get up himself.

"Can we take the bike?" I asked.

"I promised your mum I'd drive you home by car," he said.

"Do you always do what you promise?" I asked, as he locked the front door.

He turned and pulled me to his chest. "This weekend, we'll spend the day in bed. And yes, always."

He kissed the tip of my nose and opened the car door for me.

I slept like a log that night. Whether it was because I'd had that first orgasm or not, I had no idea. I knew it was rare for girls to experience that at first, or so sex-ed had suggested. Did that mean he was brilliant at sex? I hoped so.

* * *

Mum agreed to do the horses the following day for me. I'd told her all she had to do was bring them in. I'd get up super early to make sure everything was sorted for them. I packed a bag of what I thought were essential makeup items, my hairdryer, and headed into school. Tammy caught up with me at first break and confirmed we were still on that evening. Sam was going to pick us up from her house. I was elated, there had been a little part of me that thought she might be leading me on, pranking me.

She was waiting for me at the end of the day. We walked to her house, and we chatted about bands, school, what we planned for our futures. She wanted to get into fashion and would be taking her A levels in the hopes of getting into uni. I had no idea what I wanted to do.

She also told me Sam owned his own business. I knew, by then, he was a car mechanic, but I hadn't realised it was his business. He'd told me his garage was local and promised to take me there one day. He said he often worked on Saturday mornings, and I guessed it was because he was his own boss he could collect me from school.

When we got to her house, her mum was in. She didn't work, unlike mine, and fussed around us. She made us drinks and snacks. She was a lot older than my mum, and I noticed there was no man about the house. No photos of a dad anywhere. I didn't ask, obviously.

Tammy had me lean over the bath while she washed my hair. It wasn't in need of a wash, but she insisted. We laughed when soap got into my eyes. With a towel around my head, she started to look through my makeup.

"Oh, we can use this. This needs to go in the bin."

By the time she'd finished, I had a smaller makeup bag but was assured it was all I needed.

She blended some foundation over my skin, something I didn't really wear because it felt tacky and horrid. She then pressed some powder into it. She added blusher, did my eyes, tried to attach some of her fake eyelashes but I couldn't handle them, so she resorted to mascara instead.

When she was done and I looked in the mirror, I was

surprised. I'd half expected to look like a clown, but I didn't. I also looked way older than I was.

"Hair now," she said.

She foamed some mousse in her hand and scrunched it into my hair. Immediately, my curls bounced up and I hated them.

"Honestly, your hair is lovely. This is way better than a frizzy ponytail," she said.

I held my head upside down while she dried it using the diffuser. When done, I stood in front of her mirror.

"Bloody hell," I said. I looked so different.

While she did her makeup and hair, I changed out of my school uniform. I had jeans and a tight white T-shirt.

"You need some fake tits," she said, rifling through her underwear drawer.

"No, I totally draw the line at that," I said, laughing.

I'd had a great time and even though I knew Tammy didn't like Sam, I didn't know why, I saw us becoming good friends.

It was nearly seven when Sam came to collect us. He had Karl in the car with him. Us girls slid into the back and Sam looked at me in the rear-view mirror.

"How does she look?" Tammy asked, and I blushed.

"She's beautiful with or without makeup," he said, and I blushed further.

Karl handed back a bottle. I saw a vodka label but knew it wasn't neat.

"Vodka and Coke," Tammy said, taking the bottle from him and swigging from it.

She handed it to me. I looked up and saw Sam shake his head at me. It was very gentle and subtle.

"I'm good, thanks. Don't want to ruin this lipstick," I said, laughing. Thankfully, she didn't pressure me.

We went back to Karl's house. He lived with his parents in a wealthy part of town. He had a swimming pool in the back garden and a pool house that he seemed to live in. His mum kissed Tammy on the cheek and welcomed me to her house. She told us she was off out and there were beers in the fridge.

Sam grabbed two beers, one for him and Karl, and a can of Coke for me. Tammy still swigged from the bottle. Since it was a warm evening, we sat outside the pool house. It wasn't warm enough for a swim, and I was grateful.

Sam sat on a lounger and pulled me down to sit on his lap. I stretched my legs out inside his and he wrapped his arms around me.

Karl and Tammy argued over the vodka.

"Do you mind if I smoke?" Sam asked over my shoulder.

"No, of course not."

He reached over to a small table and opened a tin. He pulled out a spliff and lit it. He made an effort to blow the smoke away from me. After a few puffs, he handed it to Karl, who did the same, and he handed it to Tammy. I was intrigued. She looked at Sam and he shook his head. She gave it back to him. I guessed she'd wanted to ask if I was to have it. They did another round before it died out. Karl put some music on his record player in the pool house and we chilled out. Sam rested back and I leaned into his chest. Tammy and I chatted. We giggled and I found I was as ravenous as they were. I was light-headed. We tucked into crisps and chocolate.

"You're stoned, baby," Sam said, when I said I felt funny.

"I didn't smoke it."

"You would have breathed it in. I should have made you sit away from us for a little while." He hugged me tighter.

"I'm not a child," I said indignantly.

He chuckled. "When you're ready," he whispered, and I was starting to dislike those words.

He checked his watch and I sighed, knowing it was probably my time to leave. I didn't want to.

"Come on," he said, leaning forwards and I laughed, refusing to move.

He bit my neck, sucking on the skin, leaving a mark, and I yelped. I got up quickly then. I said my goodbyes and we left.

"Are you okay to drive?" I asked. They'd only shared the one joint, and he'd drank one beer, but I wasn't sure.

"Of course. Baby, I wouldn't put you in any danger." I liked that he called me baby.

Before we got into the car, he pulled me close. He wiped his thumbs under my eyes and then across my lips.

"You don't need this shit on your face," he said. "Unless you want to wear it, of course. You're beautiful enough without it."

I wrapped my arms around his neck. "I like it, but maybe not as heavy," I said honestly. My cheeks were beginning to feel tacky.

He smiled and nodded. Then he kissed me. I pressed myself

against him and he fisted my hair. He pulled and I moaned as my body was flooded with want for him.

"You like that, huh?" he whispered, breaking our kiss briefly.

I nodded and he pulled more. I was looking up at him and, although his pupils were small, the irises had darkened. He licked his lower lip, drawing it in his mouth and biting down on it. My legs shivered.

"I want to come again," I said, my voice cracking.

He closed his eyes and took in a deep breath. "You're going to be the death of me."

His kiss was fierce, so much so my lip bled. I ground myself against him, wanting the friction of his hard cock teasing me. He tasted of beer and dope, and it was heady.

I was bitterly disappointed, to the point I groaned and stamped my foot, when he gently pushed me away. He chuckled.

"When the time comes, when I fuck you, Hayley, you're going to come again and again."

He opened the car door for me, I doubled over holding my stomach.

"God, that is so fucking unfair," I said, stamping my feet again. He laughed and slapped my arse to get me in the car. "And I like that as well," I said, poking my tongue out at him.

He blinked a few times and grabbed for me. I laughed and fought him off. "No. Remember, *when I'm ready*."

"You really are gonna be the fucking death of me."

He slammed the car door shut and walked around the

front. I watched him, he stared at me. He continued to look at me while he turned the car on.

"There are things I want to teach you," he said quietly.

I swear I could smell myself. It was that same coppery scent he had on his fingers. I knew that to be arousal.

I nodded, and my stomach flipped. He was way more experienced than I was, obviously. And I wanted him to teach me everything. I wanted to be exactly what he needed as well.

By the time we got to my house, my dad was pulling on the drive. He worked the night shift usually, but often popped home when it was quiet for dinner with my mum.

"Fuck," I said, checking my face in the mirror in the sun visor. I grabbed a tissue from my bag and wiped away most of the makeup.

Dad stood by the front door, waiting for me. Sam got out and walked around to my door. He opened it and held out his hand for me to climb out.

"I'm sorry, I've got her home late. We were at a friends' and lost track of time," Sam said.

Dad just nodded. He looked between us. "Oh, come on, Dad," I said. "Quit with the gangster shit."

Dad laughed and beckoned us both in. "Gotta frighten the life out of this one, haven't I?" he said.

When we walked into the lounge Mum was there. She screeched and hid something behind her back.

"What's that?" I asked. Dad laughed.

"Something for your birthday," she said, and I cringed.

"It's your birthday?" Sam asked.

"She'll be sixteen next month. We're having a party for her if you want to come," Mum said.

I couldn't look at him.

"Mind you, that's if she stops playing hooky at school," Dad added.

I cringed some more. All I could do was look at my feet. The room went silent.

"Did I say something wrong?" Mum asked.

Finally, I looked up at him. He was staring at me. He then turned to my dad, and I knew it was going to be bad.

"She told me she was already sixteen. I'm sorry."

Dad frowned and opened his mouth to speak. His face was like thunder, such was his anger. Mum got up from the floor and stood beside him, her hand on his arm.

Sam turned to me. "Are you skipping school?"

I nodded. "I hate it. I'd rather be with you," I blurted out.

He raised his face to the ceiling and sighed heavily. "And you told me you were sixteen already. Do you know how much trouble I could get in?" He wasn't shouting, but there was an angry tone to his voice.

I looked over to my dad. He didn't defend me. Tears brimmed in my eyes, spilling over. Mum rushed to me.

Sam turned to my dad. "I'm in love with your daughter. So here's the deal, if you agree." He then turned back to me. "I'm not going to see you until you're sixteen, but if I hear you're still skipping school, I'm not coming back, even then. I'll call you, you call me, every night, but nothing more."

His voice shook a little, and I knew it was hard for him to say what he had.

It was even harder for me to hear it.

I screamed, letting the tears flow. "No, Sam. No. Don't do this to me."

I rushed forward and felt my mum's arms around my chest.

"Shush, baby, this is good, trust me," she whispered.

It wasn't. I wriggled in her arms reaching out to him. He stared at me, he looked pained.

"I love you," I said. "Please don't do this."

"One month, Hayley, that's all," he said. He then turned back to my dad. "In one month, I'll be back for her. I hope it's with your blessing."

My dad didn't answer, they just stared at each other.

"Dad, please!" I begged, sobbing.

Slowly, he nodded. "I appreciate what you've done here tonight. When she's sixteen she can choose. Until then, stay away. You can call her, but if I found you've met up..." Dad then looked to me. "I'll drag you away from here."

I cried.

Sam left.

I didn't see him again for one agonising month, but I did keep in contact.

Tammy would bring letters into school from him and take them back from me. He called in the evenings, every evening, to wish me a good night and I was often left in tears.

I hated it. I couldn't eat. I went back to the frizzy ponytail, and I cried in my mum's arms. I lived and slept in his sweatshirt, not allowing my mum to wash it.

"I love him, he loves me, you heard him. I don't get this."

"You lied to him, darling. He could have just walked away, but he hasn't."

That one month felt like a fucking year. The night before my sixteenth party, it changed.

"Will you come to my party?" I asked him.

"Yes, your dad gave me the details. I can't get there when it starts, but I'll be there later."

I spent ages getting ready for my party. I had my nails done, my hair cut and curled. My mum had a professional makeup artist come over and we'd shopped for the perfect outfit. I was a bag of nerves. Not for my party, but to see Sam.

Dad drove us to the hall, and I'd snuck a bag in the boot of clothes to change into. Jeans and Sam's sweatshirt, my trainers, and the packet of contraceptive pills I'd been prescribed when mum had taken me to the doctor's.

That hadn't been as ghastly as I'd thought, we talked about my options, and a pill chosen. Easy. Unbeknown to my mum, I also grabbed a handful of condoms on the way out. They sat in my bag as well.

I was pleased to see Tammy and Karl mostly. I didn't invite many people from school, just them and the few girls I sat with at lunch, her friends. The rest were family and close friends. People shouted, balloons fell from the ceiling, and the small kids spent the next half hour stamping on them. There was a large table with an amazing cake, two tiers and with horses on the top grazing on the icing. Next to it, was a table of presents.

Mum and Dad had given me a gorgeous watch. Dad had joked it was so I could know when curfew was without asking. I hoped he was joking. I had money, and some new things for the horses.

I mingled, always coming back to Tammy, though. I clock watched constantly.

Mum bought me champagne and then I was allowed that elusive vodka and Coke. I didn't really like it and was thankful for that.

"He's definitely coming, isn't he?" I asked for the thousandth time.

"Yes. He's working right now. He'll be here." Karl said. I never got to ask what he was doing so late before another cousin pulled me up for a dance.

It was getting closer to ten in the evening and my mood was slipping. I kept a fake smile on, but inside I was dying. I had expected him way before then. He'd missed my birthday, really. People were calling for me to cut my cake and reluctantly, I did. I held back the tears as I scanned the crowd before taking the knife from my mum and slicing.

"He's not coming, is he?" I asked Tammy.

"Yes, he said he was. He wouldn't let you down, Hals. I don't know why he's so late, though."

She looked to Karl, who shrugged his shoulders. I wondered if the hall had a telephone they'd let me borrow to call his house.

It was worse when the DJ started to play slow music. Tammy dragged Karl up and I was left standing alone and feeling utterly dejected. It was only when a neighbour's son started to walk over to me that I fled. I ran to the door, needing some fresh air, and straight into his chest.

"Happy birthday," he said, holding me. I slumped against his chest and cried. I buried my face and wrapped my arms around him.

"I didn't think you were coming," I said, sniffing.

"I'm so sorry, baby, I'm late. I got held up, then got a fucking puncture."

I noticed his dirty hands and nodded.

I could hear people asking who he was behind me. He nuzzled my neck and whispered, "Can we get out of here? It's been too long."

I stepped back and looked up at him. I stood on tiptoes and kissed him, not caring who saw us. It was a brief kiss, of course, I wouldn't disrespect my parents with a full-on French kiss, but it was enough to have my stomach fluttering.

My dad walked over. He held his hand out to Sam, who took it.

"You take care of my girl. Anything happens to her, you step up, or I hunt you down," he said.

"I can tell you now, whatever happens, I'm by her side. And I'm not stupid. She needs to get through sixth form and then college. I'll ensure that happens."

Mum joined us.

"I want to leave with him," I said to her. She cocked her

head to one side and placed her hand on my cheek. I was shaking. Behind us, half the hall was oblivious, the rest were staring in wonderment.

"Be safe." She then turned to my dad. "Can I have the keys?"

Dad handed over the car keys and Mum walked with us outside. I held on to Sam's hand for dear life. Mum popped the boot and pulled out the small bag I'd placed in there. She then handed me another. A small pink paper bag.

"Open it later. We'll see you tomorrow," she said.

I blinked. She was giving me permission to stay out all night. I hugged her. Sam took the bags and we left.

We didn't speak at first, not until we were both in the car. Then he turned to me. "That was the fucking hardest four weeks of my life. No more lies, Hals, ever."

"I'm sorry," I said, hiccupping my words.

He took my hand in his and brought it to his lips. "Let's go home, shall we?"

CHAPTER 7

The Past

The closer we got, the more nervous I felt, and the quieter I became. I knew what I wanted that night, I hoped he wanted the same. We parked and, as usual, he opened the door for me. He took my hand and left the bags. He kept hold of my hand all the time. When we reached his bedroom, he turned to face me.

He cupped my face with his hands and just stared. Eventually, he leaned down for a kiss. It was gentle and loving, even if I wanted more.

"Slowly," he whispered, pulling back.

He held my shoulders and turned me. He then unzipped my dress and it fell to the floor. I stepped out of it. He kissed across my shoulders and down my spine, unclipping my bra at the same time. My legs began to shake, and I became breathless. He kissed back up my spine until he was standing tall again.

Sam reached around and cupped my breasts. He rubbed his

palms over my nipples, and they hardened instantly. My stomach was in knots. He slid his hands down my side until he reached my hips. There, he grabbed the edge of my knickers and lowered. I whimpered when he kissed the cheek of my arse on the way.

I was a bundle of nerves and static. My legs and hands visibly shook, and my teeth chattered. My skin was pimpled with goosebumps and my cheeks flamed.

"I'm ready," I said quietly.

"I know."

"I've been taking the Pill for a month now."

He lifted me up and placed me on the bed. His hands slid down my legs and he removed my high-heeled shoes. I lay totally naked, and he stood at the end of the bed. He smiled, looking me up and down. I made no attempt to cover myself that time.

He pulled his T-shirt over his head, and I admired his toned stomach. I raised myself on my elbows and he kicked off his trainers and unzipped his jeans. Before he lowered them, he hopped from foot to foot to remove socks and I chuckled. I became all serious again when he walked to the side of the bed. His jeans were undone, and I stared at a trail of light hair that ran from below his belly button down. I kept my focus there as he lowered his jeans and my breath caught in my throat as his cock sprang free.

My eyes widened at the sight of a piercing in the top of his cock, and it was his turn to chuckle. He climbed on the bed beside me. I reached out for him, wanting to touch first. He lay on his back, and I traced tattoos on his chest. He had another piercing through his nipple, and I ran my finger over it. His nipple also hardened. I ran my hand down his stomach and hesitated.

"Only do what you want to do," he whispered.

"I want to touch you. I don't know how," I replied, aware my voice was hitching with fear.

He placed his hand over mine and lowered it. My palm brushed over the top of his cock, it was hot and wet, and I felt the steel bar cross my skin. He then guided my hand down his shaft. I clasped and we slid our hands up and down. I watched as his thumb ran over the tip, spreading his wetness. When he took his hand away, I continued. I loved the feel of him. I loved more that he sighed and smiled. He placed one arm around the back of my neck, holding my head with his palm, and I noticed the other grip the bedding.

When I sped up a little, his hand closed in my hair, pulling it. I was as aroused as he was. I stroked his cock, copying what he had done, catching the piercing once and causing him to wince, and then chuckle.

"Careful," he said quietly.

I started to lower my head to his cock. I wanted to taste him. As Mum had said, some of what I thought I wanted to do felt instinctive. I opened my mouth and darted out my tongue. At first, I licked over the head of his cock, then down the sides, over my own hand and to his balls.

"Jesus," he said between gritted teeth, and I wondered if I'd hurt him. I paused.

"Don't stop," he said.

That spurred me on. I closed my lips over his cock and sucked. I thought I was doing okay until he raised his hips. I pulled my head back, coughing and spluttering.

He laughed again. "I guess we have to work on your gag reflex." He pulled my head back up to his.

I was disappointed I hadn't done a good enough job but parked that thought when he kissed me hard. He rolled us over, so I was on my back, and he was to my side. His hands slid over my stomach, and I parted my legs. I placed my hand on his and felt his laugh as I pushed his hand down to my pussy. I didn't want him teasing, I wanted his fingers inside me.

It didn't take long for those feelings to overwhelm me. I panted, I moaned, even squealed. When he removed his fingers, I protested. That was until he silenced me by placing those fingers in my mouth. I wasn't sure at first. It wasn't an unpleasant taste, but it was more the thought of it. That *stuff* had come from inside my pussy.

However, I wanted to do whatever he wanted me to.

When he moved to cover my body, I swallowed hard. A pang of anxiety hit me in the chest, and I had to take in a deep breath.

"Okay?" he asked, and I nodded.

He felt between us, and his cock nudged at my entrance.

"It might sting," he said. All I could do was nod in return.

I was ready, I knew I was. I was scared also.

He was so gentle, pushing into me little by little, encouraging me to take deep breaths, and when he was fully in, he stilled.

I felt a fullness that I liked. It was odd, heat and throbbing increased as he gently rocked inside me. He moved so slowly; I hadn't noticed at first. He sped up slightly, and when I exhaled a sigh, he sped up some more.

I opened my legs farther, pulling my knees up and letting them fall to the side. I felt him more. I wrapped my arms around his body and arched my back a little. I moaned and panted, my mouth dry.

A few minutes more, and he was rocking hard into me. I loved it. I could feel wetness seeping from me. I hooked my heels over his thighs, lifting my arse off the bed. I wanted him deeper.

His face was in my neck, and he chuckled. His lips trailed up to mine. "All in good time," he whispered against my skin.

I wasn't sure how long it was, but he stopped, pulled out, and spurted his cum over my stomach. At first, I wasn't sure I liked that, but then, the thought of something so intimate on my skin pleased me. He lowered himself back down for a kiss.

We dozed for a little while after Sam wiped my stomach with a tissue. He ran his fingers up and down my stomach. I couldn't wipe the smile of my face.

"For a first time, that was good," I said, rolling to my side and placing my hand on his stomach.

"And it will only get better. That was just for starters, get you ready, so to speak," he said.

We did it again for a second time, and that one was very

different. He was harder and faster. He made me come, and when he did so, it was inside me.

At some point, Sam had retrieved my bag from the car. He handed me the small pink one and I looked at him, my brow furrowed. I delved inside to find a box. When I opened it, I took out a silver chain bracelet. There was a ruby in the middle, my birthstone.

"This is from me," he said, clasping it around my wrist. "I gave it to your mum to look after in case I forgot to bring it to your party."

I loved it so much, immediately.

It was a balmy night and I'd managed to sleep a little. I woke to an empty bed. I climbed out, naked, and walked into the living room. Sam sat in just shorts on the windowsill. He was smoking a joint.

"Can I try?" I asked.

He held out his hand and I walked forwards. I stepped between his legs, letting the cool breeze of the evening waft over me. He placed one hand on my hip and raised the joint to his lips. He took in a drag and then leaned closer. He opened his mouth and let the smoke swirl from it. Our lips were just a few centimetres apart and I breathed in deep. He closed that gap and while he kissed me his lungs emptied into mine. I exhaled through my nose.

My head swam and my heart raced. I wasn't sure whether that was the cannabis or him.

While he kissed me, I reached between us and freed his cock from his shorts. I wanted to try oral again. I lowered to my knees and sucked his cock into my mouth. I still gagged, but I was able to breathe through it. When he came into my mouth, however, he was left in fits of laughter as I heaved and spat it out.

"Yeah, maybe not ready for that just yet," he said.

* * *

"I don't want to go home," I said, whining as I dressed.

It was midday and Sam had insisted I should be with my parents to open my gifts. I hadn't been told what time to return, but I also knew I should be doing the horses as well.

When I did get home, Sam was welcomed in. Mum kept staring at me and smiling, and I wondered if she knew, could she tell what we'd done. I know I felt different.

We opened my presents, and I received some lovely gifts from friends and family. Mum offered to make a sandwich. She chuckled at his choice. His favourite, ham and crisps on white bread, with a mug of hot chocolate. He then took me to the stables, and I rode while he watched.

"I'm sore," I said, every time I passed him and winced. He laughed. "I need to sit on ice."

"I have something here you can sit on," he called out and it was my turn to laugh.

"I'll hold you to that."

"When you're..."

"Ready," I shouted, passing him again.

We put the horses to bed and sat on the bales for a little

while. It was another hot night, and I was tired. I climbed onto his lap, straddling him, he held my hips. We kissed.

"Did you mean what you said to my dad?" I asked quietly.

He stared directly at me. "Yes. I also meant what I said about skipping school."

"Why is that so important to you?" I asked.

He sighed and ran his nose over mine. "I didn't go to school, but I was lucky. I was taken on as an apprentice. Now I own the business at twenty."

"I thought you were nineteen," I asked, confused.

"It was my birthday a week before yours."

"Oh no. I missed it!" I felt awful.

"There'll be others. I don't celebrate it anyway."

"Why?"

He didn't speak immediately. "Because it was the same day I found my deadbeat dad with a bag over his head and a pile of drugs by his side. He was dead."

I had no words, but tears sprang to my eyes.

"Don't cry for him, Hals."

"I'm not, I'm crying for you."

I kissed him as passionately as I could with my limited experience. I wanted to take the hurt from his eyes. I'd seen it. I'd witnessed the fleeting pain flash across his face, causing his brow to frown and his eyes to close. He'd swallowed hard, forcing down the emotion.

"Anyway, I only own the business because I got lucky. The man, who took me on and straightened me out, started the garage years ago. I've worked for him since I was fourteen and kicked out of school."

"Where is he now?"

"Died of a heart attack a few years ago."

Everyone he loved was dead, I thought. His mum, the garage man. It didn't seem he'd loved his dad, however, but how he found him must have affected him. It was no wonder he'd gone off the rails.

"Time I got you home. I have to work later. I'll be back in the morning to take you to school."

"What do you do in the evenings?" I asked, hanging on while he stood and carried me.

"Repair race bikes at a track. Sometimes I race as well."

"Oh, I didn't know that." Why didn't I know that?

"I thought I'd told you."

"What else don't I know?" I asked as he plonked my arse on the bonnet of his car.

"Erm, I don't know what you don't know."

I squinted at him. "That's evasive."

He opened the car door. "Get in," he said, kissing my temple as I passed.

I slipped into the seat, and he leaned down. "There are things you don't know about me, Hayley, but you will. All in good time, when—"

I grabbed the car handle and pulled the door shut!

He laughed as he walked around to the driver's side. He took me home and I clung to him at the front door. I didn't want to go back to reality.

He called me at half ten and we had a brief chat, he bid me a goodnight and we arranged a time to meet in the morning.

Mum came into my bedroom as I was getting into my PJs. She sat on the bed and looked at me.

"What?" I asked.

"You look different."

I sat beside her. "I feel different."

"We're you safe?"

I nodded. Had we been? The doctor had said to wait four weeks before sex and it had been.

"Were you pressured into anything you didn't want to do?" she asked.

"No. He says... He says we can only do *things* when he knows I'm ready." I stumbled through my words.

Mum patted my leg. "Then he's a better man than your dad was at the same time."

We laughed and she kissed me goodnight.

"My baby, a young woman now," she said, as she closed the bedroom door behind her.

CHAPTER 8

The Past

E ach day Sam took me to school. He didn't always pick me up, however, it depended on his work schedule. If he wasn't overly busy, he'd pick me up as well. I spent all lunch breaks with Tammy and the girls, and we laughed and talked sex. I appreciated they didn't patronise me. They accepted I was younger and way more naïve than them. They answered some of my questions, they encouraged me to speak to my mum or Sam on others.

He came to the stables with me and then we either went back to his, or he was allowed to sit in my bedroom with me while I did homework. Of course, I didn't think the *homework* I was doing was the same kind my parents thought it was.

Soon enough it was summer break, and I couldn't wait. I'd sat my exams, I thought I'd scrape through what I needed to start a business course in sixth form and had the whole summer with Sam.

"Can I come to work with you tomorrow?" I asked.

We were lying on his bed with all the windows open.

"You'll be bored, but haven't you got to look after your brother?"

The one thing I hated about school holidays was my parents still worked so I babysat. Sometimes, Mum would take him with her, but he didn't want to be in her office all day.

"Only for the morning, then he's going to my nan's. I can get a bus down."

He brushed his lips over my shoulder and down my arm.

"If your mum says it's okay, then... Okay," he replied, chuckling.

Getting to his garage was easy on the public transport. I'd often get the bus to the shopping centre near him. Tammy and I planned to go shopping one day.

He rolled to his back and pulled me on top of him. I'd discovered I loved riding him. In fact, there was a lot I was discovering I loved.

"No, I want something else," I said, still finding it hard to actually ask for what I wanted. I slid my leg over him and turned away. I was on all fours, and I wanted him behind me.

When I did this, Sam changed. He became more dominant, he pulled my hair, forcing my head up, and that alone had me wet for him. He chuckled and kneeled up.

Sam taught me a lot about sex, my likes and dislikes. He encouraged me to explore my body and his. Jokingly, he'd tell me he'd taught me all I knew, and he had. I knew nothing about men before him. I knew nothing about my own body, and how if felt internally, before him.

While he fucked me, I teased myself.

"Save that for me," Sam growled, and the fact I could get him so aroused gave me such a sense of power.

Before he came, he pulled out and slid down the bed. I straddled his head, leaning over him to suck his cock. I was beginning to love the taste of him and his tongue inside me would bring me to an orgasm alone.

According to Sam, my body was very reactive. I had no one to compare him to, of course, and I'd have pangs of jealously knowing he'd made love to other girls. He wouldn't use those words. He'd say he fucked others but made love to me.

He made me feel like a princess. Like there was no other in the world who compared to me. He put me on a pedestal and kept me there. I fell deeper and deeper in love with him.

"Come on!" I said, shouting up the stairs for my brother.

My nan had arrived and was waiting for him, he was staying with her for a few days. Each holiday we'd do that, but that time I couldn't leave Sam, Nan understood. We'd written back and forth about mine, and her, first love. Sam was yet to meet my extended family, but it would be soon. My granddad was hitting a milestone birthday and there had been a surprise party organised for him. Poor Sam would get to meet *all* my family in one go.

As soon as I waved Nan off, I grabbed my bag and door key and set off. I walked to the bus stop. A couple of boys in a car pulled up and catcalled me. I ignored them. I was called a fucking bitch, a stuck-up whore, and spat at. I recognised one of them, he lived nearby. They drove off but I was left a little upset. When the bus came, I scuttled on and sat at the front to be close to the driver.

It only took a half an hour to get to the last stop, and I disembarked. I stopped at a sandwich shop to grab Sam and myself some lunch. I hadn't told him I was doing that.

When I walked into the garage, music was blaring. Sam was in the pit under a car and he had his overalls on. Because it was hot, the top was off and tied around his waist. He wore just a white vest. Well, a dirty, oil-stained vest.

"Hey, baby," he said, when he saw me.

He climbed from the pit and put down his spanner. He slipped off the plastic gloves and cupped my face for a kiss.

"I bought us lunch," I said, holding up the carrier bag.

"Great, I'm fucking starving."

I followed him into his office and sat on the leather sofa. He peeled off his overalls and pulled on some jeans.

"You didn't need to do that," I said, licking my lips.

He leaned down to kiss me again. "I've created a sex monster," he said, and then took a bite from the sandwich I held.

"No crisps?" he said, feigning shock.

I held up a packet of plain crisps. He took the sandwich and filled it with the snack before devouring it. He made me a coffee and sat beside me while I ate.

"Karl has invited us to a party on Saturday, at his."

"That's nice, are we going?" I asked.

"Sure, but there might be some people I don't like. If they turn up, we'll leave, is that okay?"

"Of course." I frowned at him. "We don't have to go to start with if you don't want to."

He sipped his coffee, wincing as the hot liquid burnt his lips. "I'll decide nearer the time."

I smiled at him, wondering what on earth that was about.

"Do you have any customers coming?" I asked.

He leaned towards me. "Why?"

"Because this sofa is rather comfortable. I thought you might like to take a nap."

"Take a nap?"

"That's code for have sex with me."

He laughed. "Did you close the door behind you?" he asked.

"Yes." The small door in the larger roller doors had been open when I arrived. I'd shut it behind me.

"Then get naked, baby," he said.

I put my sandwich down and we both scrambled out of our clothes. It was quick and fast, hard and delicious.

No matter where we were, I was hot for him. I wanted him constantly. I had to check myself sometimes because I was sure I was getting suffocating. I felt so insecure at times, worried he would leave me, despite his constant assurance he wouldn't.

Once we dressed, he continued with his work, and I sat reading. I answered his phone and booked in some jobs. I called home just to leave a message on the answerphone and let my parents know I was 'working.' I felt so very grown-up.

"If you sort that filing, I'll pay you a half-day wage," Sam said, laughing as he watched me clear his desk.

"You can pay me in sex," I offered, smiling sweetly at him.

He stepped closer to me. "What have I unleashed, huh?" he said, kissing the side of my neck.

"No idea, but I fucking love it."

He laughed and slapped my arse. "And I love that," I said as he walked back into the garage.

The radio blasted and I worked away. I filed everything, tutting he couldn't even grasp the alphabet. I made a pile of bills that sat in the 'to pay' tray so the oldest was at the top. I wrote out cheques and pinned them to each one, ready for signing.

Administration was easy, and fun, and I wondered if secretarial work would suit me. I could imagine sitting in this office in my smart clothes, having sex at lunchtime instead of food. I chuckled to myself.

"Are these invoices?" I waved.

By then, Sam was out of the pit and the car he was working on had been moved to rollers. He looked over at the scraps of paper.

"Yeah, need typing up," he said.

I loaded headed paper in the typewriter and copied a couple

of old invoices I'd found. I wasn't sure on numbering and laughed at his answer when I asked.

"Just make them up," he said.

I guessed admin wasn't his thing.

I swept and washed down the sofa and kitchenette areas, bleached the disgusting tea-stained cups and teaspoons. Removed clumps of coffee from the sugar, and then said I was popping to the shops. I returned quickly with some new mugs, a mug stand, a clean kettle, and tea towels. I also bought a sugar, tea, and coffee pot. I felt like I was 'homemaking' in his office.

"Wow, you can come again," Sam said, walking to the sink to wash his oily hands.

"And again, and again. You should use the bathroom to wash your hands," I replied.

He gave me a brief kiss then continued to wash his hands. He smothered them in a green gunk to remove the oil. When done, he held them up.

"Clean enough?" he said, and I stepped towards him.

I pretended to inspect his hands. His palms were rough, proper working man's hands as my dad would have called them. I loved the feel of them on my skin.

He locked up and we walked, hand in hand, to a local pub. He bought himself a beer and me a vodka and Coke.

"I don't think we should go to Karl's party," he said.

"Okay, that's fine with me."

"I had a fight with some guy and got arrested. I can't go within so many feet of him and I think he's going to be there."

"Oh, okay. Isn't Karl your friend? Why would he invite this bloke?"

"Because this bloke is his brother," he said, laughing.

"What did you fight over?"

"He was a dick to his girlfriend; I didn't like it. I beat the shit out of him, put him in the hospital, his dad called the police."

"But his mum was okay with you?" I said, remembering the time we'd been there.

"His dad lives with someone else. He's a prick as well. So, we'll skip it, yeah?"

"Totally fine with me."

"Anyway, I'm going to take you out to dinner."

I smiled. It would be the first time we'd gone out to dinner, and I checked my watch.

"I'll need to get going then. I have the horses, and then I have to get ready."

"We'll go do the horses, then you can get ready at mine."

I nodded and downed my drink.

As usual, he held my hand on the drive home. I'd look out the window as we slowed in traffic and passed people standing at bus stops. I wondered what they thought when they saw us. Young love, perhaps?

Sam pulled onto the drive behind my mum's car. I didn't wait for him to open the door for me, opting to do it myself. He tutted. He was that man who moved me to the inside of the pavement when we walked, who opened the door for me, stepping in behind me while keeping his hand on my back for guidance. Despite being only twenty in years, he was way older in his manner. I wondered if his mum had taught him to be the man he was. Despite his fights, he was *my* gentleman, for sure.

I rushed upstairs, leaving Sam chatting with my mum. Once changed, I joined them.

"Maybe tomorrow we can spend some time together," Mum said, and I looked between them. Sam was smiling.

"Okay. Have I done anything wrong?" I asked, my voice getting small.

"No, honey. I just don't get to see you anymore. I've got some time off work, we can go shopping, get our hair and nails done, girly things."

"Oh yes! Definitely."

"And I do want you home tonight, darling."

I deflated a little. It seemed staying overnight with Sam at the weekends was okay but not so much in the week, even though I didn't have school.

I nodded and handed Sam my bag of clothes. "We're going out to dinner," I said.

"Sam told me. Have a nice time and I'll see you later."

We left and while in the car I turned to him. "What was that all about?"

"Your mum thinks we're spending a lot of time together and the horses are getting neglected, for one."

"Well, one of them is her horse that she has abandoned," I said, pouting and crossing my arms.

"She has a point, Hals."

"You think we're spending too much time together?" I asked, panic flooded my voice.

"No, I'd spend every minute of the day with you, but you're sixteen. You need to do things away from me, experience life. We have a lifetime together."

"But what if I'm happy not 'experiencing life?' What if the life I want to experience is right here with you?"

He took hold of my hand and glanced at me briefly. "We'll figure it out."

We spent an hour at the stables. And I was concerned I was neglecting them. Not in the sense they weren't getting fed and watered, they were. But I wasn't spending as much time with them as I normally would. Perhaps there was a compromise to be had and I started to plan.

We headed back to Sam's, and we took a bath together. It was a tight fit, but we'd laughed as the water sploshed over the side. Having sex in a bath full of water wasn't the easiest either, but we managed it.

"We need a shower," he said, and I swelled at the 'we.'

The restaurant we headed to was a small Italian bistro. Sam seemed to know what to order, other than pizza or lasagne, I had no idea. He ordered for me. He also added a bottle of wine and a bottle of beer. I wasn't a great wine drinker, but this was a proper date, and I was going to make the most of it.

I had a lovely seafood pasta dish and garlic bread; he ordered steak and chips. I'd laughed, we were at an Italian restaurant, and he'd ordered the same food we could get at the local pub.

Sam liked what he liked. He wasn't academic at all, but

streetwise. He had grown up with a mother who bought his dope for him and let him come and go as he pleased. He fought, a lot, and he worked hard. More than anything, he cared for me with such passion. I was his queen, he'd tell me. I'd been promoted from princess, apparently. It was me and him. Him and me. Only, and forever.

CHAPTER 9

The Past

"How about this?" my mum said, holding up a dress.

"Oh, I like that." I grabbed the tag and looked. "I can't afford that," I replied, laughing.

Sam had given me fifty pounds to clothes shop. It was a vast amount of money then. He'd said part of it was 'wages,' and the rest he just wanted me to treat myself. I also had my holiday money. I was great at saving, each time I was given money, half would go into my savings account.

Sometimes, my mum and dad would add to it. I had a nice sum of money growing. I had no idea what I wanted to spend it on, perhaps a car when I could drive. Or a house if the pot ever got big enough for a deposit.

"I'll get this for you," she said.

She added the floating sundress to her basket.

I grabbed a pair of flip-flops and some new underwear. The

kind I didn't want my mum to see, so I buried them under a new T-shirt.

I made sure to go to a different till and once our items were bagged up, we headed off for lunch.

"Can we talk about you and Sam?" she said, spearing a prawn from her salad bowl.

I had been waiting for this conversation all morning. I nodded.

"Do you think you're spending a lot of time with him? Maybe to the exclusion of everything and everyone else?"

I smiled sadly at her. "Yes. I knew you would bring this up. I can't tell you how I feel about him. I don't know the proper words. But I feel like I can't breathe without him. My chest hurts at night if I'm not with him. I know I'm obsessed; Tammy tells me that, but I want to be."

She nodded. "I can understand that, darling. I felt the same way about your dad. But Tammy isn't right. You're not *obsessed*, this if your first love. But there is a risk this will burn out. He might feel suffocated at some point. You might change as you get older and drift away from him, and that's going to leave him high and dry because you've consumed all his time and he could lose his friends."

I hadn't thought about that. He hadn't seen Karl for a while, and I know Tammy said Karl had mentioned that.

"Can I propose something?" I asked.

"This isn't a business meeting, but go on," she replied, chuckling.

"What if I don't see him every day, but every other, and I can stay with him overnight those days and the weekend?"

"Assuming he is happy with that, I'd need to speak to your dad. What about the horses, darling? You had a competition you didn't get to."

I sighed. "I know. I love them. I'll make a point of picking back up there, I promise."

She nodded. "You need space to grow, Hals. Space to discover who you are without any influence. I just don't want to see you stifled in any way. And I'm not saying Sam's doing that, you're doing that to yourself."

I blinked back tears, and she reached out to hold my hand. I smiled. "Period coming, ignore me," I said.

"Well, I'm sure glad it is coming and not the alternative!"

"Mum!" We laughed. "I love you, Mum," I added.

"Good, but I'm not old enough to be a grandmother just yet."

We continued to eat and talk, then we headed to the hair salon. My hair was waist-length, brown with a reddish tint, and super curly. I'd began to love it, although it was hard work, and I wondered why I'd hated my curls for so many years. More so, Sam loved it. He loved to close his fist in my hair and pull back my head, so I had to look at him. My stomach lurched just at the thought.

Once our hair was done, we had manicures and pedicures. Mum got her legs and bikini line waxed while I read a magazine. I wasn't brave enough for that.

When we got home, Dad said he had a surprise for me and

my brother. I was showing him my new outfits, minus the underwear, of course.

He then pulled out airline tickets for a holiday in Greece. I started to jump around and scream with happiness until it hit me. I paused, and my heart raced.

"Don't panic, there are five tickets here," he said.

I rushed over and wrapped my arms around him. "Oh God, thank you, thank you," I said.

I then ran to the phone to call Sam and tell him the news.

Of course, Sam knew before me. That had been the conversation he'd had with my mum when I was getting changed the previous day.

We spoke for a little while and then he told me he was out for a beer with Karl. I was pleased and a little jealous, of course. He chuckled and detailed what he'd do to me the following day to make it up. I still didn't have permission from my dad to spend the weekday evenings with him. It had been a blazing row, me and Mum against him, to get him to agree to the weekends.

I got it, my dad was my dad, he adored me. He didn't want to think about his baby girl sleeping with a man. In our row, I'd told them I was older than my mum had been when she lost her virginity. That had sealed the argument for me.

For the next two weeks, we fell into our new pattern, and the days I didn't see him I spent at the stables. I missed him, but the nights were the worst. After that goodnight phone call, I'd often cry myself to sleep.

I still had his sweatshirt, it had been washed, and Sam had

given me the bottle of aftershave. It sat proudly on my dressing table along with some of his other toiletries. He had clothes at my house for when he came to me straight from work and showered before we went out. He hadn't been allowed to stay overnight, however.

That came the night before the holiday.

We were leaving early in the morning. A taxi was going to collect us, so Mum suggested Sam stay over.

At first, my dad had said he was to sleep on the sofa until Mum pointed out there was nothing stopping me sneaking down, or him sneaking up. Unless he wanted to be on patrol all night, he was just to grin and bear it.

He grumbled, we laughed, I hugged him and kissed his cheek, then called Sam. He brought his case round and we all had dinner together. I loved the way Sam interacted with my parents, joked with my dad, and my brother seemed to idolise him.

We didn't have sex that night, it felt wrong in my parents' house, and Mother Nature had decided to visit. But that didn't stop Sam teasing my clitoris, fingering me. I loved he didn't care if I was on or not. My 'silent' orgasm eased my stomach cramps.

It was just messy and after seeing some blood on the sheets, I vowed to lay on a towel next time!

* * *

We had one whole week on an island off Greece together. Dad had rented a villa with a pool, and the best part was there were only three bedrooms so Sam and I shared. No mention was made of him on a sofa at all. We sunbathed a lot, we swam in the sea, went on boat trips, and sat by the pool. When my parents and brother went off sightseeing, we made love. Both indoors and in the pool. Each new experience with Sam was better than the last.

"I have a feeling we're building up to something, sexually," I said, lying on the sunbed with my eyes closed.

Sam was on the bed next to me, on his side with his hand on my stomach. We'd just gotten out of the pool after fucking again.

"And if you say, 'when I'm ready,' I'm going to throat punch you," I added.

He laughed, and then propped himself up on one elbow.

"There are things I like to do that satisfy me sexually, and I'd like for you to experience. But I don't want to rush you into them."

"Like what?" I asked, also turning on my side, curiosity running through me.

"I want to tie you up. I want you in a position so you can't move, and I can do whatever I want to you," he said, his voice lowering.

My stomach flipped.

"And?" I asked.

"I want to fuck your arse," he said.

"Ouch, not sure about that one," I replied, and he laughed. "What else?"

"I want to spank you."

"Now, I can get on board with that, for sure," I said, aware my voice had taken on a husky tone.

"Are you aroused now?" he asked.

I nodded. "Then maybe we'll try some things when we get home."

"Why not now?" I asked.

"Because if your dad found you bound, I think he'd beat the shit out of me, don't you?"

"Probably. Although, I think I'd be more scared of my mum."

"When we get home." He flipped over, lying on his back, and his erection strained against the fabric of his swimming shorts.

"I can't wait," I said, also lying back. "Also, can we drop the, 'when you're ready'? I trust you, Sam. I want to do all the things with you."

He reached over to take my hand. Since we hadn't gotten a lot of sleep that night, we dozed off, only to be woken when I heard a tinkle of laughter and woke to see my parents on sunbeds the other side of the pool.

It was idyllic. He tanned, I burned, and it was way too soon that we were packing up to leave. I wanted to shed tears and I stripped the bed for the cleaners. I wasn't going to spend every night with him anymore.

"Why are you so moody?" my brother asked as we ate our last meal on the terrace.

"I'm not, fuck off," I said, and earned a slap on my thigh from Sam.

I looked at him and scowled. Mum and Dad were in the kitchen bringing out food.

"I don't want to leave," I said quietly.

"We have all the time in the world, remember?" Sam whispered in my ear.

"I want it all now," I replied, pouting.

"You need to learn to be patient," he replied.

Our conversation ended when the food arrived.

"Sam slapped Hals," my brother blurted out. My dad half rose from his seat.

"Hold on, that's not true," I said, glaring at my brother. "I swore at this shithead and Sam *tapped* me on the leg to tell me off. No big deal," I added.

Dad slowly sat down. "Thanks, Sam, I don't want to hear her swearing."

"Neither do I," he said.

I pinched his thigh, fucking liar. He chuckled.

We arrived home and fell into bed. It was with dismay that Sam had already left by the time I woke the following morning. Mum and I walked to the yard and did the horses together, it was nice. We'd had a friend covering for the week we were away, and although she'd do the basics, she didn't clean the yard the way I liked. We rode, taking the two out of a hack around the lanes, and then turned them out. Since the weather was heating up, the horses would live out for the summer. We mucked out, removing all the straw, and then scrubbed down the rubber matting on the floor and walls. We cleaned water troughs and buckets and feed bins. I removed everything from the tack and feed shed, and we gave that a good clean as well. I was dirty and sweaty by the time we finished a few hours later.

We sat in the yard on camping chairs and drank cold drinks, admiring our spotless yard.

"I think, when I get a job, we're going to have to get a groom or move to a livery yard," I said sadly.

She nodded. "Yeah, I was thinking about that. I was also thinking Alfie might go to Henry."

I looked quickly at her. "You'd give him away?" I asked.

"Henry needs to move up to a horse now, and his family doesn't have the money to buy one. Alfie would be perfect for him."

Henry was a pony club member with me. One time, we thought we might be boyfriend and girlfriend, but I was convinced he'd rather be boyfriend and boyfriend. We'd been good friends for a long time, but I didn't see him that often. His family had moved away and, I guessed, we'd moved in different directions as well.

"I think he'll love Alfie, but Sov will be sad." Sovereign had never been on his own and I wondered how he'd fare.

"Maybe, it might be time for you to consider loaning him out. You're not doing as much with him anymore," Mum said gently.

I didn't want to give up horses, but I wanted to spend all my time with Sam. It was conflicting. I knew I'd have to decide come college because the hours were much longer than school.

"I'll have a think," I said.

By the time we'd washed up our glasses and locked up the

yard, Sam had arrived. I wasn't expecting him, but he'd decided to finish up early. It was way too hot to be under cars, he'd said.

He drove us home, Mum sat in the front and me in the back. I was glad, because I spotted a pair of my knickers on the floor and blushed. I picked them up and caught Sam glance at me in the rear-view mirror. I held them up and he chuckled. I pocketed them quickly before Mum could see.

I had a quick shower and changed. I put on a bikini and then shorts and a T-shirt. Sam had said we might go to the river. It wasn't my day to see him, but Mum waved me off after a promise to return home that night.

Locally, there was a pub next to a river with a ford. As kids, we'd been there with our parents and stood in the river waiting for cars to drive through and splash us. We'd fished for stickle-backs with nets on poles. As an adult, or rather a teen, Sam and I sat on the bank dangling our feet with a beer and vodka.

I paddled and he watched. It was also the first time I witnessed him fight.

Karl and Tammy joined us, so did a couple more of their friends. I'd met them all but there was one I wasn't comfortable with. Tammy and I sat together with another girlfriend; one I hadn't met. Her name was Sandy. She reminded me of me when I first came into the group. She was shy and wanted to cling to Harry's side all the time. We encouraged her to sit with us, slightly apart from the boys, but she constantly looked over to him.

"He isn't going anywhere," Tammy said, and I poked her subtly. It was a little harsh.

"So, where do you go to school, Sandy?" I asked.

She'd recently moved to the area and was in sixth form already. She'd done her first year and was waiting to start the second. Then she was off to university. She was super intelligent, wanting to go into medicine, and I think that was why Tammy was off with her. I liked her though.

Once she started to talk, she opened up a little. Tammy yawned and lay back on the grass. I ignored her.

It was her wide-eyed stare that puzzled me. I had my back to the boys, and she was looking over my shoulder. I turned and froze.

Sam had jumped up and had one of the lads by the throat. He punched him straight in the face. The lad punched back, catching Sam in the jaw but it didn't even rock him from his feet.

Sam punched and punched so quickly it was terrifying. I rushed to him, grabbing his T-shirt to try and pull him back. He had no idea who it was and twisted his body away. I shouted his name.

"Sam!"

He ignored me. Blood poured from a broken nose and Sam was splattered with it. He had a split lip, where the other lad had got one shot on target, but it wasn't an even fight at all.

Karl managed to separate them, and both stood panting. The place had been packed, there had been families and children who had scattered. Some stared, one man shouted at the pair, telling them what a disgrace they were, fighting like that in front of kids. I told him to fuck off, he didn't know the circum-

2

stances of the fight. Not that I did either, but I was protecting my man.

Karl walked Sam backwards and away, the other lad lay on the ground. I heard someone say an ambulance was needed, and I wanted to cry.

"Go, now," Karl said.

Without speaking, Sam grabbed my wrist and we walked to the car.

I hadn't got my seat belt in properly before we'd roared off. We didn't speak for a while, I just watched him dab at the split lip, running his tongue over it to clean up the blood, and for some reason that aroused me. It shouldn't have, and I wondered if that was part fright as well.

His knuckles were busted, bloodied, and he had a blood splatter across his cheek. I grabbed a tissue from my bag and while he focussed on the road, I cleaned his face. We pulled up at his flat and he turned the engine off. He just sat.

"Are you okay?" I asked, knowing it to be a stupid question.

He finally turned to me. His look was feverish, and my legs began to shake. He didn't see me at all. I climbed across the seat and straddled him. Holding his head between my hands, I kissed his lips gently. He dug his fingers into my hips. When I tasted his blood, I kissed him harder.

His blood smeared on my lips and then my cheek when he moved his head to kiss the side of my neck. I ground myself into him, wanting him to know how aroused I was.

I realised I wasn't aroused at the sight of him fighting, or his blood, it felt more empowering than that. I could take his mind off whatever it was that had caused the fight. I could get his focus back on me. He stared straight into my eyes, and I saw him change, his shoulders relaxed and he sighed. It was heady to know I wielded that power over him.

"Are you back with me?" I whispered, and he nodded. He rested his forehead against mine. "Want to tell me what happened?"

"Let's get in, shall we? I imagine the police will be here soon."

He opened the door, and I climbed out first.

I made him sit on the sofa and wetted a flannel in cold water. As I knelt in front of him, I gently rubbed that over his face and hands, cleaning him. I held ice to his lip to stop any swelling and I kissed him again.

He blew out a lungful of air. "His name is Ken. He's a fucking arsehole and I hate him."

"Why?"

"He slagged off my mother once and I beat the shit out of him then. When she lost all her hair from chemo, he took the piss."

"What did he say to kick you off this time?" I asked.

"He said you were fuckable and when I was done with you, he wanted a go."

My eyes widened in shock. "He said what?"

Sam just nodded. "I won't have anyone talk about you like that, ever, Hayley."

It was my turn to nod. I thought what he'd done was rather extreme, but I couldn't lie. There was a little part of me that swelled with delight and pride he'd beaten a man for me.

"Probably best just to have given him a little slap, don't you think?" I said, partly in jest.

He grabbed my wrists, pulling me towards him. "No." His pupils were back to dilated. "Are you turned on? Because I can fucking smell you."

The Sam in front of me was different, more... manly, more alpha.

He stood still holding my wrists and walked me backwards until I was against the wall. I whimpered, partly in fear, mostly in arousal.

He held my hands above my head and kissed me. His tongue demanded, claimed. He took my breath away. His lip started to bleed and that spurred him on more. My legs shook as I took everything he could give me. He ground his erection into my stomach, and I parted my legs so his thigh could press onto my crotch.

When he stopped kissing me, I was breathless. More so when he kissed and licked the skin down my neck. He nipped and it was both painful and arousing. I moaned out his name, moving my head so he could have more access. I could feel myself getting wetter and was desperate for some form of touch. I forced myself down on his thigh, needing the pressure on my clitoris to ease the ache in my stomach.

"No," he said, moving his leg back. "You only get what you want when I decide you can."

I swallowed hard.

"Please?" I whispered; my voice shook.

He winked. "Trust me," he whispered.

It was fucking agony. When he stepped away, he lowered my arms. My shoulders ached. He walked us to the bedroom and without another word he removed my clothes. He instructed me to lie on the bed and to raise my arms above my head. While I lay there, he walked to a drawer in his wardrobe. He returned with handcuffs. Except, they weren't the usual type the police would have. These were leather with a longer chain. He cuffed both wrists and raised my arms to the headboard where he hung the chain over a metal hook.

I nodded, giving him the consent he was seeking.

With both arms tied and then both ankles, I was unable to move. I could only watch as he undressed himself and closed his fist around his cock. I closed my eyes.

"Look at me!" he said, his voice harsh.

I whimpered again and tears filled my eyes. I wasn't crying because I was sad or angry but frustrated beyond belief. The need for him to touch me was so powerful. And when that need wasn't fulfilled, I wanted to thrash on the bed. I growled at him! Actually growled. I felt carnal. The want was escalating, heat was chasing ice over my skin.

He stopped playing with himself and stepped forward to the end of the bed. He knelt on it, his hands on my thighs. My skin scorched under his touch, and I lifted my arse off the bed. He buried his face in my pussy.

He licked and sucked, and what had me screaming out his name was when he held my clitoris between his teeth. He alternated the pressure, and his fingers dug into my skin. I needed the pain from his grip to stop me falling off the ledge I was balancing on.

I moaned and cried out his name. Begging for more. When I thought I was about to come, he pulled away.

"No!" I screamed out loud and was rewarded with a chuckle.

"Fucking painful, isn't it?"

I wasn't sure exactly what he was referring to but, yes, it was.

"Orgasm denial. Don't worry, you will come, and it will be the best relief you've ever felt," he said, sliding back off the end of the bed.

His mouth and chin glistened, and I wanted to lick that from him.

He walked back to the wardrobe and the drawer. He picked up a bottle of liquid he squirted over my pussy. It ran down to my arse. It cooled me, although I didn't think that was the intent. When he climbed on the bed beside me, I found out.

He ran his fingers over my opening, smearing the lubricant. I tensed as he closed in on my arse.

"Breathe," Sam said.

I nodded. I was panting like a dog, not getting enough oxygen into my system. Tears had fallen and rolled down the side of my face.

He slid one finger just inside my arse and paused. "Big breath," he said, and I complied.

I liked it, and I didn't. I wasn't sure. What I was sure of

though, was when he used his other hand to push two fingers into my pussy, I nearly leapt of the bed. Only my restraints kept me there.

It was the most delicious feeling in the world. The pressure was amazing. I felt fuller than ever before. I relaxed, which was hard considering he was inside me giving me what I wanted. And I guessed that was part of the plan. I couldn't move, I couldn't demand harder and faster, because this was new. I needed more, much, much more.

When I came, it was both powerful and painful at the same time. It was exhausting and I could feel fluid leak from me. My stomach muscles rolled with 'contractions,' and pulled at my restraints.

"You want out?" Sam said, and I shook my head.

"No, I want more!" I shouted the words at him, and he chuckled.

Being fucked while restrained was probably one of the best things. I couldn't hold him. I couldn't wrap my legs around him to encourage him deeper. All I could do was raise my hips. He nibbled on my skin, biting my nipples, taking pleasure to the brink of pain, and then bringing me back down again.

I came for a second time, and it was my first from penetrative sex. He was slow, fast, hard, deep, light, and just brushing across me. Sweat rolled from his forehead, dripping down on my skin.

I was hot, so very hot, and could taste my own sweat on my upper lip. My mouth was dry, and my voice was hoarse. I didn't think I'd cried out as much.

When he finally came, it was with some relief. I wasn't sure how much longer I could carry on. His body shuddered; he bit down hard on his split lip until blood dripped to my chest. His arms shook. He slumped down on top of me and, for a moment, just rested there.

He reached up to undo my wrist restraints and I wrapped my sore arms around him.

I cried.

He let me.

When I was spent emotionally, he slid from the bed and released my ankles. I curled into a ball on my side. He pulled a blanket from the top of the wardrobe and wrapped it around me. He sat on the edge of the bed.

"Thank you," he said. I opened my eyes to look at him. "You are so fucking amazing." He leant down to kiss my forehead. "Sleep for a little while."

I closed my eyes and felt him leave the bed. He was back in the room in about five minutes, and he picked up my arm, placing a cold flannel around my wrist. He held it there, not talking. When it warmed up, he left and returned with it freshly cooled for the other wrist. He did the same to my ankles.

The last time he came back it was with a warm flannel. He gently pulled the blanket away and encouraged me onto my back. He wiped between my legs, cleaning me. He then wrapped me back in the blanket.

I slept, although, I was sure I felt and heard him every time he came into the room to check on me.

It was early hours of the morning that I woke. Sam was lying beside me.

"Shit," I said, aloud. "I was meant to go home."

"Chill, I called your mum," he mumbled.

"So she knows I'm here?"

"Yes, you have an upset stomach, I said," he told me.

"You lied to my mum?" I asked, giggling.

He opened his eyes fully. "I could hardly tell her I'd fucked you so hard I'd exhausted you, could I?"

I giggled some more. I stretched and heard my back click. I pushed the blanket off me and snuggled into his side. I was naked, he was in shorts. I raised up a little so he could slide an arm under my neck, and we settled back down.

We only woke because someone was banging on the door, and it was mid-morning.

"Okay, okay!" Sam shouted. "Quit with the fucking banging."

He climbed from the bed and closed the bedroom door behind him.

I heard raised voices and shouting. I jumped out of bed and pulled on my shorts and T-shirt. When I opened the door, I saw the police pinning Sam to the floor.

"Don't fight, baby," I shouted to him.

The more he fought them, the more they hurt him.

"Leave him alone, you bastards," I screamed. I was pushed out of the way, which escalated Sam's anger.

I ran back into the room and slammed the door. A minute or so later, a policeman walked in.

"Can I take your name?" he asked.

"Why?"

"Because I want it," he replied cockily.

"Let me call my dad first, he should be here with me."

"You can do that from the station," he said.

I stood. "Then I guess you need to arrest me as well. But before you do, you need to tell me what for. It's not a crime to withhold personal information until I have a representative with me."

He laughed. "Someone watched too many cop shows."

"No, someone has a lawyer as a mother."

He stopped laughing and walked out. I slumped onto the bed and sighed, then panicked and cried. When the car taking Sam away had left, I called my mum.

"Dawn Reynold's office," I heard.

"Hi, Jan, I need to speak to my mum," I said, sniffing back the tears.

"You okay, honey?" she asked.

"Yeah, just something has happened, and I need my mum."

"Hold on."

My mum was a lawyer, a corporate one, but it had done the trick in getting the policeman to leave me alone.

"Hayley, what has happened?" Her voice was laced with panic.

"Sam has been arrested. Mum, I need your help," I said.

"What do you mean, he's been arrested?"

"The police came this morning and beat him up."

"Are you at his flat now?"

"Yeah."

"Stay there. Do not answer the door or phone, do not talk to anyone. Do not give any details out."

She put the phone down before I could reply.

I paced the flat, tidied up, not that it was untidy, and made the bed. I remembered the restraints and ran back into the bedroom. They were still hanging from the head and footboard. I opened the drawer and stilled.

"Blimey," I whispered. There was an array of toys. Most of which were in their wrappers and I was grateful for that. I replaced the handcuffs and shut it.

It took Mum just over an hour to get to me. When I opened the front door, I fell sobbing into her arms.

"Come on, darling, tell me what happened?"

She followed me into the living room, and I remembered the ashtray with the joint on the windowsill. I prayed she hadn't seen it.

"He got into a fight yesterday, so I'm guessing that's why the police came," I said, terrified of my mum's reaction.

She stayed cool. "What was the fight over?"

I told her about the lad and what he'd said about Sam's mum and me. I saw my mother's eyebrows raise.

"He beat the crap out of someone just for that?"

I swallowed hard. "It was pretty horrible, Mum," I said.

"Yes, it was. But did it warrant this?"

I shook my head, not because I agreed with her, because that was what she wanted to see.

"What can we do?" I asked.

"I'll go to the station and see what I can find out. I'm not a criminal lawyer, Hals, so I'll need to get a colleague involved."

"Please don't tell Dad?" I asked.

She chuckled. "I've bailed your dad out more times than I've had hot dinners, he hasn't a leg to stand on. One day I'll tell you why I didn't become a criminal lawyer. It's not the done thing when you're married to one!"

My dad had always been a bit of a *lad,* but I'd never known to what degree.

"I'm coming with you," I said.

"You'll stay in the car," she replied.

I nodded.

I grabbed Sam's keys from the side, and we left. Once I was settled in her Mercedes, she started the car.

"Don't suppose you know what station he's at?" she said.

"No, I didn't get a chance to ask," I replied.

"We'll try the local. Oh, how's your stomach?" she asked, glancing over to me.

"My...? Oh, fine, must have been something I ate."

That glance was accompanied by raised eyebrows. "Don't start lying to me, okay?"

"I'm sorry. I fell asleep and that's the truth. Sam didn't want to wake me because I was exhausted and, after his fight, I just wanted to be with him."

It wasn't a lie. Thankfully, she just nodded her head.

We pulled up into the local station. I was instructed to wait in the car. I watched her walk in, she wore her blue suit, and her hair was in a bun. She looked formidable.

I knew how hard she'd worked to get where she was. She'd dropped out of school because she was pregnant with me, and everything she'd done after had been through sheer determination to have a career. She went to night school, college, and then university. We had a picture of her in her gown and cap, holding her scroll in the hallway. I wish I had some of her drive for a career, but I just didn't know what I wanted to be.

She was taking too long, I thought. If he wasn't there, she'd have been out by now. I waited until a half hour had passed. When I got too impatient, I climbed out of the car. I stood outside and then saw her come back through the door. Sam followed.

I ran to him, flinging my arms around his waist. He had a black eye and I cursed whoever had done that to him.

"Let's get home, Hayley," Mum said rather sternly.

I climbed in the back and Sam in the front. At first, we were silent.

"Do you have legal representation, Sam?" she asked. He shook his head. "I'll have David meet with you. I have no idea what his diary is like, but he's a good bloke, very experienced."

"What's happening?" I asked, leaning between the seats.

"I've been bailed out, thanks to your mum. I'm being done for assault, they can't decide if it's GBH or ABH," Sam replied.

"What's...?

"Grievous bodily harm or actual bodily harm," he replied.

"What happens now?"

"Now, I have to get a lawyer and wait for a court date."

"What happens then?" I asked, my voice getting small.

Mum looked at me in the rear-view mirror. "Sit back and put your belt on."

"I think you should press charges," Mum said to him.

He shook his head and chuckled. "This is nothing, you should have seen what they did to me last time."

I so wished he hadn't said that.

"You know I have to say this, don't you?" Mum started.

"Mum!"

"Be quiet, Hayley," she replied, and I shut up immediately.

"I don't want my daughter around that level of violence, Sam. I understand you were angry at what was said, but you've inflicted a lot of injuries. I know he doesn't want to press charges, but that's not the point. He doesn't get a say in the matter, even as a victim. It might save your arse, however. But, as I said, I do not want my daughter exposed to that."

Neither of us spoke for a little while.

"There's no point in me promising it won't happen again. I don't think that's something I can keep to. And that's not to say I'll go out and find a fight. I only ever defend myself or mine. I can't promise I won't do that again. I can promise she will never come to harm when she's with me. Ever. I'd die rather than let her get hurt."

Mum glanced at him. "Well, that's a little extreme, but I get the gesture."

We pulled up outside Sam's flat. Both he and I got out. I stood not knowing what to do. I wanted to be with him. I handed him his keys and he kissed me on the forehead. He walked away and I stood staring after him, tears rolling down my cheeks.

"Oh for fuck's sake, Hals. Go after him. I'll go and feed the horses, because I bet you haven't, and you make sure you are home tomorrow."

I smiled and blew her a kiss, then ran up the path and banged on the door. She waited until it was opened, and I stepped in.

"I think your mum is pissed off with me," he said, as I flung myself at him.

"She is, but she knows how much I love you."

"I need an ice pack for this," he said, pointing to his closing eye.

"You sit and I'll fuss over you."

I made up an ice pack by crushing some ice cubes with a rolling pin I'd found and placing them in a small plastic Ziploc bag. I wrapped that in a thin tea towel and then handed it to him. He held it to his eye. I climbed on the sofa beside him, curled my legs underneath me, and leaned into his side.

"I found your drawer," I said quietly. "I thought I ought to put the handcuffs away before my mum came." I chuckled.

He turned to face me and smiled. "And?"

"And I can't wait to try more."

He leaned down to briefly kiss my lips. It was awkward with him holding one hand over his eye.

"I think I need some pain relief," he said. He stood and walked to the window. He opened it and lit his spliff.

"Shall I make some lunch?" I glanced at my watch. "Afternoon tea even?"

He nodded. I left him to his pain relief and made him his favourite sandwich and mug of hot chocolate. It dawned on me he wasn't joking when he referred to his joints as pain relief. He wasn't just in physical pain, but the mental pain from his life and the deaths of his parents had to hurt.

He'd told me he used cannabis to relax his mind. Without it, he'd be angry all the time. I hoped he never ran out of it.

It was an agonised six-week wait before we found out all charges had been dropped. No one was going to testify against Sam, and all the witnesses had told the police Sam hadn't started it. I'd breathed out a sigh of relief. He could have gone to jail and that would have killed me.

CHAPTER 10
The Past

My seventeenth birthday came, and I was woken up with coffee and pastries. Sam and I had spent the night together, obviously. I was spending more and more nights at his house. So much so I didn't need to take clothes with me. Most were already there.

We were a firmly established couple at that point. Everyone who knew us individually, knew of the other. We were rarely apart. I'd worked hard through sixth form first year and was on track to get a distinction in my business studies course. I also found I was loving the business law side of it, much to my mum's delight.

Sam presented me with a card, which I opened. It was huge and one of those real soppy ones. I climbed out of bed and placed it on the windowsill next to the one I'd bought him the week before.

We hadn't celebrated his birthday, he hadn't wanted to, and

that was fine. I just cooked him a nice meal, and we got stoned. The best present I gave him, so he said, was a blow job that knocked his socks off.

"I have a day planned for you," he said.

"Oh, that sounds good. What are we doing?"

"Not telling you."

Both horses had recently gone and I'd been devastated but knew it was the right idea. It wasn't because of Sam, however. The landowner had sold up to a property developer, we were being kicked off anyway. Alfie was given to Henry, and Sovereign was loaned out to another member of the pony club. I knew they'd both had wonderful homes and when the loan term was up, I'd have Sov back.

I hadn't needed to rush to get up since it was the weekend.

Sam ran me a bath and sat on the edge while I washed. He held out a towel for me, wrapping me up in it. He led me back to the bedroom and while I dried, he picked out my clothes.

"I can choose my own outfit," I said, laughing.

"Yeah, but then you might get a hint at what we're doing."

He laid jeans and a T-shirt on the bed. I could gain nothing from those.

I dressed and pulled my hair into a ponytail. He then told me we had to leave. Sam had sold his Capri by that point. It had been worth a lot of money as a collector's piece. He opened the door to his soft-top Mercedes, and I climbed in. It was warm enough to have the roof down, and I rifled around in the glovebox looking for my sunglasses.

"Where are my glasses?" I asked, they were always there, usually.

"No idea, now buckle up."

We drove for a couple of hours. I had no idea where to. We stopped for diesel and to grab something from a fast-food drive-through, and then carried on. The scenery changed from grey motorway to green fields once we turned off. I saw signposts for the New Forest. I'd always wanted to go there and see the ponies but had never had the chance.

"Are we...?"

He smiled. "Yep."

He pulled up outside a small cottage. He was met by a man who seemed a little taken aback at first. Sam often looked intimidating. But he handed over the keys and we unpacked the car.

"Happy birthday," he said, and I laughed.

"When did you do all this?" I asked, looking into the boot.

There was a holdall and some bags of food and drink.

"Last night, while you were sleeping."

We carried the bags into the cottage and then had a walk around. It was tiny, just the one bedroom, but had a gorgeous garden.

"Could only get the one night, but we can take a drive through the forest, if you want."

I nodded. He fished out my glasses from the holdall and I laughed, taking them from him.

We returned to the car and drove. The roof was down, and it was glorious. We drove along lanes that had the trees meet above us creating a natural tunnel. We stopped when we saw horses and he handed me my camera. I took lots of pictures, of us, him, the scenery, and the horses.

We found a pub and stopped for lunch. We walked hand in hand along a riverbank and back and then headed back to the cottage. We sat in the garden with a beer, and he rolled a joint. I still wasn't smoking them myself, I didn't want to, but he'd give me the smoke from his lungs. It was smoother, so I was told, and it felt ritualistic. I'd sit on his lap and inhale and kiss him at the same time.

Sam was cooking dinner for me. He liked to cook and was way better than I was at it. He poured me a glass of wine and I returned to the garden. When the meal was cooked, he called me. He'd set the table with candles he'd brought and rose petals. There were flowers in a vase for me.

"I missed your last birthday, sort of. I wanted to make it up to you with this one."

He pulled out my chair and then brought my meal. He'd cooked steak, a jacket potato, and prepared a small salad. I laughed; it was my favourite meal. He wished me a happy birthday again, and we ate. For dessert, he told me to stand in the living room. He placed a blindfold over my eyes. He said we were going to taste test and if I got it right, it was mine to eat. I stood, smiling, excited to know what was coming.

"Balls, hold on. Take off the mask," he said.

When I did, he was knelt in front of me holding out a ring. I clasped my hands over my mouth.

"Hayley, will you marry me? I did prepare a whole speech, but I'm too nervous for it."

I nodded, tears blurred my vision, and I held out my hand.

"Is that a yes?" he asked, and I laughed.

"Yes!"

He stood and I flung my arms around his neck. I kissed him through my tears. When I stepped back, he put the ring on my finger.

"It belonged to my mum. If you don't like it, it's fine. I'll buy you a different one."

I looked at the antique rose gold ring with the ruby on the top. It matched the bracelet he'd given me.

"That was my mum's as well. She was a July baby, same as us."

He hadn't told me that.

"I love it. I love you," I said, and I threw myself at him.

He caught me and I wrapped my legs around his waist. "I love you," I said repeatedly and peppered his face with kisses.

"I love you too, Hals. I want to spend the rest of my life with you."

"And kids? We'll have kids, and when should we get married? Soon? Can we do it soon? I don't want to wait. Where will we live? Oh my God, wait until Tammy knows. Oh, shit, wait until my dad knows."

I fired so many questions at him and he spun me around laughing.

"No, not soon. We're not rushing. You have to go to college. No kids, not yet, Not until you've decided on a career or not. And your dad knows. I asked for your hand in marriage."

"You did what?" I melted. My old-fashioned, bad boy

boyfriend had asked my dad for my hand in marriage. "What did he say?"

"No." Sam then laughed.

"Did he?"

He nodded. "Yep, he said no. I said, 'Tough, I'm asking her on her seventeenth birthday.'"

"What did he say to that?"

"Nothing, he laughed."

"We don't need permission from anyone, anyway."

That evening I got my dessert. I got to have three orgasms that wrecked me. We fucked, we made love, we dozed, we *played* with sex toys, and then he restrained and totally dominated my body.

"I love Alpha Sam more than regular Sam, and I love regular Sam more than the universe," I said afterwards.

He squinted at me. "I think I get what you mean."

"Am I ready for more?" I asked.

He nodded. "You are. But we need some discussions first."

"Like what?"

"What level of pain you can tolerate?"

"Lots, I broke my leg falling off a horse and walked home," I said.

"Not quite the same thing. You'll be in a heightened environment. You won't be able to rely on adrenalin to get you home. I'll take your senses away from you, so pain is all you'll feel. But it will be beautiful and sensual at the same time."

I was aroused again.

"What started this... you know, for you?"

"What got me into this kind of sex, do you mean?"

I nodded. I didn't want to know the *who*, just the *what*.

He shrugged his shoulders. "I guess regular sex was okay, it was just a fuck. It didn't mean much. This? This is different. To know you trust me so much to guide you, turns me on more than anything. To see you unable to move and still give yourself to me is mind-blowing."

I stilled for a while, just looking at him.

"Is it about the trust for you?"

He nodded. "I've never trusted because no one has been around for me. To see some...you, submit to me, fills me with hope and love."

I noticed he'd quickly corrected himself from saying 'someone' to 'you.' I didn't push that though.

"You like regular sex with me though, right?"

"Yes. I love all sorts of sex with you."

I slid over him, lying on top. "Can we have regular sex now?"

I rode him until we both came again, and I was so sore my pussy felt on fire. We slept in the following morning.

I was gutted we only had the one night together but thrilled that we had. It had been the most magical night. I couldn't stop looking at the ring. I held my hand up and took photographs of it. I set the timer so we could have pictures of us together with my hand facing out on his chest.

We packed up the cottage and then left. We drove farther into the New Forest and spent the rest of the day walking some trails. We found horses, campers, the river again, and another pub. It was with reluctance that it was time to leave.

I dozed in the car on the way home and was woken by him when we pulled up outside my house. Suddenly, I felt nervous.

"What shall we say?" I asked.

"What do you want to say?"

"I want to tell my mum, but I don't know if my dad might kick off."

"If he does, we'll leave. You don't have school tomorrow."

I took a deep breath. "Right, let's do this."

We strode hand in hand to the front door and I unlocked it. Mum was in the kitchen and Dad in the living room. We headed for the kitchen first.

Mum was swaying her hips to some song on the radio as they counted down the charts, and my brother was drying up. I guessed, they'd just had dinner.

"Mum?" I called.

She turned, her hands all soapy. I held up my hand to show her my ring.

She screamed and jumped up and down. "Oh, my baby, that's amazing," she said, wrapping me and Sam in her arms and splattering us with washing up bubbles.

"When? How? Oh my God, and happy birthday, we have presents."

She was in a tizz and Sam laughed. I guessed she had sounded the same as I had.

Dad came into the kitchen. "What's all the racket?"

"Look, they got engaged," Mum said, waving my hand around.

Dad looked at Sam and Sam just shrugged his shoulders. "I did ask you."

"And I didn't give my blessing," Dad said, the kitchen quieted, and I held my breath.

"I told you I didn't care. I'm marrying your daughter," Sam replied.

They stared at each other and then Dad broke first.

"What the fuck, get the champagne out, Dan," he said.

He hugged Sam and then me.

When Mum handed us glasses of bubbly, we sat down at the table.

"I'm trusting my daughter in your hands, Sam. How do I know you'll step up to that? We don't know a lot about you, really," Dad asked.

Although Sam and I had been dating for a year, excluding the weeks prior to our forced separation, Dad was right. My parents didn't know what I did because I worried they would not understand Sam. He placed his glass on the table.

"My father, someone I knew as my uncle as well," he said, shrugging his shoulders again. "Was a deadbeat arsehole. He was never around; he was a drunk and a drug addict. My mum brought me up, and my aunt brought up her sons. They're my half-brothers, and I don't see them anymore. My aunt never forgave my mum for taking her man. I have no idea if that's accurate."

He paused to sip his champagne and then winced, not liking it.

"Would you prefer a beer?" I asked him and he nodded.

I rushed to the fridge to grab a bottle.

"Anyway. He took his own life. I walked into my bedroom, and he was on my bed with a bag over his head. There were drugs everywhere. Cocaine, heroin, pills, you name it, it was scattered over the bed."

"Do you do drugs, Sam?" my mum asked, and I held my breath.

"I smoke dope. She doesn't, I don't let her smoke it, but she does experience the high. I do it because it settles me. It chases the nightmares away."

No one spoke, my mum looked at me, I looked down at the table.

"Go on," my dad said.

"My mum received a pay-out. Seems the old bastard had life insurance and he'd named her and me. She didn't want it; I took it all. And I bought a two-bedroomed flat with it. We lived in that flat until my mum died of cancer. I didn't want to stay there so I sold it and moved. I don't have a mortgage, I earn well most years, and when I don't, I have savings. It's not enough to live on for the rest of our lives, but enough to pay for our wedding."

"I'll be paying for the wedding," Dad said, and a smile tugged at my lips. "One engagement party, and one wedding. Any more, you can fucking pay for that yourself," he said, directing his statement at me.

"There will only be the one," I replied.

"I'm so sorry to hear all that, Sam, and it must have been awful to have lost your mother. I do want to get back to the drugs."

"Danielle, I *only* smoke dope. Years ago, especially when I found my dad, sure. Other than the heroin, I kept most of what I found on the bed and worked my way through it. My mum was a hippy, she bought dope for her and me. When she died, I blamed all the drugs and I stopped taking them, other than the weed."

"And you?" she asked, turning to me.

"I don't smoke cigarettes, Mum. I could never smoke a joint. Yes, I inhale the smoke. I... I like it," I said, deciding to be honest.

"I don't, but I guess there's not much I can do about that." She reached over to take my hand. "You are so grown-up already."

"There is another thing," Sam said. "I'd like Hayley to live with me at some point. I'm not suggesting right now, but I'm serious about this. There isn't anyone else for me. I'm twenty-one now. I know she's only seventeen and I wish she was older, but this is a proper relationship."

I reached out for his hand. He raised it and kissed my knuckles.

"I want this, Dad," I said. "I know exactly what I'm getting into."

He shook his head. "I can't agree to that, not yet. But I can't legally stop you, baby girl, either. So it's your decision."

"I'd rather it be with your blessing," I said.

He slowly shook his head. "You do what you need to do, and when you have kids yourself, you'll understand. I love you, and I'll be here always if you need me. That's all I can offer you right now."

I moved in with Sam. I was seventeen years old and living a married woman's life.

CHAPTER 11
The Past

As Dad had said, he paid for our engagement party. It was epic. We got totally drunk on shots, even my mum, and we danced. Tammy and Karl celebrated with us, as did some friends and family. It was kept small because most didn't approve, and my mum got some stick. She'd been sent a message at work to condemn my life and question what kind of a mother she was to allow it. My nan was the only one who gave her blessing.

I'd taken great delight in having her over for Sunday dinner. Sam picked her up while I cooked. We'd borrowed a table and some chairs and set it up in the living room, the kitchen wasn't big enough.

I cooked a chicken, not confident to try anything else, roast potatoes, and veg. We had a bottle of wine and Nan and I toasted.

Sam loved her, and she loved him. She'd hug him, more so

than me. She bought him gifts all the time. Socks, pants, T-shirts. He thanked her and reminded her that he could afford to buy his own. She bought me notepads, envelopes, stamps, and diaries. I appreciated that way more than he had his socks.

When it was time to leave, she hugged me and told me to look out for her next letter. We never exchanged them, they always had to go in the post. Sam took her home while I cleared up. I folded the table back down and stacked the chairs. I rolled a joint for Sam, for when he got home, and I sat in the small, grassed garden with my wine.

I felt so grown-up.

Sam was paying for me to have driving lessons, and he was doing up a car for me. I loved to help him but had said I'd rather have a motorbike. I could get that on a provisional licence and ride to college instead of getting the bus every day.

He would have none of it. We regularly went out on his motorbike, and at that time, he had a road bike and a trials bike. But he wouldn't allow me one of my own. He feared I'd kill myself or be killed.

There was nothing I could put my finger on, but I was feeling unsettled. I didn't like college that much, but I persevered. I also decided Business Law wasn't for me. I wasn't academic enough. I switched to marketing.

"Why can't I just work for you?" I asked.

On days when I wasn't at college full time, I was at the

garage, and I loved it. I had started to work on the tools as well. Sam was teaching me how to maintain my car. I could change a tyre, spark plugs, check oil and water.

"Because I want more for you," he said gently.

"What about what I want?" I asked.

Sam and I rowed, just like any normal couple, and we always made a point of solving our issue before we went to bed. It was something I insisted on. There had been one argument where he'd stomped out and didn't come home until the early hours, stinking of alcohol and weed. I'd gone ballistic, throwing things at him and screaming abuse. I'd called him a coward for running away instead of dealing with the issue.

He had picked me up, thrown me over his shoulder, and then onto the bed. He hovered over me, pinning me to the mattress.

"I'm fucking sorry, I'm not saying it again. I'm here, aren't I?"

I'd fucked him that night. I'd rode him so hard he came twice. I didn't make a habit of winding him up so we could have great sex, but it was often how we solved our problems. We talked, of course, and we genuinely did resolve our differences.

I could hear him sigh from inside the car, he was installing a new radio.

"What about what I want?" I repeated.

He climbed from the car and stalked towards me. I stared at him. I had leaned against the bonnet, and he placed his hands at either side of me.

"What do you want?" he asked.

"To get married, have your babies, and live happily ever after."

"And we will, but not yet. You're fucking seventeen, Hals. Give us some time, for Christ's sake."

"I could just come off the Pill," I said, and then instantly regretted it. He stepped back and shook his head. "I'm sorry, I didn't mean that."

He snorted. "I don't believe you meant it, you're not that fucking devious. But know this, if you ever did, I'd leave, Hayley. If I can't trust you, I can't be with you."

Shit!

Trust was his biggest issue, and the last thing I wanted to do was to put any kind to kink in that.

"I didn't mean it. I would never do that to you. I'm so sorry, Sam. I'm just desperate to have a family with you."

I walked towards him and lifted his arms; he wrapped them around me and sighed. "I know you are. So am I. But I also know there might come a day when you regret that. I can't take the risk."

"So how do we move past this?" I asked, tears brimming in my eyes.

"We set our wedding date, how about that?"

I smiled and squealed. I kissed him and he laughed.

That evening we chose a date two years in the future. I thought I would be a perfect age, and by then I'd have finished college. We could get married; I'd get a job, and then I made him promise I would be a mum by the time I was twenty.

It didn't work out that way.

I'd felt poorly for a couple of weeks and finally, I visited the doctor. I confessed I was having the worst period, seriously heavy and prolonged. I was sent for some blood tests and scans.

Sam came with me for the results. It seemed I had fallen pregnant, much to our surprise, and had miscarried. I needed to attend hospital for a D&C. I was told my cervix would be expanded, and any remaining tissue would be sucked out. It sounded bloody awful.

"I didn't even know I was pregnant and I'm on the Pill," I'd said.

I knew it wasn't one-hundred-percent safe, of course, but for the amount of sex we had, it seemed odd.

I learned that while I'd been poorly one time with a gastric issue, the Pill had failed.

"Why have I miscarried?" I asked.

"That's not something we're going to know just now. If you are trying for children, then continue to do so. We don't start to test after the first miscarriage." The doctor was brutal, and I could feel Sam bristle beside me.

I was told to go home and wait for an appointment. I was distraught. Sam had held me while I cried for a baby I didn't know I was carrying. I kept questioning myself.

What had I done wrong?

My immaturity really showed at that point. I was so inconsolable that Sam called my mum to come over. She sat with me while I told her how I must have been diseased or something. I'd killed my baby.

She did her best to comfort me and talk some sense into my brain. She only managed that after about three hours.

I was so exhausted that I slept.

When I woke some hours later, I tried to convince Sam to have sex with me.

"No, Hals. Not until after the procedure."

I had started to convince myself he didn't fancy me anymore.

I drank more. I demanded weed, and I dropped out of college. I'd missed so many classes there was no point in attending, I'd never catch up. Sam was annoyed with me, as were my parents. My mum was the only understanding one among them.

I was grieving, whether I knew I was carrying a child or not.

I drank too much. I picked fights with Sam constantly.

And then one day he snapped.

"I can't do this right now, Hals. I'm going to stay with Karl for a couple of days, we need some space to think."

I panicked.

"Think about what? You're running away again," I said, slurring my words.

"Yeah, I am. Just for a couple of days. I need to clear my mind and I can't fucking do that here."

"Don't leave me," I said, collapsing to the floor and sobbing.

"I'm not leaving you. I love you, baby, but this is killing me. I need to clear my head. Can't you just give me that?"

I shook my head. "You can do that here."

"No, I can't because you won't let me."

I grabbed at him, and he stepped away.

He walked away from me, and I clawed at the floor, bashing it with my fists. I heard his car drive away. The only time I moved from that spot was to throw up, get more vodka that I drank straight from the bottle, and change my piss-soaked jeans.

I was a mess. There was a part of my brain that knew I hadn't handled my grief well. I'd refused all help, even anti-depressants. I'd pushed everyone away, not seeing any of our friends.

It was two days later I finally realised. I rose and the stench from sick on the floor overpowered me. I bathed, put all my clothes in the washing machine, and scrubbed the carpet. I was ashamed with the number of empty bottles on the side, and I put them in the bin. I then called my mum.

She hadn't been aware Sam had left and wanted to come round straightaway. I told her not to. I needed to deal with the mess. She was annoyed with Sam, but I knew I had to take some responsibility. I pushed and pushed to get married, to have a family. I knew what I was doing when I dropped out of college, I was trying to escalate things. And I also knew my reaction to my miscarriage was normal, but I'd needed to have spoken to Sam rather than drown myself in vodka and harsh words.

I waited for him.

He came home later that evening, and by the sight and smell, he'd come straight from work.

It killed me to see him hesitate before walking into the

living room, half expecting something to be thrown at him, I guessed. I stood. I was nervous.

"I'm sorry," I said, and I found I couldn't say any more. I swallowed back tears, unsuccessfully.

"So am I. Yes, I ran away, and I shouldn't have," he said, rushing towards me. He wrapped his arms around me, and I cried into his chest.

We sat and talked, he told me his mum had pushed him away when she was sick, and he hadn't dealt with that very well. He said it wasn't an excuse, and he didn't understand my grief. He should have helped me more. I reminded him that he had tried, I'd refused all help.

We made love that night, and the following morning he took me to the hospital for my appointment.

I started to look for a job. I had passed my Business Studies with distinction, and I could put Sam on my CV. I sent out loads, not getting anywhere. It was horrible being constantly rejected, and I did more and more with Sam. Mum offered me a junior position in her company, and I jumped at the chance. It wasn't in her department, but the criminal side and I loved it.

I wore suits to work and high heels. When work was over, I'd get the bus to the garage to meet Sam. I'd walk across the concrete floor and pretend to be a new client. I'd hitch my skirt up as I sat, cross my legs and role-play.

Then I'd laugh, change, and help him with my car.

I wasn't a natural driver at all. I hated it. I persevered, going through three instructors and my mum before I decided it wasn't for me. I was happy to get the bus, and Mum and I shopped together on a Friday night after work.

We had developed more of a friendship over the time I'd lived with Sam. It was nice, I was also closer to my brother, having him over to stay on occasions.

We often dined out with my parents and with Tammy and Karl. It was one such meal out that Tammy dropped her news.

"I'm pregnant," she said at the dinner table.

Everyone congratulated her, I swallowed down the most awful feeling of instant jealousy. Sam stared at me. I planted a smile on my face and ran around the table to congratulate her.

"Oh my God, that's bloody brilliant," I said, laughing with her.

We'd become best friends over the past year, and I was thrilled for her, I really was. But I was also envious.

We talked babies and she wanted me to be so involved. I nodded and agreed to everything, knowing I doubted I could. I felt sick in my stomach.

I'd wanted a baby so much and was being denied that, and now my best friend was pregnant. I felt life wasn't fair.

I was a little quiet on the way home. Sam had held my hand as he drove, and he rubbed his thumb over my knuckles.

"Talk to me, Hals," he said when we got home.

"I'm okay, just jealous and I feel so awful about that," I said.

He pulled me into a hug. I kissed his chin and then his throat. "If I can't have a baby, can I get a tattoo?" I asked.

He laughed. "We can both get a tattoo. What do you want?"

"I want your name somewhere."

"Then I'll get your name as well."

Neither of us considered the fact we might not last and would then have to do something to cover them up.

It was the following weekend we turned up at the tattoo parlour he used. I was bloody terrified and kept covering my face with my hands, screeching, and moaning about how painful it was.

"It's three fucking letters," Sam said, and he and the tattooist laughed.

I was having his name in a heart on my hip. Since it was a bony part of my body, it hurt. Sam opted to have my name across his chest. I had loved to see that; I was going to be there forever.

Sam was racing the following day. My dad had taken it upon himself to become part of the team. He'd tow the trailer with both Karl and Sam's dirt bikes on them. They'd head off to tracks all over Kent for race meets. Tammy, who was getting bigger by the minute, and I would follow. Sometimes with my mum, other times in Tammy's car. She had bought the car Sam had allocated for me.

"You need to get your licence. What's going to happen

when I give birth and Karl isn't around?" she asked, reversing into her parking place at the track.

"Why wouldn't he be around?"

"Because he's a fuckwit who's likely to be stoned somewhere with your man." She laughed, joking. But not.

I had spoken to Sam about Karl. He seemed to be more and more at our place, stoned in the garden and then passing out on the sofa. At first, Sam wasn't concerned, but then, after a conversation with Sam, it turned out Karl was having cold feet about the baby. Neither of us could tell Tammy and hoped, once the baby was born, he'd come round.

Because Sam won most of his races, he was always surrounded by people. It irritated me, especially the women who flung themselves at him. It was a source of tension between us, more so when he didn't flick them off quick enough. They'd drape their arms over him, pouting, knowing he had a partner. Often Sam felt uncomfortable with the women, but he never told them to fuck off. I did, of course, and that tension would increase. Sam would say I had embarrassed him, but I didn't see that.

Those women made me feel insecure. They were older and more beautiful than I was. I didn't like to feel insecure.

Tammy would tell me to ignore them, but it was hard.

Sam had never given me any cause to be jealous. He'd laugh and joke with other women but there was never more than that. He didn't flirt at all. He'd also make a show he was with me, hug and kiss me in front of them. He did that to comfort me, and that made me feel worse.

Once the women were finally brushed off, I helped get the bike ready. I zipped up Sam's jacket and helped him on with his gloves.

"Be careful," I said, as I always did, then he pulled his helmet over his head. Tammy did the same with Karl.

They set off down to the start line. I'd hug my dad and bury my face into his side when they started. It was a free-for-all and if there was going to be an accident, it was there.

"Yes!" Dad shouted and I looked up. Sam had started in the lead. Karl was about three places behind. We watched until they rounded a corner and were out of sight.

Dad wanted Sam to try out for the Highcross Dirt Bike team. It would mean travelling through Europe to race. I wasn't so sure about it. It was dangerous. The guys raced on dirt tracks, through woods, up mountainsides, over rocky ground. There were always accidents. Five hundred would start, only twenty or so would finish, and they'd have to do that twice in a competition.

The races usually lasted thirty minutes and we would expect them to pass us soon. I leaned over the side of the railings and screamed as I saw Sam come into view. He had my name on his race suit and across his helmet.

We watched the bikes speed past. "I didn't see Karl," Tammy said.

"He was probably in there," I replied.

We heard an announcement over the tannoy that the race was being paused and that usually meant someone was bent into a tree and causing a blockage on the track. The riders kept their positions and slowed down. When they got round to the start/finish, the red flag was waved. That meant the race was over. The bikes came to a halt and riders started to talk among themselves. Sam removed his helmet and team members climbed over the rails.

I followed Dad.

"What's happening?" Sam asked.

"No idea. I'll go and find out."

Dad left us. "You were winning as well," I said.

"Must be bad to halt the race. Usually they pull the casualty out of the way," Sam replied and then laughed.

Tammy joined us. "Karl isn't here," she said, and her voice quivered.

Sam kicked his stand down and climbed off his bike. He handed his helmet to me and started to walk back up the line of bikes. He asked after Karl.

I saw one rider talk to him. He pointed up into the woods, and then rested his forehead on his handlebars. Sam started to run. He scrambled over the barriers and headed up the hill. I could hear marshals calling him back and then one ran towards him. He wrestled Sam to the ground.

"Shit," I said, knowing Sam would fight.

I then saw my dad running up the hill as well. We all watched in silence as my dad pushed the marshal off Sam. Sam jumped up and my dad held on to him. The marshal was talking, and then I saw Sam fall to his knees. It was some minutes later the wail of an ambulance was heard.

"It's Karl, isn't it?" Tammy shouted, frantic.

One of the other riders' wives came over. "Come with us, honey," she said. Tammy and I followed her and her husband to the marshal's office.

"There's been an accident, a bad one," we were told.

"What do you mean?" Tammy asked.

He wouldn't tell her any more.

She became frantic, screaming and crying. I became concerned for the baby. We tried to get her to sit, more so when we saw the medical team bring down a person on a stretcher. They rushed to the ambulance and the back doors were closed.

Tammy ran, I followed. We met my dad and Sam at the ambulance. Sam banged on the door.

"This is his wife," he said when the door was opened.

"One minute." It was closed again and we were left outside, not knowing what the fuck was happening.

"Man, it was bad," I heard.

Another rider had approached us. My dad shook his head, but the guy didn't get the message.

"He went straight off the edge. Smashed against a tree. He was dead before he hit the ground," he said.

Sam punched him, knocked him clean out, and Tammy started to scream. She banged on the door, and then clutched her stomach.

The door opened and she was allowed in the ambulance. Blue lights flashed, the siren sounded, and it sped off. We were left watching and not knowing if the speed was for her or him.

"I need to get to him," Sam said. His eyes were full of tears, his face dirty.

"Take Tammy's car," I said, handing him the keys from Tammy's bag.

He started to run and then stopped. He ran back to me. He held my face and while a lone tear ran down his cheek, he kissed me.

"Come home when you can. I'll wait for you there," I said, my voice cracking.

Karl had been my friend as well, but nowhere near as close as Sam. They were like brothers.

Dad and I loaded Sam's bike on the trailer, having no idea where Karl's was. We were all told a notification would be sent out with regards to what happened. An investigation would need to take place.

We left. I cried all the way home.

CHAPTER 12
The Past

K arl died early hours the following morning. He had been breathing but unconscious and had massive internal injuries. His mum, Sam, and Tammy were by his side. His dad hadn't made it in time and a row ensued beside his bed. Sam went to punch him, and the dad was removed. Thankfully, Sam got to stay for a little longer and said goodbye to his friend.

He called my dad and was picked up from the hospital while I waited at our flat. He looked wretched when he walked in. Dad hugged him and then left us after ensuring I would be okay. I thought Sam might need some quiet to process. He stripped out of his racewear, and I ran a bath for him. He hadn't spoken one word. He sank under the water, holding his breath, just staring up at me. When I started to worry, I placed my hand in the water and touched his hand. He raised himself.

I spread soap over a sponge and washed the dirt from his

face and hands and his neck. I then sponged water over his head. Water ran down his face and I was aware it was mixing with his tears.

Sam climbed from the bath and wrapped a towel around his waist. He walked into the bedroom and sat. I used another towel to rub his hair dry, then his back and chest.

When he was dry, I knelt in front of him. I placed my hands on his thighs, and he covered them with his own.

"What can I do?" I asked gently.

He shook his head. "I don't know." His voice was hoarse, and I imagined he'd cried a lot.

"Why don't you lie down?"

He did so and I climbed on beside him. I held him in my arms until he fell asleep.

Sam was up and out before I woke. He left me a note in the kitchen.

Morning, beautiful. Gone to work, I have to keep busy. I'll call later. Sam xxx

I would have preferred he stayed home so I could look after him, but that was Sam all over. He had to keep busy.

He worked all the hours, not coming home until eight or nine at night. He visited Karl's mum and agreed to be a coffin bearer at his funeral. He also wrote the eulogy. I was concerned he was burning himself out.

He smoked more dope, it was the only way he could sleep, he told me.

He drank more beers, it was the only way he didn't think, he told me.

He didn't shed one more tear, he closed down.

I got it. It was his way of dealing with the pain of loss. I couldn't help but feel pushed to the side, excluded. He spent time with Tammy, and that hurt.

He was the one who called me from the hospital to say she'd gone into labour.

He was the one who drove her back to Karl's since she'd moved in with his mum.

He was the one who bought a large teddy for the baby, also named Karl.

He was acting like a dad, and that killed me.

I couldn't say or do anything. I knew it was still grief and his way to keep that connection with Karl. I died a little inside though.

On the day of the funeral, I had to make my own way there. He was in the lead car with Karl's mum and Tammy. My dad drove me after asking how I was getting there and receiving just a shrug of shoulders. I could see the worried look on my mum's face. Mum and Dad had grown close to Karl because of the racing, so they wanted to attend to pay their respects as well. I was extremely grateful. The thought of having to get there on my own was causing me untold anxiety.

I didn't say anything to Sam in the run up to the funeral. He spent long hours at Karl's planning, and I spent long hours waiting for him with cold meals in the bin.

"You need to say something, darling," Mum said.

"I will, trust me. Just after the funeral."

She had grown even more concerned about my exclusion. I

wasn't backwards at coming forwards. Sam and I could have some blazing rows, real screaming matches, door-slamming, plate-smashing arguments. But I didn't want that before laying Karl to rest.

My patience wore very thin on the day.

My parents and I were waiting at the crematorium when the hearse and limousine pulled up. Sam held Tammy's hand. I wasn't sure where the baby was, I hadn't seen him at all. I took a deep breath to quell the sickness that rose in my stomach, and Mum took hold of my hand.

Sam didn't even look my way.

I watched him join other friends as coffin bearers and walk Karl through the room to the stands. All the boys then took the first row opposite the family. Karl's parents had Tammy between them, and I thought that was more so they were kept apart than comforting her. His father had his new partner to his side.

Mum, Dad, and I slipped into seats halfway down. I sidled up next to Sandy, a girlfriend of one of the friends.

"How are you doing?" she asked. "I called you last night to see if you wanted company."

"Not good, and I'm sorry, I ended up staying at my parents' since... Well, you know."

I swallowed back the tears. "I know, honey. Get him back on track tomorrow," she said, nodding towards the front of the room. "He loves you, remember that."

So it was noticeable to everyone Sam had all but abandoned me. I squeezed her hand.

When it was Sam's turn to speak, he stood. He looked so smart in his suit and white shirt; he must have bought that recently since he didn't own a suit. I wondered where he'd kept it. His hands shook. He scanned the room, twice. Then, he finally found me. He stared at me, swallowing hard, his eyes brimmed with tears. His brow was furrowed, and he looked so sad.

I smiled at him and nodded in encouragement.

When he spoke his voice was strained, it cracked, and he had to pause a few times to regain his composure. He talked about times when he and Karl were in school, from primary to secondary. He talked about their love of motorbikes and racing. He talked about Karl's love for his mother and Tammy, and then he talked about the baby and how he looked just like his daddy. He didn't mention Karl's father at all. He talked about other friends, and he turned to the coffin and made a promise to Karl that he would always look out for his son.

That was like a nail in mine.

When the service was over, Sam finally came to find me.

"Hey," he said hesitantly.

"You spoke well," I replied, not really knowing what I could say.

"It was hard. I'm glad I found you, I could focus on your face."

So, I was found not because he missed me but to help with his speech?

"I have to head back to the house to help set up for the wake. I'll see you there?"

He had looked around while he spoke.

I nodded. He gave me a brief kiss on the lips and then left.

I didn't go to the house. Mum and Dad dropped me off home after I insisted I wanted to be there alone than with them.

Sam came home the following morning hungover.

* * *

I was woken by Sam sitting on the side of the bed. He looked down at me. His eyes were bloodshot.

"I'm sorry, Hals," he said.

"For what, Sam?" I wanted to hear exactly what he was sorry for. I didn't expect it to be what came next.

"I kissed her. I was drunk, that's not an excuse. I don't want her, I love you. I didn't go any further, I can promise you that. And I won't see her again, at all."

Ice ran through my veins.

I sat up and stared at him. A tear ran down his cheek.

"You...?"

He nodded.

"Tammy?"

He nodded again.

I didn't react. I didn't scream or shout. I was numb. I climbed from the bed and walked to the kitchen. My hands shook as I made myself a cup of tea. Sam walked in and stood by the doorway.

"Please say something?" he said, so quietly I'd only just heard him.

I couldn't look at him.

"Why?" I asked.

"Because I was sad, angry, drunk, but none of that is an excuse. I've been that way before and never cheated on you. I can't answer exactly why. I guess I needed some comfort, she hugged me, she kissed me, and then I kissed her back."

I spun around. "Comfort? You needed some comfort?" I whispered, but with such anger I spat the words at him.

"I should have come to you. I should have been here. Yet again, I've abandoned you when you needed me. I fully understand if you want me to leave. You can stay here."

"So what, you can see her?"

"No. I meant what I said, I won't ever see her again."

I snorted a laugh. "You made a promise to Karl, remember? Or has he gone out the window as well now?"

Sam didn't reply initially, he just stared at me. "You are more important than any promise I've made to anyone else. I'll live in regret for not doing what I thought I should, but I won't compromise us."

"You just did!" I shouted.

We fell silent. Sam ran his hand over the stubble around his chin. He looked way older than his twenty-one years in that moment.

"Where were you last night?" I asked.

"I slept in my car. I started to drive home, then realised how fucking stupid that was, I couldn't even see the road. So I pulled up and fell asleep."

"Not with her?"

"No. As soon as...it happened, I left."

"Did she try to stop you?"

"No, she was as mortified as me."

I sighed. "I guess that's something."

"I told her I was going to tell you immediately."

"Well, that's grand of you."

"What do I need to do, Hals, to make it up to you?" His voice cracked.

"I don't know. Right now I can't be in the same room as you. This is your flat, so I'll go back home."

"Would it help if I begged you not to? I'll keep out of your way. I'll sleep on the sofa or at the garage. If you move out, I'm scared you won't come back."

"Good, be fucking scared, Sam. I'm hurt. I gave you space to do what you needed to. I sat here day and night without you, not for me, because I wanted to comfort you. I wanted to be the one to kiss away your tears. I knew you were grieving, and I wanted to hold your hand and stand beside you while you did. You didn't give me the fucking chance. Instead, you closed down and shut me out."

"I know I did. I'm so sorry."

"You didn't even think of how I was getting to the funeral, did you?"

He winced, closing his eyes, and shook his head.

"I got it, you were consumed and for you, doing things, keeping busy, is what you do. But when you can't even think about us, that's a problem."

I sipped my tea, needing some warmth inside of me. I

started to cry. Sam walked towards me, and I held up my hand. I didn't want his cuddle. He bowed his head and bit down on his lower lip.

"Do you want me to leave you alone for a few hours?"

I nodded.

"Can I at least touch you before?"

I closed my eyes, desperately trying to get the tears to stop. I nodded.

He stepped closer and placed one hand on my cheek, I leaned into it. When I looked at him, his tears matched mine.

"I love you so much, baby," he whispered. "I'll give you a couple of hours and whatever you decide for us, I'll accept. I won't like it, and I hope you can forgive me. I won't patronise you with promises, you've seen me break two now, but this won't ever happen again."

I stayed in the kitchen while he changed out of the crumpled suit. He pulled on jeans, a T-shirt, his biker boots, and a leather jacket. He grabbed his helmet from the hall cupboard and with one last glance at me, he opened the front door and left. I heard his motorbike start up. It was the first time he'd ridden one since race day.

I walked into the living room, curled up on the sofa, and sobbed. The phone rang a couple of times, I let it go to answerphone. One was my mum checking I was okay, and one was Tammy.

"I wonder if you could call me, Hals. I... Hopefully, I'll hear from you soon."

Did she know he'd already told me? Did she think she

would be the one to tell me? I shook my head.

I just sat and thought. I loved Sam with all my being. He was my soulmate, the man I wanted to spend my whole life with. I had no experience with any other man, and I didn't want to. I knew it was just him. But could I get past this? I'd have to, I guessed.

In my young brain, I tried to rationalise it. She hugged him; she kissed him first. I wasn't blaming her, he could have pulled away, he didn't. He kissed her back. Was it cheating?

It wasn't that he'd kissed her that hurt the most. It was the way I'd been pushed aside completely. He'd found solace in being at Karl's house with his mum and Tammy to the exclusion of me. That stung, a lot.

I closed my eyes against a building headache and pinched the bridge of my nose. I plumped up the cushions and lay down my head. I slept.

Sam came home a couple of hours later. I heard him creep about and put the kettle on. He took the cup from the floor in front of me and replaced it with a cup of tea. He sat on the other end of the sofa. I opened my eyes; they were puffy and sore. I shuffled up.

"Thank you," I said, my voice croaky as I reached for the tea.

He didn't say anything.

"Where did you go?" I asked.

"The coast. Just sat on the beach and thought."

"About what?"

"Us, me, my mum. I'm going to get counselling. I've been

offered it before."

I nodded, it was a good idea, one I'd brought up before.

"I love you, Hals. I don't want to lose you."

I sighed. "You're not going to lose me. I just need to find a way to work through this."

He nodded. "Can I hold you?"

I then nodded. He slid up the sofa and opened his arms, I leaned into his chest, and he wrapped them around me. He sighed.

"I'm only ever at home when you're in my arms," he whispered.

* * *

We talked and talked, and we made love. I took Tammy's third or fourth call, I can't remember which, and she cried and apologised. She promised it was all her and it wasn't because it was Sam. It was because Sam was the closest she could get to Karl. I understood. I couldn't forgive them both at that time, but I could park it and move on.

I even arranged to visit and see the baby.

I started to take up my driving lessons again. I knew I needed to be more independent. And I never told my parents.

Sam was overly attentive initially, but after a couple of weeks of him suffocating me, we fell back into our usual routine.

I went to work at the office, Sam to the garage, and we started to plan our wedding.

CHAPTER 13
The Past

"You are never going to believe what has happened!" I said, getting home from work one day.

"What?" Sam was in the kitchen preparing our dinner.

"I've been headhunted." I smiled so broadly, my cheeks hurt.

"What?"

I waved a piece of paper around. I'd received an email at work from a company in London I'd had some brief dealings with. It probably wasn't the done thing to email my work address, but we didn't have private emails.

"This company of lawyers in London wants me to talk to them about a position. A PA for one of the partners."

He took the paper from me.

"That's bloody amazing. What did you say?"

"I said I'd meet them to talk. I can't believe it. It's got to be way more salary than I'm now, hasn't it?"

"Yeah, I imagine so."

"And think about working in London. Oh my God, Sam. I can go to wine bars and all that stuff," I said, excited.

He blinked a few times and paused before answering. "It would be fantastic for you."

I was so caught up in the moment I didn't see the bite of the lower lip, something Sam did when anxious.

"I'm going to call Mum and tell her. I didn't see her today."

I spent half an hour on the phone to my mum while Sam cooked. She was as excited for me. She knew the firm and told me they were one of London's top criminal lawyers, with barristers and some top clients. Celebrities, royalty, and big names in business. I'd need new clothes, she said. Proper suits and high heels. We said we'd shop together to get me kitted out. I only cut off the call when Sam came in with dinner.

I talked constantly about the job, about London, who I might meet. I'd have to get a train ticket; I could walk to the train station from where we lived. All the while he just listened. He smiled and when dinner was done, I took the plates to the kitchen and washed up. I made him a coffee and we sat on the windowsill. I'd progressed to smoking my joint at that point, although I still found the exchange of his inhaled smoke erotic and arousing.

That night, buoyed up by the excitement of a new job, we played hard.

Sam had me lie on the stomach with my restraints on both

wrists and ankles but with longer chains. He spanked me until my arse stung and I was dripping with arousal. He nipped my skin, from the back of my neck to my thighs, marking me, and he pulled at my hips, so I raised my arse in the air. He fucked me from behind, it was one of my favourite positions. He would fist my hair, pulling my head back hard. He reached underneath and while he fucked me, he would tease my clitoris until I came.

Alpha Sam was in the room, and he growled out my name when he came.

After we'd fucked, we rested and then always made love. He was softer, gentle and loving. He held me in his arms, and we fell asleep.

The closer to my interview we got, the more excited I became. Sam took me shopping and I paraded up and down in new suits and high heels.

Mum took me to get my hair and nails done, and Dad put some money in my account for travel. I didn't need his money, I earned, and Sam earned well, but he felt he wanted to do something.

I travelled to London by myself, took a taxi to their offices, and waited in reception. I was terrified. I played with my engagement ring, twisting and twisting it. Eventually, I was met by a youngish man, the partner I would be working for.

"Hi, Hayley? I'm Toby. Do you want to follow me?"

I had expected a secretary or HR to come and get me. Not the man himself. I followed him into the lift, and he asked about my journey.

"Have you come far?"

"No, not really. It's only a half hour on the train. I got a taxi here because I wasn't sure of the way and didn't want to be late."

I rambled a little, nervous.

"Always good to be early," he said, smiling at me.

I couldn't place his age, perhaps thirtyish. I knew he was young to be a partner, but Mum had checked him out. He'd recently won some huge case, defending a celebrity who had been wrongly, I hoped, accused of rape.

We walked across an open plan office. Some people acknowledged me, some didn't, not because they were being rude, but busy, I assumed.

I sat in his office in front of his large wooden desk.

I retrieved a copy of my CV from my bag and handed that over to him. He didn't look at it, just kept his hand on the page.

"Tell me about yourself?"

"Erm, I've been working at Thompson and Thompson for nearly a year now. I earned a distinction in my BTEC Business Studies, but I confess to flunking out of college," I chuckled, and he smiled. "I wanted to work; I love working."

"Any hobbies?"

I paused. It had occurred to me when I was typing up my CV that I didn't do much beyond Sam.

"I used to own horses and I'd like to get back to that at some point. I live with my fiancé, and right now, we're planning our wedding. May I ask why you chose me?"

I decided to move off me since I couldn't really answer his question.

"Good diversion, I like that," he said, laughing. "I chose you after the Hearns versus Hearns case. Our admin team screwed up, and although we were on opposing sides, you came through for us. That's unheard of. I was impressed with your organisation skills, your presentation, and how you handled yourself in court."

I'd attended a case as admin and remembered it well. One of his team had forgotten documentation that had been shared, she was in tears. This was just before the case started. It would delay it. I took it upon myself to get her copies. It wasn't a big deal, and my team was happy about it. They didn't want the delay. I hadn't thought any more about it.

I nodded, pleased that small act had made such an impression.

"Here's what I have on offer. I'd like to have you here four days a week, the fifth will be at university. I want a legal PA, and there are areas that you need to catch up on. I'm sure you're doing well where you are, but this is a different level." He looked up at someone who had come to the door.

"Tea? Coffee?" I heard. He ordered coffee, I did the same.

"There is a salary on offer of twenty-five thousand pounds per annum, that will increase once you've completed your course."

I had to make a real effort not to react to that. It was a huge sum of money. I'd heard of 'London wages' but hadn't expected that.

"You'll get twenty-five days holiday, but there could be times I'd want you on call and that might be weekends. If something happens to an existing client, they expect us to respond."

He stopped again as a girl, about the same age as me, walked in. She placed the coffees on the desk.

"This is Pam. She's the team secretary."

He went to explain what he believed his PA should be doing and it wasn't much different to what I did generally. I would type up his client documents, but Pam would deal with everything else. It felt odd because we were the same age, but I'd be higher up the ladder than her.

He showed me around the office and where I'd be potentially sitting, which was right outside his office. He asked me to let him know what notice period I had to give and to let him know a preferred start date.

I shook his hand and Pam escorted me back down to reception.

"What's it like here?" I asked.

"Good, honestly, he's a dream to work for. I was hoping for the job," she said, laughing.

"Oh, I'm so sorry," I replied, mortified and unsure what else to say.

"Ah, it's okay. I'll grab another partner someday. I don't have your experience. He is dreamy, isn't he?"

Dreamy? I don't think I'd used that word since I was seven and it was over Bay City Rollers!

"Erm, I guess so."

We said goodbye and I headed to the corner of the road. I was unsure which way I needed to go and vowed to print out a map next time. I'd also need to check out bus and train times. I flagged down a black cab and was taken the ten-minute drive to the station. The driver was amazing, he told me it was a quick walk, but because of the one-way system, it was longer to drive.

I paid and added a tip and then walked into the train station. I passed some builders and one whistled.

"All right, love?" he shouted out. "You can walk all over me in those heels."

I laughed, more because I didn't know how to respond. I'd been catcalled a couple of times and the advice was always to just ignore it, but it wasn't nice. I scanned the train board until I found one that took me home and waited.

My feet were killing me by the time I got to my home station, and I still had a bus ride to do. I found a payphone and called Sam.

"Sam's Garage," he said, when he answered.

"Hi, I'm back."

"Hey, baby, how did it go? Why didn't you call me when you finished? I could have picked you up."

"It's too far, but I would appreciate being picked up now, if you can. And remind me never to wear high heels again!"

He laughed. "Go get a coffee, I'll be twenty minutes."

I thanked him and did as he suggested. When twenty minutes had passed, I walked outside. I only had to wait another five when he turned up in a car I didn't recognise. I slid in the passenger seat and handed him a coffee.

"Whose car?" I asked.

"Customer's. Needed a test drive so killed two birds and all that. Did they love you? I bet they did. When do you start?"

I laughed. "Yes, they loved me, I think. I'm to find out what notice period I have to give and then let them know. I'll be working for a partner and, get this, I'm starting on twenty-five thousand!"

He looked over to me. "No fucking way?"

"Yes, I know. I thought I'd misheard him. I'll go to uni one day a week and when I'm qualified as a legal secretary, or whatever it's called, my wages will go up."

"We'll move, get a bigger house," he said, and I nodded.

"We can have a holiday," I added.

He put his hand on my leg. "I'm so fucking proud of you," he said.

I leaned over and kissed his cheek.

While he finished up at work, I did some paperwork for him. I was still encouraging him to bring it home. I was trying to convince him to buy a computer, we'd had them installed at work and they'd made life so much easier.

When we finally got home, he took a bath, I changed out of my suit and started to make dinner.

Sam came up behind me and wrapped his arms around my waist. He nuzzled into my neck.

"Let's go out and celebrate," he said. I readily agreed.

We headed to the local pub and bumped into a couple of friends. Sam told them all about my new job in the city, he was so proud of me. The only time his smile slipped was when someone joked that I might run off with a *suit*.

* * *

I started work in London one month later. I loved it. The job was so satisfying and varied, and I adored working for Toby. He wasn't like any lawyer I'd ever come across. First, he was young. Second, he included me in everything. We laughed and visited wine bars in our lunchtime. In the evenings I was full of talk about work, and I missed Sam getting less enthusiastic.

"Your voice is changing," he said, one evening. We were sitting in the garden smoking and drinking wine.

"What do you mean?" I asked.

"You're getting posher," he said, chuckling slightly.

"Oh, am I? I didn't realise."

I actually felt a little embarrassed he'd said that. I had tried to change my accent; I was talking to posh people and I didn't want to sound common.

"You're changing," he said gently.

"Is that a bad thing?" I asked.

"No." He smiled, and I scooted over to sit on his lap.

"You'll still love me even if I talk posh, won't you?" I was half jesting.

"I'd love you if you spoke a foreign language."

I kissed him and laughed.

"I can put those shoes on and talk posh for you," I said seductively.

He stood, placing me on my feet. "Go and do that," he replied.

I rushed to the bedroom. I stripped out of my sweat pants

and T-shirt and pulled on the tightest skirt. I left my underwear off. I pulled a white shirt on and tucked it in but left it unbuttoned. I pulled my hair into a bun and then slowly walked back into the living room.

"Ah, Miss Adams. I want you to take some dick...tation."

I struggled not to laugh. "Where would you like me, Mr. Weston?" I asked.

I stood before him, parting my legs a little. He reached out and placed his hands on my thighs. He slid them up and shifted my skirt to my waist.

With my heels, and him sitting, my pussy was near enough at head height. He dug his fingers into my arse and licked over my opening. I held on to his head, scratching over his scalp. He could bring me to my knees with his tongue and fingers. He nipped at my skin.

When he sat back, I reached down and unzipped his jeans. I reached in and pulled his cock free. I straddled him, positioning him at my entrance.

"Miss Adams, I think you're taking advantage of me," he said, running his hand down over my calves.

"Yep. Are you complaining?"

I lowered and sighed. "I love you inside me," I whispered. Before I rocked against him, I untucked the shirt, letting it flap open. He palmed my breasts and kissed my chest.

I rode him, gently at first, and then as hard as I could. I came first and slid from his lap. I kneeled and wrapped my lips around his cock. I sucked him, taking him as deep to my throat as I could. I'd trained my gag reflex over the years and, according to Sam, I was an expert at blow jobs.

He came and I swallowed. I looked up at him and smiled. "I'm still the same person, Sam. The one who loves you and your cock."

He laughed and kissed my lips, then cringed at the taste.

I bathed and by the time I was in my PJs, he was sitting on the windowsill smoking. I wiggled my way between his legs and when he opened his mouth, I breathed in the smoke. We got high together.

CHAPTER 14

The Past

O n his twenty-third birthday, I was working. I also had to work late. I'd called him to let him know and he said he'd collect me from the office. He'd taken to driving up when he wasn't too busy, and I loved that. That evening, I saw him out of the window and rushed down to open the door for him. I wanted to show him around my office. I was excited.

We took the lift up and I led him across the room. I introduced him to Pam, who was also working late with me. And then Toby came in from grabbing us a coffee each. Sam instantly tensed.

"Hi, I'm Toby. Hayley has told us so much about you," he said, holding out his hand.

Sam looked at the hand before he took it. My cheeks flushed with embarrassment. Toby wasn't sure what to do.

"Hi," was all Sam said.

"Okay. If you want to leave, Hals, you can," Toby said.

"No, I'll finish up," I replied. Sam stared at me. He had a look on his face that worried me. "But if you don't mind, maybe I will," I added.

I said goodbye and grabbed my bag. We didn't speak until the lift doors closed.

"Hals?" Sam said.

"What the fuck was that all about?" I asked, at the same time as he'd spoken.

"He called you Hals."

"It's my name!" I replied.

"No, it's what I call you."

"And my mum and my dad and my brother."

"So family, then," Sam added.

"So you've got the hump because I've given him permission to call me Hals? Can you hear how stupid that is?"

"So I'm stupid, am I? Not as educated as your city boys. Just a grease monkey here."

I stared at him, frowning. "Where is this coming from?" I asked gently.

Sam had a jealous streak but not to that degree. If he thought a man was getting too close to me, he'd intervene but I often liked that.

"Toby is my boss."

"It's my birthday today, and you want to spend time with him?"

My mouth fell open. "Remind me when you have ever acknowledged your birthday? I gave you a card this morning, I

172

woke you up with a fucking blow job, Sam," I hissed, aware we were reaching the ground floor.

He didn't answer.

"Well?" I asked, as the lift doors opened.

He stomped out and I sighed, following him. I hated when Sam was in a mood, he could be super childish sometimes. He was four years older than me, but you'd never know it.

He opened the passenger door, and I slipped in. If he wanted to give me the silent treatment, then so be it. I turned on the radio. When he got in, he turned off the radio.

"You're changing," he said.

"Is that a bad thing? I'm fucking growing up, maybe you want to do the same."

He pulled out into the traffic too fast and gave the finger to the car behind that beeped him.

We drove home in silence and slept back-to-back. Well, he slept, I lay there thinking. Yes, I was changing, and I was growing up, I thought he'd like that. I was just shy of nineteen and that was the year we were meant to get married.

I started to think about the wedding. We hadn't booked anything at that time, and I thought it might be best to delay for a little while. I hadn't earned all the holiday I would be entitled to, and it was my last year in training. Once I was qualified, I'd be earning more, and we could afford a better wedding.

Sam had left before I finally woke the following morning.

I had the agonising situation of having to apologise to Toby the following morning.

He held up his hand. "Don't worry about it, honestly. I'm guessing he's a little upset about you working late, huh?"

I shrugged my shoulder. "I think it's more that I'm growing up and he's still in the same place."

I hadn't meant to confess that thought to Toby, and I felt very uncomfortable.

"If there's anything I can do, let me know," he said, smiling. "In the meantime, we have a court case to prepare for."

I worked solidly all day, no break, and I slumped onto the train exhausted.

"I made dinner," Sam said, when I walked through the door.

I kissed him. "Thank you." I took that to be his apology. "I'm going to have a bath, do I have time?"

"Sure, I might join you."

I smiled at him and raised my eyebrows. "I'd like that."

We had sex, ate, and then fell into bed. He wrapped his arms around me, and we fell asleep.

That was the pattern for a few weeks. On my nineteenth birthday, he went all out. He booked a restaurant in London; I had a new outfit to wear. We had cocktails and wine, and food we'd never seen before. I had loved it, he, not so much. London was becoming *my place*. I loved the buzz, the lights, the atmosphere. I loved the wine bars and pubs, the clubs. The architecture amazed me, the money attracted me.

* * *

"Are we finalising a date?" Sam asked, I'd pulled out a box of wedding items I'd been collecting.

"We should, but I think it should be next year now. I'll be qualified and on more money. What do you think?"

"I think I can afford a wedding without your money anyway. Why the wait?"

I stared at him. This was the man who insisted we waited.

"No reason. I thought it might be easier. I'll be able to take full leave for a honeymoon and we'll be able to afford a few things we can't right now. That's all," I said, not wanting an argument.

He shrugged his shoulders, and I sighed.

"Guess being a city girl now is a priority."

I closed my eyes. "Yes, Sam, it's a priority for me. Stop being jealous. Who do I live with? Who do I love?"

He snorted. "You think I'm jealous? Of what?"

"Because I'm moving up the ladder, I guess. I don't know, why don't you tell me?"

He laughed and it irritated me.

"Grow up, Sam. I'm too tired for this."

I left him to his joint and headed to bed.

Things settled down for a little while and it was nice. We did set a date and it was for the year after. We even booked a venue, and I ordered invitations. That seemed to satisfy Sam. I worried though.

I was seeing Tammy that evening. We'd long got over what had happened, and she'd asked me and Sam to be godparents.

He had stuck to his promise to not see her, but we had compromised, and he only saw her if I was there as well.

"You look stressed," she said, handing me Karl.

I bounced him on my lap. "I am."

"Wanna tell me about it?"

Tammy lived in the pool house Karl had once lived in. Karl's mum had unofficially adopted her, since her parents had kicked her out when they'd found out she was pregnant.

"I don't know what's going on with Sam. He seems really jealous of my job."

"Is he threatened by this new you?"

"What do you mean, *new you*?"

"You're way more confident than you were. You're more gorgeous, always got your nails done and your makeup is perfect. Maybe he worries you'll leave him."

I rolled my eyes and sighed. "I dress the way my job dictates. Trust me, Tams, if I could wear flats or trainers, I would," I said, laughing.

It was the done thing to look good, to wear the heels and makeup. I was even getting my eyebrows shaped.

"What are you going to do?" she asked.

"I'm not leaving. I asked him to employ me a couple of years ago, he didn't. So, I got a job and then another. I don't understand why he wouldn't be happy for me about that. He was thrilled when I had the interview."

"Does he think you're moving up in the world and he isn't?"

"I said that, albeit in a nasty way, because I think that. He's a business owner, I'd love to do that. Why would he feel that way?"

"You've changed so much since you both met. You look and act different, maybe he feels you're going to outgrow him."

I fell silent. Tammy had hit the nail on the head, I thought.

"I love him, but, and please don't tell him this, I do feel a little stuck. Like, he doesn't want to travel or do things I see my friends at work doing, and I get a little jealous of them."

When I'd first met Sam, my mum had told me to be aware of our love burning out. I didn't believe that was the case at all, but I was beginning to think, as I was growing up, I wanted different things in life than Sam.

"You know you can't get married feeling like that, don't you?" she said gently.

I nodded and sighed. "I put it off for a year already. I'm so confused, Tams," I said, and I felt the tears falling.

"Why not tell him this?"

"He's too insecure, really. You know that."

"Then why not do it slowly. Book a holiday as a surprise."

"Yeah, that's a good idea. He loved going to Greece with my parents that time, and they're always inviting us wherever they go."

Karl decided to shit at that point, and I screwed my nose up. "Here, I think you need your child back."

She laughed. "What are you going to do when you have your own?" she said.

I kept quiet. That was another thing. Over the past year, the thought of having a child was getting pushed farther and farther back in my mind.

I snuggled into Sam that night, feeling clingy and needy. I loved him more than life, I wanted him to embrace the journey I was on. I wanted him on that journey with me.

He kissed the hand I'd wrapped around him, and I vowed to spoil him that weekend.

"I love you so much it hurts," I whispered. He kissed my hand again.

The following day I was up before him. I cooked him a nice breakfast, made a coffee, and took it into the bedroom on a tray.

"Hey, sleepyhead," I said gently.

I loved looking at Sam when he slept. I'd taken hundreds of photographs of him like that. He would start on his side, spooning me, then slide to his back at some point. He would have one arm across the pillow over his head, and the other over his chest, as if he was holding his heart. I thought he was protecting it.

The tattoo of my name was always visible.

"What time is it?" he mumbled, opening his eyes.

"Time for breakfast," I said, and smiled.

He slid up the bed. "What do I owe this to?"

"Nothing, I want to spoil you today. I have plans. We're going to spend the weekend doing all the fun things you love."

"Mmm, I like the sound of that," he said.

I placed the tray on the bed and climbed on beside him. I sipped my tea while he ate.

"We need this, don't we?" he said quietly.

"I think so."

"It's been a strange few months, baby."

"You know what I think we should do? We should get the bike out and go down the coast today. Get fish and chips, and talk. Lots of talking."

He nodded and smiled at me. "I love you, you do know that, don't you?"

"Absolutely, and you should never question that. Now eat."

Being on the back of his bike with him was one of the best places in the world for me. I loved the sound and smell. I loved holding on to him, and him placing his hand over mine when we were on a long stretch of road. A thought came to me. We could do a road trip by bike, get a tent, and tour around Europe. I was sure he'd love that idea.

We headed towards Camber Sands, one of his favourite places, and drove along the coast road. There was something about being by the coast for him. It buoyed him up, the smell and sounds of the waves were soothing for him. As much as I liked it, I preferred the city lights.

Once we'd parked and secured the helmets to the handlebars, he took my hand and we walked. It was autumn and although still a lovely day, the beach wasn't as crowded as it could be.

We found a place to sit and settled down. I kicked off my boots and removed my jacket. He did the same. We lay side by side.

"See those clouds?" he said, looking up. "That one's an elephant, see?"

I had no idea what he was looking at. "No." I laughed.

"Look closer. I used to do this with my mum when I was a kid. We'd lie down and make shapes from the clouds."

I turned on my side and rested on one elbow.

"When are you going to start that therapy you said about?" I asked.

"Do you think I need it?"

"Yes. I think you have unresolved issues about your parents, and it might be good to talk to someone neutral about that."

"Is that our problem?" he asked.

I frowned. "Our problem?"

He turned on his side and rested on one elbow as well.

"Yes." He reached forward and pushed some hair behind my ear. "We haven't been right for a while. We know we love each other, but we're a bit lost at the moment, aren't we?"

I hadn't thought of it that way. We were moving in different directions, and we needed to find a way back to each other, for sure. I nodded.

"I love you, Sam. I can't bear the thought of losing you."

"I feel the same, baby. But we are. We are losing each other and maybe that was how it was meant to be."

I blinked back tears and shook my head. "No, I won't let that happen to us. We have to stop that."

He nodded and wrapped an arm under my neck. He pulled me to him, and we cuddled silently on the sand.

"Do you want to put off the wedding until you're settled at work?" he whispered.

I nodded. "Not because I don't want to marry you, you

know that, right? I just want to get my career off the ground without having to take any time out."

"Then we need to do the same about kids. Call me old-fashioned, but I'd rather we were married first," he said.

He sounded sad but I couldn't tell him to change his mind because it was what I wanted. I was the one who wanted the delay and he, bless him, was just giving me a way out, allowing me to save my face and not have to be the one to broach the subject.

"We will be fine," I said, hoping that would be the case. "We could start looking for a larger place, if you like. You said you wanted to move."

He looked down at me and smiled. "Yeah, we'll rent that flat out. It can be our kids' inheritance, and we'll buy something bigger. A house with a garden, maybe.

We started to plan, talk about the wish list we'd make. He wanted a den, a man-shed of some kind. I thought that was a cracking idea. I didn't cherish the idea of us smoking in the house anymore. I'd started to notice the smell lingering.

"I'd love a dining room, a proper one," I said.

"Why, you can't cook," he replied, laughing.

"I can learn. So, it has to be two bedrooms."

"Minimum," he added.

"A garage for the bike?"

"Yep, and maybe you can get that one you've always wanted."

"I prefer to be on the back of yours. I'd be terrified."

I had quit my driving lessons for the second time because I just hated being in control of a vehicle on the road.

"We need to be somewhere on a good bus route, so I can get to work," I said.

"So not in the countryside, or by the coast?"

I knew those would be his favoured spots. I decided just to go along with it. "As long as I can get to work okay," I replied.

He sighed and smiled. It was a contented sigh rather than an exasperated or sad one. He kissed the top of my head and we fell silent. I dozed; I was sure he had as well. It was the breeze picking up that stirred me.

"Do you want fish and chips?" I asked, sitting up and looking over at the kiosk. "It doesn't look open."

"We'll find one along the coast."

"I had an idea for a holiday. I thought we could get a tent and do a road trip on the bike. Can you imagine, just pulling up and camping somewhere?"

He cocked his head to one side and nodded. "Yeah, that could be fun. When do you want to go?"

The one thing about Sam was, if a suggestion was agreed on, he wanted it firmed up. I understood a lot of that was because of work. He had customers he needed to work around, and he had to blank himself out in the diary. Nothing could be done last minute unless he had a free few days.

"You check your diary on Monday, and I'll request the time off."

We both sounded enthusiastic about something. There wasn't the low, bored, or irritated tone to our voices.

We walked back to the bike and headed a little way up the coast. We were in no rush to get home, and it would be nice to spend the evening on the beach as well. Sam found a fish and chip shop and I rushed in. I got us some food and stuffed it in my backpack. I then shot into the mini supermarket next door and grabbed a couple of beers and some soft drinks.

We were back on the coast road, just for a little way, when we found a small bay unoccupied. It had looked like someone had a barbecue there, there was a fire pit with charcoal.

Sam dragged a log closer; he gathered some dried grasses and relit the fire pit. It took him a few minutes.

"My Boy Scout. You are clever," I said, laughing.

We sat on the sand and leant against the log, eating our fish and chips and drinking our beer. When we were done, Sam pulled a joint from the inside of his jacket and lit it. We rested back, smoked, and watched the night draw in.

I could have stayed there for hours, just looking at the stars. Maybe Sam had the right idea about not being in town. There was way too much light pollution to see anything.

We chatted about nothing, really. Until he mentioned his mother. I didn't know a great deal about her, other than I didn't think she had the greatest parenting skills. He did, so I never said anything. I couldn't imagine buying dope for my son's birthday or Christmas present!

"My mum ran away when she was young. She's the only person I know for a fact who ran away and joined a circus," he laughed as he spoke. "Straight up, she did the tickets, or something."

"Did your dad ever live with you?" I asked.

"Not that I remember. He might have when I was young. He was married to my aunt first, had two sons. I used to be close to them, but when our mums fell out, they moved away, and we lost contact."

"We could try to find them if you wanted to."

"Nah. When someone moves on, that's it. I prefer a clean cut."

"You've been alone for a lot of your life, haven't you?"

I knew his mum left him as a young teen for days on end. He never said where she'd go, but she'd come back and shower him with gifts... and drugs.

"I've managed."

"Where is she buried? Would you take me there one day?"

"I've never been myself. She was cremated and then her ashes scatter by whoever does that. There was some talk of a tree, but I bet that's a load of bollocks. Probably washed her down the drain. Can you imagine hundreds of people's ashes around a fucking tree. It would kill it! Especially the drugs, legal and illegal, in my mum's system."

It was a funny statement, made all the more hilarious the more stoned I became. Sam was way more tolerant than me. He'd been smoking for years.

And the more stoned I became, the hornier I was.

When the joint was done, I rolled over to lie on top of him. "Wanna make out?" I said.

He placed his hands on my arse cheeks. "Yep."

We kissed, a deep and slow kiss. I cupped his cheeks and

ground myself into him. I only stopped so I could take my jacket and boots off and slip off my jeans and knickers.

"Don't get sand in my whatsit," I said, chuckling and looking around to make sure we really were alone.

I freed his cock from his jeans, pushed them down a little and guided it inside me. I sighed with contentment. I leaned down to kiss him again and rode him gently.

"Remember the first time I did this?" I whispered and Sam laughed.

"Yeah, you bounced up so high you nearly got my cock in your arse. And we're still going there one day."

I laughed and shook my head. "One for in, one for out."

Joking over, I started to ride him hard. I spread my legs so I could feel him deeper inside. He came before me, something he hated, but I didn't mind. I knew he'd always make it up to me.

"I'm sorry, baby," he said. "You're too good at this now."

"That's okay. You can owe me one."

I slid to the side, and then wondered what on earth I was going to clean myself up with. I rifled through my backpack and found an old tissue. It would have to do. Once dressed, Sam kicked sand over the coals, we poured one bottle of water over it, so it was cold, and shared the other as we walked back to the bike.

Sam drove home slowly and I leaned against his back. He would pat my thigh every now and again to make sure I was still awake, and I would tap his stomach in reply.

We arrived home at gone midnight, and although tired, Sam paid what he owed.

CHAPTER 15

The Past

We bumbled along for the next couple of months, redecorating the flat and house-hunting. Mum and Dad wanted to give us a gift, some money towards the deposit since we'd told Dad he wasn't to pay for the wedding. We'd saved a lot ourselves; we didn't want a massive mortgage if we could help it.

It took a year, but we found a lovely two-bedroomed new build that suited us both. It was a half hour from where we lived, on the edge of the town. The station was within a short bus ride, and farmland was behind us. We guessed the farmer had sold off some of his land. I could also get the bus to my parents' and to the nearest supermarket.

Usually Sam always took me shopping, he hated shopping, of course, and sometimes just stayed in the car. Other times, I'd get a cab. It didn't bother me using public transport, but if I was ever late, he always collected me. He wouldn't allow me on the train or bus at night, terrified something would happen to me.

We found a tenant for the flat, an elderly man who had lost his wife and wanted to downsize. He was perfect and a customer of Sam's already. It had been a chance chat while Sam was giving his car a service about moving that had Alfred asking about the flat. His daughter came to view it with him, and other than wanting to change the bathroom to a shower room, they thought it was perfect. Sam told them they could do what they wanted.

We ended up having to move our furniture to the garage for a couple of weeks and living with my parents because our new house was delayed, but once we got it, we settled straight away. I took endless photographs, spending a fortune at getting them developed to the point that, as a surprise for my twentieth birthday, Sam converted the spare room into a studio for me. I could develop my own photographs.

We built a shed, his man cave as we called it. He built a bar, we put in a sofa, a television, and it became our smoking room. He grew a few cannabis plants in pots at the old flat and he tended to them lovingly in his man cave. I used to laugh; he was as caring with them as he was with me sometimes.

Things were good, I felt. It seemed we'd found a compromise we were both happy with. I got my London fix with work, and then one night out a week with the girls, and sometimes blokes, in a wine bar, and Sam got the country living he desired.

He had even talked about moving work. His garage was too small really for what he wanted, and I encouraged him to talk to the farm owner to see if perhaps he had a small yard for rent. It would cost a fortune to set up the pit and ramps, but I thought it would be worth it. He'd be closer to home, in fact, he could walk to work if he wanted to. I could help out easier, we could have the office at home, share the spare bedroom.

We started to plan.

It all started to go tits up when I was invited to Pam's wedding.

Pam and Sam had met loads of times. He'd dropped her off home when he'd picked me up. They got on. She'd visited us for a barbecue with her boyfriend, someone Sam wasn't overly fond of but could tolerate.

Pam was marrying Gregg, who was lovely, if a bit of a *wet lettuce* as my dad would say. He worked in sales, had slicked back hair, and a weak handshake. He sold photocopiers and would spend ages telling us all about them. All Sam wanted to do was pop him over the head with his beer bottle. I would work so hard to contain my laughter when Sam's eyes glossed over. Gregg's only saving grace was he liked a little dope himself. And once he was stoned, he was hilarious. He'd still talk about photocopiers, but how stupid they were.

Pam loved him, and that was all that mattered.

"Do I look okay?" I asked, standing in front of the sliding wardrobe door mirror.

"You look beautiful," Sam replied, lounging on the bed.

He wore a new suit I'd bought him, and only after an argument and me telling him he couldn't come. He hated suits, only owned the one he'd worn to Karl's funeral and refused to wear that again. I left that at a charity shop and bought a new grey one.

"So do you," I said, when he stood. "Honestly, Sam, you don't know how handsome you are, and how amazing you look in a suit. I'm going to have my hands full keeping women off you!"

He shook his head and laughed.

We got to the church, and I reintroduced Sam to Toby and a few of my colleagues. He was polite and not arsy that time. Jenny, one of the juniors, was all flustered by Sam and blushed scarlet when he spoke to her. I nudged him in a 'I told you so' way.

We sat through the service and then hung around for photographs. Sam and I took Jenny to the reception since she didn't have a lift, and we grabbed some champagne while we waited for the bride and groom. Sam bought himself a beer. We were soon joined by Toby, Pedro, and Del. Del was an arsehole and someone I didn't like. He wasn't a partner but working his way up the ladder. He was sexist, racist, every *ist* you could imagine. Worse when he was drunk. He'd been thrown out of our regular wine bar so many times, he was then banned. He was also in the middle of a disciplinary. Why Pam had invited him, I had no idea, she hated him as much as I did.

"So you brought the grease monkey?" I heard, praying Sam hadn't.

I slipped my hand in Sam's and squeezed. Sam was ordering another beer and a wine for me.

"Hayley," Del said, dragging out my name. "You ignoring me?"

"I have this," I whispered to Sam, noticing the tension causing his jaw to tighten.

"Yes, Del. And I'd appreciate you don't refer to my fiancé in that way."

"Can't he speak for himself?" I turned to face him. Del was swaying and it seemed he was already drunk.

Toby had his hand on Del's chest and was pushing him away.

"What?" Del said to Toby. "I'm only joking with her."

Sam slowly turned. He handed me the wine glass. "Ooohh, scary," Del said, waving his hands in the air.

I stepped in front of Sam and placed one hand on his cheek. I needed to get his attention on me, immediately. The fucking bride and groom hadn't arrived, and it was kicking off!

"Sam, please. For me, we'll have the meal and then leave," I whispered.

He looked down at me and nodded. His jaw was so tense, and I knew his teeth would be gritted together.

We walked away, and I think it was the first time that had ever happened.

"Thank you," I said as we decided to look at the table plan. I groaned when I saw Del was at the same table. "He's sitting with us."

"I'll behave, don't worry. These are your friends; I can stomach that cunt for a couple of hours."

When Sam used the C word, I knew he was super mad. I also knew if Del started, a fight would follow.

I tried to catch Toby's eye, I wanted to have a quiet word, but I didn't want to leave Sam alone. He didn't know anyone; it had been a struggle to get him to come. He didn't do mixing with strangers usually. The last thing I could do was leave him on his own at the bar.

My heart was thumping in my chest when we were called to sit. Luckily, any interaction was stopped when the bride and groom entered. And more so when the meal was served. Del was sitting opposite Sam, and I hoped he'd just concentrate on the nice woman beside him. I hadn't been introduced to her, she was Pedro's plus one, and I felt terrible she'd get the brunt of him, but it saved a fight.

Or so I thought.

After the meal Sam was happy to stay for a little while so I could chat to Pam. He went out to the car park to have a cigarette, and I hadn't noticed Del also left. I only knew that had happened when I heard a woman scream.

I knew, without anyone telling me, Sam was in a fight.

I ran, Pam and Gregg ran, as did some of the guests. We bundled outside and saw Sam sitting astride Del punching his face. Blood was everywhere and I knew Sam wouldn't have seen anything other than the red mist that descended over him. Toby ran and rugby tackled Sam off Del. He wasn't strong enough to hold him down, however. I screamed, shouting at Toby to move away, and Sam to look at me, focus on me. Del lay unconscious on the ground.

It took three men to hold Sam back, and then eventually, the police. He was handcuffed and driven away. He'd *come to* at that point and stared at me through the window.

"I'm sorry," he mouthed. I nodded.

"What a fucking animal," someone said, as Del was being loaded into an ambulance.

"No, he isn't. You have no idea what started that." I started to cry. "I need to call my dad," I said.

Toby put his arm around my shoulders. "Let's find a phone."

"I'll have him come and collect me and take me to the station," I said.

"I can do that. Remember who I am?" he said, smiling gently at me.

"You don't want to step into my shit. Fucking Del, why did he have to start?"

"Come on, get your bag and let's go. Enough people are staring at us," he said, chuckling.

"Don't laugh, this isn't funny," I replied.

"I know. Come on."

I walked in knowing people were gossiping. Pam rushed over and hugged me. "I am so sorry. I've ruined your wedding."

"No, honey, *you* haven't at all."

Gregg joined her. "What's a wedding without a good fight anyway?" he said. "Let us know what happens to Sam, won't you?"

I nodded.

I joined Toby in his car, a top of the range Mercedes with a white leather interior. I was frightened of marking the leather with my tears and running makeup.

"I'm so sorry, Toby. I'll resign on Monday," I said.

He looked sharply at me. "Whatever for?"

"For the embarrassment I've caused you and the company."

"*You* haven't done anything. Del and Sam are the culprits. Del is going to lose his job; he knew that already. It's a shame Sam bit so easily though."

I nodded. "He'll go away this time," I said softly.

"This time?"

"This isn't his first fight. The last one that was this bad, admittedly, the guy didn't want to press charges, so they were dropped, but he has a restraining order against him for something else. Surely, that will mean he'll go to jail, won't it?"

"No, not necessarily. I'll represent him, I'll get him off, but you must do whatever I say, okay?"

I nodded. "Thank you. I can pay you; I have savings."

"Call this a quid pro quo," he said, smiling at me.

"Well, I'll work it off, then."

"First, we need to find out where he is. So, back to your house?"

I lived closer to Pam than he did, so it made sense. He needed a telephone to work from.

Toby spent a half hour ringing police stations to find out where he was, and eventually did. I was told to wait at home, and he'd go and see if he could get him bailed out.

I watched him leave and waited. And waited.

I took a shower, wanting to get out of the silly wedding clothes. I slipped on some jeans and a jumper and made tea. My stomach was in knots, and I felt sick.

I sat and thought. Sam couldn't continue to behave that way. He might have had full justification to be pissed off, I had no idea what started the fight. But when he fought, it was like he wanted to kill someone. He lost control. He was going to end up in prison if he wasn't careful.

I must have fallen asleep because I woke when the front door slammed. I heard Sam and Toby walk into the hall. I jumped up from the sofa and rushed out.

"Sam?"

"Hey, baby," he said.

"What the fuck?"

I came to an abrupt halt.

"Told you last time, they don't like me," he said, laughing.

"It's no fucking laughing matter," I said, holding his chin and moving his face from side to side. He winced. "What did they do to you?"

"Beat him good. We'll file a complaint for that. Sam, we're going to need to get prepared for court." We continued into the living room.

"Court?" I asked.

Toby looked at me. "There's no doubt Del will press charges. I'll see you on Monday. Unless you need some time off?"

I shook my head. "I'll see you Monday and thank you. I can't tell you how much I appreciate your help, Toby."

He stared at me a little too long, I thought, for Sam's liking. "Let me show you out."

I walked Toby to the front door and stood just outside it. "What does it look like?" I asked.

He shrugged his shoulders. "Depends on Del's injuries right now. And I don't know what that is. So we wait. The police will interview Del when they can. I've registered as his lawyer. I also suggest we keep that among ourselves, no talk about it at work."

I nodded, thanked him yet again, and closed the door behind him. I then joined Sam in the living room. He was sparking up a joint.

"Don't smoke that in here," I said. He laughed and ignored me. "So what happened?" I asked gently, diffusing anything coming.

"He's a fucking prick. Got what he deserved."

I sighed. "Sam, what happened?"

"He took the piss, I shut his mouth for him."

I sat and stared at him. Eventually, he turned to me. "Took the piss out of my cheap suit, my job, how I look, that kind of thing. Prick got in my face, squared up to me, so I put him on his arse."

I sighed a little too loudly.

"What? You don't think I should have done that, huh? He your work buddy, is he?"

"No, and no." He stared at me. "Someone takes the piss out of you, you don't need to pulverise them, Sam. When are you going to learn that? You could have walked away, laughed at him, anything other than do what you did and spoil someone's wedding."

When Sam was mad, and he still was, he was unreasonable. Often, there was no getting through to him and mostly, I'd leave him be. He had embarrassed me in front of my colleagues twice now. I worked for one of London's top lawyers, there would be an impact on me.

"So sorry I spoiled your friend's wedding," he said sarcastically.

He was picking at the scabs on his knuckles and dripping blood over the cream carpet. I walked to the kitchen and grabbed a tea towel.

"Here," I said, handing it to him. He didn't take it, I let it drop. Instead he just let his blood drip on the floor.

"I guess I'll just leave you alone, shall I?"

I huffed, shook my head, and stormed off.

Sam didn't come to bed that night. I found him asleep on the sofa the following morning. There was a burn hole where he'd dropped his joint, blood and empty bottles of beer on the cream carpet. I was furious with him. I slapped his leg.

"Sam, wake up," I said loudly.

He stirred. When he woke, his face was encrusted with blood, and I softened.

"You need to get in the shower," I added.

He stood and stretched. I could see the bruises on his side when his shirt rose. He gave me a small smile as he walked past and climbed the stairs.

I put the bottles in the bin and scrubbed at the carpet. There was nothing I could do about the burn mark, but I managed to get most of the blood up. I'd always know it was there but didn't think anyone else would. As a last resort, I could move the sofa forwards a little.

I made him a coffee and took it upstairs. He was sitting on the edge of our bed, looking at the floor. I sat beside him and handed him the coffee.

"He said when you grew bored of me, he was going to fuck you. Whether you wanted him to or not."

"What? He said, what?"

"What he said, what he meant, was that he'd quite happily rape you when you left me."

"You didn't say," I said. He just shrugged his shoulders.

"What did Toby say?" I asked.

"He's going to defend me, this will go to court, and I could get put away. I guess we'll see if he's right."

"What happens next?"

"Toby will come here and do whatever it is he does."

"I offered to pay him. He didn't want any, so I've said I'll work it off."

"I can fucking pay for my own counsel, Hayley."

"Do you know how much he charges, Sam?"

He sneered at me. "No, but I'm sure you're about to tell me."

I took a moment to breathe deeply. "I'm not the enemy, Sam," I said quietly.

He placed an arm around me and pulled me to his side. We sat that way for a little while.

"Have I fucked it up for you at work?"

"I doubt it. But it's going to be hard to go in on Monday and face people. I can bet Pedro would have already called everyone he could. It's Pam and Gregg I feel sorry for."

"I'll apologise to them." He made no mention of apologising to my work colleagues.

Sam spent the rest of the day fixing up motorbikes in the garage. I called my mum and told her what had happened.

"Hals, I'm getting a little concerned about his temper," she said.

"There's no need to be concerned about me. He has never hurt me in anyway. I think he might go to prison this time."

"Hayley, come home, please."

"I can't just walk out, not at the minute. I just wanted to talk to someone. I'm going to ask you something, please don't tell Dad."

"Oh, darling, I won't, but only for the minute. You need to get your life sorted. Sam needs to get on an anger management programme. I know what he was told was awful, but highly unlikely to ever happen. It was to wind him up, and it did the trick."

"What do you think the worst outcome would be?" I asked.

"I don't know, certainly jail time. I'm sure Toby will do his best. Even if he gets off, you have to push him to get therapy. We love him like a son, but I can't have you at risk in any way. You also have to work out, can you afford the house if he's in prison and not earning?"

I knew I couldn't. I had finished uni, I was on the higher salary, but the cost of the mortgage and travel to London, the bills, would probably clean me out each month.

"I'll sell up, go back to the flat while I wait…"

"While you wait for him?"

"I don't know. I need to speak to Toby and then see what happens."

"You know you can always come home."

We said goodbye. The next call I made was to Toby. I had his home number because I'd had to call him on the rare occasion he worked from home for some reason.

"Hi, it's me," I said.

"Hey, Hals. How are you holding up?"

I sighed. "Okay. I think. I just spoke to my mum about what I'll do if Sam goes to prison. I know it's too hard to say, but what do you think his chances are."

"Right now, fifty-fifty. What is it that you'll do?"

"I'll have to sell the house. Sam owns a flat I can stay at until he gets out, I guess."

"That could be some time."

"I know. I'll have to just take it day by day."

"Want to meet up tomorrow?" he asked.

"Sam said you'd come here," I replied.

"No, I mean you and me. Maybe we can go through some things so you can prepare."

I nodded, then remembered he couldn't see me. "Okay, that would be good if you're not too busy."

"How about at the wine bar?"

"That would be lovely. Say, about twelve?"

We confirmed our plan and I put the phone down. When I looked up, Sam was standing in the doorway.

"Hey, that was Toby. I'm going to meet him tomorrow to talk about planning," I said, standing.

"I heard. Does he want to see me?"

"No, just me tomorrow. I'll go to the wine bar we visit."

"I'll drive you."

"You don't have to do that; I don't know how long I'll be."

He bit the inside of his cheek and didn't respond.

"Unless you drive me, and I'll call you when I'm ready to leave? I just don't want you sitting around for a couple of hours."

"I'll find a pub."

"Is that wise?"

"I'll drink a fucking Coke, Hals."

"Don't, Sam. I'm doing this for you."

He sighed. "I know. I don't want you worrying about getting there and home on a bank holiday."

"I appreciate that. And I'd love a lift there and I'll call you when I'm ready to come home."

CHAPTER 16

The Past

I walked into the bar, spotting him straightaway.

Toby sat in a booth in jeans and a polo shirt. I walked to the bar and grabbed two bottles of beer.

"Hi, here. I got these." I handed him one bottle.

"Nice, thank you," he said, taking the bottle from me and taking a sip. "How was your evening?"

"Strained. Sam wouldn't talk at first. He slept on the sofa, stoned and drunk, I think."

"Not good. Did Sam tell you what Del said?"

I nodded. "Not straightaway. He said that to wind him up, didn't he?"

"Don't know, to be honest. He has a rape charge pending that we weren't aware of, and that's why he's losing his job."

"*Losing*, as in, it hasn't happened yet?"

"Correct. He hasn't stood trial. Innocent until proven guilty, remember?"

"I don't understand."

"Del told Sam he was going to rape you once Sam was out of the way. Now, he may not have meant it literally, but knowing what we do about him... This could very well be our get out of jail card."

"Oh," I replied, not sure what to add.

"It's not enough to get him off, but I'm hoping for a suspended sentence. Maybe a little community service."

"You haven't lost a case yet, Toby. This won't be good for you, will it?"

I knew it wouldn't. Defence lawyers relied on their 'get out of jail' record.

He shrugged his shoulder. "Gotta lose one, I guess. And I'd rather it be for you than anyone else." He sipped his beer, looking over the bottle at me.

His voice had changed, and I held my breath.

"Don't worry, I'm not hitting on you. Well, I am showing my hand, but that's all. I can see how in love with Sam you are. And for him to jeopardise his freedom for you shows me his depth of love."

"Now this is going to be awkward," I said.

"No. Only if we let it. We're friends, right? As well as boss and whatever. We're adults, we can work through this. How old are you now?"

"Twenty-four. I've worked for you since I was eighteen."

"Time goes so fast, doesn't it? I have something else to tell you. I'm leaving the firm. Which is why I guess I'm speaking more openly than I should. Sam will be a private case, the first in my own practice."

"You can't leave!"

"I want to branch out on my own. You can come with me," he said quietly.

"Erm, Jesus. I don't know if I'm even going to be able to carry on working at the firm, do I?"

"I highly doubt you'll lose your job, Hals. And if you do, you have options. You can come with me."

"Where will you work?"

"From home, in Dulwich Village."

"When are you leaving?"

"I'm on garden leave from a week on Monday. I have one week to hand over my clients and update Mark on all open cases."

Mark was another partner; one I didn't like. He was so miserable and had gone through tons of PAs since I'd been there.

"How long do I have to think about it?" I asked.

"A week, maybe two. I'm sure I can cope without you for one week. It'll be hard, but I'll manage," he said, giving me a fake whimper.

I laughed. I'd loved working with him, but the line had now been blurred. How could I work with him in his house after his confession?

If I wasn't confused before, I certainly was then.

"Now, back to you. You need to convince Sam to get anger

management. He's dangerous, Hals. If he doesn't end up in jail next time, I'll be surprised."

I bristled a little. "You're assuming there will be a next time."

"Come on. You're not silly. He has one heck of a temper."

I slumped a little. Toby called for two more beers; I hadn't finished my first.

"What do I do?" I asked, my voice small.

"Assume Sam is going to prison. I advise my clients to prepare for the worst, hope for the best. I like to make sure the partners of my clients are prepared and understand the process."

He then went through what was likely to happen. He also told me what he expected of me. How I was to act in court, cry when prompted. I hadn't realised it was all so theatrical! I'd been to court with him, I hadn't thought twice about any of it being staged. I wasn't sure to be shocked or not.

"I also want you to prepare to be alone, Hals. At some point Del will leave hospital. He knows where you work, but not where you live. So perhaps you should make sure to get security."

"Hold on. Are you suggesting he could come after me?"

"No, I'm suggesting that you need to prepare to be alone. If Sam is found guilty, he goes there and then. There's no going home. You'll get, like, ten minutes with him if I can wrangle that. I, me, your friend, not your boss, would like to know you're safe at home, and I know Sam will too. For someone like him, being away from you and not being able to help or do anything to protect you is going to drive him mad. He can't afford to fight in prison, he can't lose his rag. If he's found guilty, we'll go straight for appeal but if he's inside punching the shit out of people, he stays in there longer."

I closed my eyes. "I can't bear all this," I said.

He reached across the table and took both my hands in his. I let him. I wasn't sure why, but I needed some contact right then. For me, there was nothing in it. He was my boss, and a friend. Nothing more.

"I'm here for you as well. I know what I said earlier, but I can keep myself in check." He smiled and I knew he was telling me the truth. Or his truth.

He was a lawyer, after all!

I called Sam from a payphone and said I was ready. It would take him a half an hour, which was enough time to finish our beers.

"I don't know how to thank you, Toby, for all you're doing."

"There's no need to thank me. If you're really troubled about how to pay me back, just remember how shite my filing was before you came, and how bad it's going to get."

He cocked his head to one side and widened his eyes. I laughed.

"I'll think about it. I don't know how on earth I'd get to Dulwich Village, and I might be doing that without Sam driving me, remember?"

Finally, we came off the subject and chatted about Pedro's plus one. "I thought he was gay," Toby said.

"So did I. Maybe she was his sister? Did anyone ask?"

"We didn't really get the chance," he said, then winked.

I rolled my eyes. We talked about his new venture and the kind of clients he wanted to take on. Toby was a great lawyer. Young*ish*, dynamic, and knew the law like the back of his hand. Like most lawyers, he took on cases he thought he could win, but every now and again, he'd coach a lower graded lawyer through a difficult case to get the best result for the client. That didn't always sit well with me. They believed the client was guilty, but they deserved a fair trial.

Sam arrived a little later than I expected, but I was pleased to see him. He shook Toby's hand, and I gave Toby a hug. I thanked him, yet again, and told him I'd see him on Monday with his usual coffee.

"That was a bit *friendly,* wasn't it?" Sam said, as he opened my car door.

"He is a friend, as well as a boss. He's leaving the company and he offered me a job."

"He said he was leaving, but didn't mention anything about you," he replied.

"Maybe he didn't think about it then."

"Or maybe he didn't want me to know at first."

"You are not my keeper, Sam. I'm old enough to make decisions for myself, especially where my career is concerned."

He chuckled, knowing he'd stepped over a line and was doing damage control. I took hold of his hand.

"Let's get home and I'll tell you all about the meeting," I said.

* * *

It was weeks before the court case. It was agonising. The closer it had gotten; the worse Sam was behaving. Especially since I'd taken up the job offer with Toby and was leaving earlier and arriving home later because of the travelling distance. His jealousy was getting a little out of hand, and I constantly pulled him up on that.

In the beginning, when I was a kid, I'd loved his jealous streak. I'd felt treasured and protected. As I'd gotten older, it irritated. It was unwarranted, and I started to feel smothered by him. I was doing things simply to keep the peace, having to pre-empt how Sam would react to a situation.

I was back having those feelings that I was moving on a different trajectory to Sam.

He had stagnated, I was climbing, and yet again, a gap was opening up. We were aware, we saw it happening, but we didn't have the energy to deal with it. We had far more important things to worry about.

Del had wanted Sam charged with attempted murder. I'd nearly died when I heard that. Instead, however, he was charged with Section 20 GBH. Had he been charged with the more serious Section 18 GBH, he could face life imprisonment. As it was, he could be facing up to five years in prison.

Del had suffered some cuts and bruises, a split eyebrow, lip, and broken nose. I was stunned that was all he'd suffered considering how pummelled he'd been. His injuries were enough to warrant a grievous bodily harm charge. And it would be the second one he'd been charged with. Albeit the first had been dropped. I knew that couldn't be mentioned in court, but I was sure it would come up. The prosecution would want to tear Sam's character apart. Paint him as violent.

I hated that first day in court. I had my mum and dad with me, and we sat just behind Sam. He gave his name, confirmed his date of birth and address, and pled not guilty to GBH. Toby was pushing for ABH, citing that Del very well could have sustained the broken nose prior to the fight with Sam. If there were no broken bones, he was hoping to down charge. No medic could categorically state Del's nose had been broken in the fight because, and we all knew this, he had a broken nose from a rugby match he'd played in the weekend before the wedding.

After that, I didn't go back to court.

I'd sit at home with Mum and wait. Dad was in court every day and he'd bring Sam home, who was still on bail. Again, how Toby had managed that, was beyond me. Anyone on a Section 18 would instantly be on remand. And often anyone on a Section 20 would be joining them.

We went through a whole week of stress, anxiety, tension, tears, and arguing. I began to resent Sam for putting me through it all. He had aged the past few months. He wasn't even thirty and looking ten years older.

When Del was on the stand to give evidence, Toby ripped him to shreds, according to my dad. He told the jury how Del had told Sam that he intended to rape me. He left out any reference that it could have been simply to wind Sam up, of course.

In his summing up, which I was there for, he told the jury how that had affected my mental health, how Sam was fearful for me. He explained any man would have done the same in that situation and he was thrilled to see all the men on the jury nod.

Sam was found not guilty.

Even Toby was stunned.

Del screamed at the injustice and threatened a civil action. Toby said we'd deal with that when it happened.

Right or wrong, we celebrated, hard. We partied at home, got drunk, got stoned, fucked hard, and crashed. We slept on and off for a couple of days, exhausted by the whole procedure. Sam's business had suffered, and when we finally got ourselves together, he threw himself back into work.

I'd lost him for a while during the court case, and then I lost him to work. He had certainly withdrawn a lot, and I wasn't sure why.

What saddened me the most was I wasn't sure I wanted to know why.

"I need to talk; can we meet up?" I asked Tammy when she answered her phone.

"Sure, want to come to the park for a walk with me and Karl?"

I agreed and jumped on the bus to meet her. As usual, Sam was in the garage fixing something and it was a lovely Sunday morning. I wouldn't see him until he was hungry, normally.

I met Tammy at the park, and we walked for a while. We found a lovely bench and sat.

"I don't think Sam and I are going to make it," I said slowly.

"Make what?" she asked, staring, and frowning at me.

"I think we've come to the end. I love him, I know he loves me, but we're on totally different paths now. We've grown apart, and I'm not sure either of us wants to fix it."

"Have you spoken to him about that?"

"I don't see him, Tams. He hides away in the garage. I think as a means to not have to deal with this."

"You have to talk to him!"

"I'm going to. But I'm going to ask something of you."

She didn't speak. "When I'm gone, make sure you check on him for me?"

"Wait, what do you mean by that?"

"I mean, when I leave him, he will cut me off dead. It's what he does. I need to know you'll be there for him. He won't have anyone."

"Whoa, no. Hals, you can't be thinking straight."

"I'm thinking perfectly straight," I said, looking at the ground and watching my tears form a puddle. "I love him. I don't love our life together. We've grown apart."

"If this has anything to do with Toby…"

She didn't finish her sentence and I hoped it was the outrage she saw in my face that had caused that.

"Don't go there! I mean it. I am not like you, or Sam. I wouldn't dream of anything happening between me and Toby. We are friends, colleagues, nothing more."

She gasped at my statement and stood. "That wasn't called for. I think I need to go home."

I reached out for her. "I'm sorry, you're right, that wasn't called for."

She sat again and handed me a tissue.

"Is there any way I can change your mind?"

I shook my head. "No. This time, I think my mind is made up. I think his is, as well. And if we're going to separate, I'd rather do it now than stay together, hate each other, and get old and bitter."

I hugged her and left. Hoping she'd do that one thing I asked of her. She did owe me, after all.

Later that evening when Sam came home, I let him shower, reheat his cold meal, and then he headed to his shed to smoke his joint. I joined him.

"Can we talk?" I asked.

He nodded and patted the seat beside him. He smiled and handed me his joint.

"I need to talk as well," he said.

"You go first," I said.

He looked at me, kissed my forehead and I closed my eyes.

"You're stifled here. I can see that. I see that light in your eyes getting dimmer. You're tired. Tired of us, and that's okay. You need to spread your wings and fly, baby. I can't do that with you. You were right, that time. I'm stuck here, I like here, so I'm letting you go."

I couldn't speak. Tears flowed from my eyes and the largest lump had settled in my throat.

"It kills me to do this, Hals, and know I will always love you, way more than I'll ever love another. And I'm not just saying that. I know it in my heart. I also know, if we carry on, that love is going to tarnish. I think you and I would rather go out at the top, wouldn't we?"

He offered a smile, but I could see the pain behind it.

I nodded. "I love you, Sam. I always will. Thank you. Thank you for making this easy. Is there any way we could stay in touch? Stay friends?"

He shook his head. "It would kill me, Hals. Clean cut, you know me."

He swallowed hard, and I caught the lone tear that rolled down his cheek on my thumb.

"I'll move out," he said.

I shook my head. "No, I'll do that. You have your work here. I'll pay half the mortgage and we'll worry about the house another time."

"I can buy you out if you want."

"I don't want... I don't want to think about that just yet."

He wrapped his arms around me, and I sobbed. I sobbed so hard against his chest. I gripped his T-shirt in my fists.

"Can I keep your sweatshirt?" I whimpered and he nodded.

"Shall I take you to your parents?"

I nodded. Still crying I packed a bag, just an overnight one, and hand in hand we walked to the car.

I cried the whole way. I nearly changed my mind and begged him to take me home.

We'd been together eight years. Not far short of a decade.

He'd taught me everything I knew. I had been a kid when I'd met him. I was leaving him a confident woman and I only had him to thank for that.

When we arrived, I waited until he opened the car door. The lights on the drive had alerted my parents, and both came to the door. I saw my mum frown, and then my dad touched her arm, holding her back.

I slumped in Sam's arms. He kissed my forehead, and then my lips so softly. He looked up at my dad who came down the drive.

He handed me back.

"I love her. So I'm letting her go."

When his voice broke, then his legs shook and he stumbled against the car, I broke. I screamed out his name, I reached for him. My dad held me up. I was fifteen years old again. I begged him to come back.

Then he left.

And I didn't see him again.

Until I received a message some twenty-five years later.

CHAPTER 17

Present Day

I scrolled through my diary; I had a book signing the following weekend I couldn't miss. It was in London, in a bookstore and only for the Saturday, but I had a sense of urgency. I composed my message back to Alison.

Hi, Alison. I'm in London this Saturday, I'm staying overnight on the Friday, but I can meet your dad on Sunday. That would be the 12th. Other than that, I' available any day next week. I'll make the time.

I had a full diary of meetings, but I'd move one or two. I wanted to see him. I wasn't sure of his reaction though. Although Alison said he had wanted to apologise, and I still didn't know what for, I wonder if he also hated me.

It had been Tammy who had told me that. She, however, had ulterior motives by that point, I believed.

She'd kept in touch for a little while, chastising me constantly for how broken he was and reminding me I was the one who asked her to check on him. According to her, it took him a year to get over me, not that he ever really did, she'd said. She made her move on him, and he'd fallen for it, and that was okay.

They had dated for a little while and she'd made a point of telling me all the fun things they did, and how he'd grown to dislike me for wasting his time. If I'd have told him I'd fallen out of love with him earlier, he could have settled down, had a family with someone else. That had hurt and, although, deep down, I knew that wasn't him talking, I had a blazing row with her. Eventually, I had to block her. It was killing me.

Alison replied almost immediately.

I can't tell you what this means to me. We lost Mum a long time ago now, and although Mum knew Dad loved her, we all knew he still held feelings for you. I don't want Dad to go without seeing you. Sunday will be fine; I just know it. Where would you like to meet?'

Hi, Alison. Ask your dad if he remembers the pond on Blackheath where we used to sit? Tell him, I'll meet him there at 10 a.m. We can always take a walk to the shack and grab a coffee, if it's still there. Please tell him I can't wait to see him. Tell him I still have the sweatshirt; he'll know what that means.

I was nervous, I had to shut down my laptop so I didn't see her reply. Sam and I had often walked over Blackheath, through Greenwich Park. It had been one of our favourite places to visit. We'd grab a coffee and burger from the shack that the taxis all visited. That was before it all got serious, of course.

He understood and he laughed. He said he'd bring the aftershave and you'd know what that meant. I feel like I'm on some dating show ha ha ha. Sunday at ten. He drives a blue Jaguar. He hasn't changed at all, just a little grey. I'm so happy and I'd love to meet you some time as well.

I picked up my mobile.

"Hi, guess what?" I said when Pam answered.

"You won the lottery? You got abducted by aliens? You finally fucking finished those edits?"

"No. I'm meeting Sam on Sunday."

She went quiet for a moment. "Are you sure that's a good idea?"

I frowned, surprised by her comment. "Yes, I'm sure. Aren't you?"

She'd forgiven Sam for the fight at her wedding, or so I thought. Once they'd gotten back from their honeymoon, they'd come over and Gregg was laughing with Sam about it. They came to court with me.

"Okay, here's where I'm at and call me a bitch if you want. You never got over him. He never got over you. Your lives are so far apart now, you're on different fucking planets. What happens if that connection is still there? Who has to give to fit the other?"

"Oh, Pam. I can't imagine anything will happen, and we're both twenty-five years older now. What I wanted back then, I detest now."

The mere thought of heading into London gave me palpitations. I hated the pollution, traffic, the number of ignorant and rude people who bustled and jostled and didn't speak. It was the last place I liked to visit, unless it was strictly work and for a limited time only.

"You know I will always worry about you. I was with you when you split up. I don't want to go through that again. I don't want you to."

"Hello, earth to Pam? I repeat. I am twenty-five years older."

She chuckled. "We'll talk more about this on Saturday. Although, it would make a fantastic book."

I laughed and cut off the call. If I wrote my and Sam's story, I was sure it would be banned. Readers would be all up in arms about young sex and dope smoking, I imagined. I continued to laugh and shook my head.

I didn't speak to Alison again until the Saturday and I couldn't reply immediately because I was in London at my signing.

Hi, Hayley, are you still okay for tomorrow? Just wanted to check.

It was later that night that I replied.

Yes, Alison. Just got home so going to have an early night. I'll be there, don't worry. Tell him, I'm the one with the straight hair now.

She didn't reply. I grabbed Ursa's lead, and we walked around the fields. He was happy to see me, of course, he'd been with the house sitter overnight and as much as he loved her, he much preferred to be with me.

A pang of nerves settled in my stomach, and I chuckled. I had no idea why I was nervous. I recalled lots of fun memories, things we'd done and that very first meeting. I also remembered the very last day and the year that followed.

Pam had been right; it had been awful. I'd stopped eating, the weight dropped off me. I took so much time off work I was worried I might lose my job. Toby became extremely concerned, and it was him who finally booked me into a hospital and paid for it. I recovered, eventually, and Toby and I did end up together.

We often wondered if that was more gratitude or loneliness. I grew to love him, and we'd married, but it wasn't the heart-stopping love I'd had with Sam. We both knew that. We had been, and still were, great friends.

I decided to call him. We hadn't spoken for a few weeks, he'd recently married the love of his life, I'd been at their wedding, and they'd honeymooned in the Maldives.

"Hey, you, how are you?" he said, when he answered.

"Good, how was the honeymoon?" I asked.

"Bloody amazing, you should go there. Sally put all your books in the library," he answered chuckling.

I heard her shout hello in the background.

"Oh gawd! You won't be allowed back."

"It was amazing, I'm sure Sally will email over some photos. Don't suppose you fancy coming back to work, do you? Heidi left."

"Why did she leave? Were you a shit to her? And no, I don't have time."

Over the years, between fostering kids and writing, I'd helped out in his office. He still lived in Dulwich Village, but I drove by then. It was way easier getting to him, and I could have kicked myself for quitting so often.

"God knows, having a kid, I think."

I laughed. Toby was an old man now, so I reminded him. He had kids and grandkids. He and Sally had been together for years, they had no desire to make it official, and we had never gotten around to divorcing. That was until I decided they, and us, were being silly. We got the quickest divorce we could, they got married the same day.

"Guess what?"

"You know I'm shit at guessing anything. What?"

"I got a strange message the other day. A woman asking me if I knew her dad."

"Sam?"

"Yeah, his daughter. Apparently he is ill, and he has a list of things he wants to do. One is to apologise to me."

"Wow, for what?"

"No idea. I'm meeting him tomorrow and I'm so nervous."

"Oh, Hals. I highly doubt there will be anything to be nervous about. He was, still is, I bet, your *best love*."

I chuckled. Toby had always said Sam was my best love, and he was my second love.

"Isn't it odd, after all these years?" I asked.

"If the man has a list, he has a list. If I remember, he wasn't someone to do anything he didn't want to do. How ill is he?"

"I think very ill, like *dying* ill." I found my voice had cracked and emotion welled up inside me.

"Oh, Hals, I'm so sorry to hear that. Want me to come over?"

"No, don't be daft, I'm fine."

"He can come over, honey," I heard Sally shout and assumed she was beside him and listening.

"Thanks, Sal. But you've just got back from your honeymoon, it's not necessary."

"Honey, I've had to endure him for two solid weeks, day in and day out, you can have him for a couple of hours."

I loved her. "Thanks, but it's late, and I'm going to have an early night. I am fifty, a big girl now."

"You'll never be a big girl to me," he said affectionately.

"I'm lucky to have you both in my life," I said.

"Will you let us know what happens?"

"I will."

"Have you told your dad?"

"No, I don't know if he'd remember Sam." I sighed. My dad was in a home suffering dementia. My mum had passed away a year ago.

"Thanks for listening, and I'm so glad you had a lovely time. I want to see some pics and when you're both free, come down for dinner."

"Love you, Hals. Let me know what happens, okay?"

I smiled, he always said that but we, and more importantly, Sally, knew it was the love of friends only.

I showered and took myself off to bed. While I lay in the

dark, I remembered the sex. I'd never had sex like it with Toby, who was more conservative than me. I missed the level of play Sam and I had. I found myself aroused and reached into my bedside drawer. In the absence of a man, it was a BOB that had to do.

* * *

I woke early and walked Ursa. I found I was shaking with nerves. I kept laughing to myself, knowing how ridiculous that was. My heart kept missing a beat and continued to do so all the while I showered and dressed. I was even being stupid about my outfits. I had on jeans, then a skirt, then trousers, then jeans again. I lived in jeans mostly. I spent ages choosing a T-shirt, but what went on top was quick to decide. I grabbed Sam's sweatshirt from my wardrobe and slipped it on. I often wore it, it had faded, most of the writing had disappeared, but it still fit, and it still gave me comfort. I tied my laces and then I was ready.

My hair was straight and shoulder-length, not the long curls he would remember. I didn't wear as much makeup as I had, but then it had been the eighties and nineties, red lipstick and shoulder pads had been all the rage! I seemed to have been blessed with good skin and had nowhere near the wrinkles Pam had.

I drove, aware I was going to be early, hoping I might find somewhere to grab a coffee, my stomach was too knotted to eat. I pulled onto the motorway and headed towards London. I turned on the radio, changed channels, then turned it off.

A half hour later, I was coming off the motorway towards Blackheath. My palms sweated and my heart raced. I slowed down. The road system had changed a little and I found myself diverted into the village and then had to make my way back out. Soon enough, I was pulling up alongside a blue top-of-the-range Jag. I sat for a minute, holding my breath.

I could see him. He had his back to me, and I wondered, since my car was electric, whether he'd heard me. He straightened his back. He still had the buzz cut but tinged with a little grey.

As I exited my car, he stood.

As I took one step towards him, he took two.

We didn't speak at all, not even after he wrapped his arms around me, and I melted into his chest.

I was home.

I could breathe, and my heart settled into a steady beat.

He kissed the top of my head.

"Hello, Hals," he whispered.

I looked up at him. "Hello, Sam."

I wanted to tell him I'd missed him. I wanted to tell him I still loved him. I wanted to tell him all the things immediately, but we had time.

Instead, he held my hand. "Cup of coffee?" he said, smiling with that same cheeky grin he'd always had.

I nodded.

We walked to the tea hut, and he bought two coffees, we then strode back to the pond and sat on the bench.

"I didn't think you'd answer Alison. I didn't tell her to do that, by the way. Although I'm glad she did. She's a cow, that one."

I laughed. "I'm glad she did. My heart stopped when I saw her message. I often think of you, I did try to find you once."

"I moved, as you know. I went back to the flat for a little while, but then, when Alison came along it was too small. So I moved again. I still have the flat, though. You won't believe who lives in it now?"

I shook my head. "Who?"

"Karl."

"No way. Gosh, how old is he now?"

"Early thirties. He's taken over my business."

"That's amazing."

"Tammy left him with me, I brought him up."

"What happened to her?"

He shook his head. "Fuck knows, fell in love with someone who didn't want her kid." He turned to face me. "You haven't changed one bit, other than the hair."

"Neither have you. Still handsome, still a bad boy," I said, laughing.

"Don't know so much about the bad boy part, but yeah, even if I do say so."

"Still vain," I added, and he laughed. "I can't believe we're here."

"Do you remember when we said, if we split up and when I reached forty, we'd meet here?"

I nodded. "I do. And I came."

He stared at me. "So did I?" He frowned. "You weren't here."

"When I got to forty...?" I said.

"No, when I got to forty."

"Are you sure about that?" I asked.

"Positive, I remember you reminding me I didn't do anything on my birthday, so why mine?" he chuckled.

"Fuck!"

We fell silent. I wondered what would have happened if we'd arrived on the same day.

"How long do you have?" he asked.

"All day," I said.

"Good. Come with me?"

He stood and held out his hand. We walked back to the car. "Do you want to come in my car or follow me?"

"What's best?" I asked.

"Follow me, then you'll have the car when you need it."

"You're being cryptic," I said.

"Yep." He gave me that lopsided grin. He still had the chipped tooth and the scar in his eyebrow. He still had the beautiful eyes.

I followed him across Blackheath and out towards Kent. When he turned off the motorway, I wanted to cry. It was one turning after mine. We pulled up to electric gates and waited while they swung open.

"You live no more than a half hour from me," I said, when I got out of the car.

He snorted a laugh and shook his head. His house was stunning, so not what I would have thought Sam would live in. All modern: white render, grey window frames, and lots of glass. We didn't walk to the house though, we headed towards the garage. He pushed a button on the key fob and the door rolled up.

I started to laugh. Lined up were his bikes. Even the one he'd had when we'd been together. There were small kiddie bikes and powerful drop handlebar road bikes. He walked to a rack and grabbed two helmets, he handed me one and I readily took it.

He tightened the strap under my chin and then handed me a leather jacket.

"I won't get into that," I said, laughing. "I haven't worn that in twenty-five years!" It was my jacket, the one I wore whenever I was on his bike. He swapped it for another.

"Camber Sands?" he said.

"Fish and chips on the beach?" I replied.

We laughed and he rolled one of the bikes out. He climbed on and patted the seat behind him. I quickly joined him. I wrapped my hands around his waist and gripped his jacket. All that was missing was his combat jacket and we could have gone back thirty-five years.

I screamed as he pulled back the throttle and we roared off. We hit the motorway and weaved among the traffic. I loved every second of it.

Once we were on a straight run, he placed his hand over mine, and we cruised until we came into Camber. We made our way into the car park, and he stopped the bike. I climbed off, and then he did. He secured our helmets to the handlebars, and he took hold of my hand again. We walked, and we talked.

He told me all about his life, how his business had gone from strength to strength, especially with the advent of newer and electric cars. He specialised in *vintage*, as he called it.

"Still a grease monkey," he said.

I told him about leaving work and fostering kids, and then my writing.

Neither of us mentioned any previous partners.

We sat on the sand, laying our jackets down first so as not to get damp arses.

"So, we could have met ten years ago," he said, referring to the mix-up on dates.

"We could have. Is it worth worrying about that now?"

"Nope." He turned to face me. His eyes searched mine. He looked healthy and I was too afraid to bring up whatever illness it was. "I'm sorry," he said.

It was there, out in the open, his list, the reason we were meeting.

"For what, Sam? I owe you, not the other way round."

"I should have gone on that journey with you. I know why I didn't now, of course. I was terrified of moving forward anywhere, it was as if I was frozen in time, back in the days where I couldn't get hurt. I didn't want to venture into the unknown. I was wrong. I don't know if we'd have still been together, but... Well, sometimes I'd believe we would have been."

"I should have seen that and not been so selfish. I demanded you come with me without any thought on how that affected you."

He shook his head and wrinkled his nose. "We both know it was me. It's okay. I've dealt with it. I understand it. I grieved for you, and I resolved it. I never got over you though."

"Alison said. I bet that was hard for you... Your wife?"

I felt I needed to bring it up.

"Yes, it was. I was honest with her from the start. Alison was a failed condom, but a welcomed one," he laughed. "And you? Did you end up with Toby?"

I didn't speak to start with. I bit down on my lower lip instead.

"It's okay. I stalked you for a little while," he said with a wink.

"You did what?" I asked, laughing.

"Not like in a creepy way, just making sure you were okay."

"Yes, we ended up together and it wasn't right. We both knew I didn't love him in the way he needed me to. I loved you. We split up about twenty years ago, but we only got divorced recently. We are still really good friends and he recently married."

"So, had we met, you would have been single?"

I nodded. "My wife died when Alison was a baby. I bought her and Karl up together as brother and sister, on my own."

"So, had we met, you would have been single." I echoed his words with sadness in my voice.

"Spilt milk and all that." He took hold of my hand and kissed my knuckles.

We reminisced, talked about the old days of riding his bike over the Mad Mile. How he'd help me with the horses, and then confessed to being absolutely terrified of the things and thankful I gave them up.

We laughed at silly things, we laughed at some of the rows we had and the man cave.

"Still smoke?" I asked.

"Sometimes. Keeps me calm," he replied.

"Still fighting?"

He laughed. "I'd get my arsed kicked nowadays. No, Karl is the boxer in the family now. I had to put him in a club to focus his anger in a more positive way. He went totally off the rails for a while, especially when his mum came back one time, wanting him back. He was early teens then. He's a great man now. You'd love him."

"Tell me about Alison."

His smile melted my heart when he thought about his daughter.

"Fuck knows where she comes from, she has the kindest heart ever. All she does is care and fuss over everyone, mostly me. She has a couple of kids; can you believe I'm a fucking granddad at my age?"

"A dashing one, at that," I said, raising my eyebrows.

"If you say so. She's amazing, Hals. She works in a care home with dementia patients."

"Where?" I asked.

"Longfield."

"Don't tell me it's Honeygrove?"

"Yeah, something like that, anyway. Why?"

"My dad is in there?"

He stared at me. "No way!"

I nodded and laughed. "Fate?"

"Didn't believe in it until now, so yeah. Wait until I tell her."

She wouldn't have known my maiden name to connect us. Even if she had, Smith was about the most common name in the world.

It dawned on me then. When I'd looked at her image on social media, I thought she was familiar. At first, I thought it was because she looked so much like Sam, then I realised, it was because I'd seen her at the home. I told Sam that.

"I have to call her."

He FaceTimed her and gave her the news. "No way, I know him! He's not on my floor but he wanders down every now and again. How strange is that. I can't believe it. Jesus, Dad. You could have found her years ago," she said, maybe not realising I was sitting beside him. He angled the camera so she could see me, and she laughed. "It's so good to finally see you. I had a picture of you in my head for years. Dad has photographs, but..."

"Yeah, all right. Time to go before you spill all my secrets." He cut off the call.

"You have photographs?"

"Lots. Now, I have somewhere else I want to visit."

I wanted to ask if this was on his list, but I didn't. We walked back to the bike and drove up the coast. I laughed as he stopped at the fish and chip shop. I had no backpack that time, so stuffed our food down the front of my jacket complaining that my sweatshirt would stink.

"My sweatshirt," he said.

"Mine, you don't get it back after all these years."

We carried on to the cove. There were no logs that time, and no fire pit. But we sat with our backs against the rocks, and we ate, we drank a beer, and he sparked up a joint.

"I can't believe we're doing this," I said, taking it from him.

I hadn't smoked in years, and I spluttered and coughed my guts up. My eyes watered and I handed it back to him.

"Other way?"

I paused. My heart didn't, it raced. My hands shook as he took a drag, filled his lungs with smoke. My stomach flipped as I leaned in close. My pussy throbbed as he opened his mouth, mine just millimetres away and I inhaled. He placed his hands on the side of my head and closed that gap.

His kiss was tender to start, growing more passionate with every passing second. I breathed out through my nose, emptying my lungs. It wasn't the cannabis that made my eyes water, it was tears. They rolled down my cheeks.

When he pulled away, and it was with great reluctance on both parties, I thought. He stared at me.

"It's still there, isn't it, baby?" he whispered.

I nodded and closed my eyes. He kissed each eyelid, my nose, and forehead.

"It's still there," I replied.

CHAPTER 18
Present Day

W e sat and chatted, but there was a shift, for sure. He had his arm around me, and I snuggled into his side.

We'd have periods of silence, and it was comfortable.

"Remember when we had sex here?" I asked.

"Often," he replied, laughing.

"We did some amazing things. You taught me a lot," I said.

"You taught me how to love, Hals. I think that far outweighs anything I did."

I started to laugh. "Do you remember when the police came round to arrest you? I hid in the bedroom and when the policeman came in, I saw him glance at those cuffs we had. I had to run around and get them off the bed before my mum came."

He joined in my laughter. "Jesus, you didn't tell me the cops saw them," he said.

"I think I probably had more important things on my mind at the time."

"Yeah, well, let's get off that subject. I haven't had sex in a while; I don't want to embarrass myself here."

I spat my drink out with laughter. That was Sam, the Sam I remembered. So quick with a dry wit.

"Why no kids?" he asked.

"It just never happened. Unknown Infertility, it's called."

"But you were pregnant once."

"Maybe whatever is wrong, is the reason I lost that baby." I shrugged my shoulders.

"I'm sorry, baby," he whispered, and then kissed the top of my head.

"It's okay. I have twenty foster kids."

"Not all at the same time!"

"No, over the years. I still see some of them."

"You'll have to tell me about them one day."

I stilled. "Will there be another day?"

He looked down at me. "You don't think I'm letting you go again, do you?"

I smiled. "Ah, Alpha Sam, glad to see he's still in there." I raised my eyebrows.

He rolled himself over, pushing me to the sand and leaning over me. "Yeah, baby, he's still here working fine."

That kiss was passionate and full of want, from both of us. Twenty-five years ago I would have damned the consequences and fucked him there and then. Instead, I wrapped my arms around him and held him close. He felt the same, everything about him was as I remembered, and it was comforting, it was perfect. And it was just right.

He slid his body more, so he was totally covering me, and I hooked one of my legs over his. His moan caused my core to tighten.

"Get a room!" I heard, and Sam pulled his head up. Someone was walking a dog along the beach.

He slid to the side of me, and we laughed.

"Fucking hell, but probably for the best," he said, tugging at the front of his crotch.

"We better go," I replied.

"So you can ravish my body?"

"No, in case he calls the police. I don't work for a lawyer anymore and my mum is... My mum died a little while ago." I sniffed as I spoke.

"I'm so sorry. I loved your parents. I kept in touch for a while, I know they never told you because I asked them not to. I thought that was the best thing at the time. I know you were ill, and I caused that."

"You didn't cause anything. No more going back, Sam, okay?"

We walked back to the bike and took a slow ride back to his house.

He parked the bike in the garage and asked if I wanted to come in.

"I need to get back for my dog," I said. In truth I was feeling overwhelmed.

"This isn't a one-off, is it?" he asked.

I stepped closer and wrapped my arms around his waist.

"Hell, no." I pulled my phone from my pocket and handed it to him. He frowned.

"Put your number in there," I said.

"Oh." Then he laughed. Once he had, I called him.

"Now you have my number. I'm feeling a little overwhelmed right now. I'm also feeling that I want to jump your bones, but we shouldn't do that. Not yet, at least," I said, laughing.

"Does this mean we're back together? Or whatever the term is nowadays."

I wasn't sure what to say so just nodded. Yes, I wanted that to be the case, but we still had a lot of ground to cover. There was the illness to talk about, for one thing.

"Alison is staring from the upstairs window. Don't look though," he said.

I chuckled. "This feels like when we snuck around before my parents knew."

"Thank you for today. This means everything to me," he said, and he stepped back.

"And me. Will you call me later, like you used to? I imagine you'll have the Spanish Inquisition when you get in."

"What do I tell her?" he asked.

"You tell her you didn't get your sweatshirt back, so you need to see me again."

"Oh, wait." He ran to his car and returned with a bottle of aftershave.

I laughed and unboxed it, then sprayed myself liberally.

"Tomorrow," I said, finally walking towards my car.

He opened the gates, and I started the journey home. I laughed and smiled the whole way. My lips tingled and felt so very different. I couldn't put my finger on it.

When I got home, I walked Ursa and ignored all phone calls from Pam and Toby. I didn't want to share my day. The call I waited on came later in the evening. About half ten.

"Is this still your bedtime?" he said, not announcing himself.

"Believe it or not, yes, although I've been in bed for a half hour already, reading. I had a delayed munchies when I got home," I laughed.

"Thank you for today," he repeated.

"That's one off your list," I said.

He didn't reply at first. "You didn't think I just wanted to meet to tick you off my list, did you?"

"No... Well, maybe, but who cares what the reason was."

"I care. I've wanted to find you again for years. I tracked down Toby, he wasn't hard to find but there was no mention of you in his company, so I guessed you'd moved on. Your parents moved; it was like you just disappeared."

"And yet, we're a half hour apart. Alison works at my dad's home. I bet we've been to the same places at the same time loads. Can I ask, why the list?"

I thought it might be easier for him to talk about his illness if we weren't face-to-face. He sighed, however.

"We don't have to talk about that," I added.

"Can we not, just for a little while? I'd like to talk about us."

"I have your sweatshirt in bed with me," I said, changing the subject.

"I'd rather it was me, but I'm glad," he replied, chuckling. When he was flirting he'd lower his tone of voice. It caused my stomach to clench, and he knew it.

"You're not playing fair," I said.

"Have I ever?"

"Nope, you could make me come just by talking to me."

We fell silent and I could hear him breathe in deep.

"Do you want to come now?" he whispered.

I wetted my lips; my mouth had dried. "Yes," I answered quietly.

"Get naked, Hals."

I pulled off my vest top and pushed down my shorts.

"Are you wet?"

I nodded, then remembered I needed to speak. "I am."

"Touch yourself. Tell me what you're doing, how you feel. Describe it to me."

My voice hitched when I did. I told him how hot I was, how engorged my clitoris was, and how hard my nipples were. I stroked and probed, not getting anywhere close enough to where I wanted to be. He coached me, told me to hook my fingers, to raise my upper body. He did so in that sultry voice he had, breathless and low.

"Oh, Sam," I whispered, getting more aroused.

"I can remember your smell. Your taste is on my tongue right now."

I moaned some more.

"I'd like to tie your hands and feet. I want you so you can't move, you can't run away. You have to endure all I want to give you."

My stomach lurched with want.

"I want to tease you until you're begging me to fuck you. Remember that?"

"Yes." My voice was croaky.

"When I do fuck you, Hals, it will be in every way I can. I want you not being able to walk the next day."

He became breathless himself and I knew he would be stroking his cock. That thought turned me on further.

I came, as did he. I let the phone fall to the side of the pillow, and I closed my eyes. Tears ran down my cheeks, not because it was the most amazing orgasm, although it was the best I'd produced myself, but because the memories of our passion floored me.

"Good night, baby," I heard, and the call disconnected.

* * *

I finally took Pam's call the following morning.

"Well?" she said curtly.

"We got a coffee, talked, it was like old times. We went and got one of his bikes and drove down to Camber. Got fish and chips."

"And?"

"And we kissed."

"And?"

241

"And I came home."

"And!" She was getting more demanding with each 'and.'
I chuckled.

"And I never stopped loving him, and that was obvious. He never stopped loving me, it's still there. That flame was just dormant for twenty-five years. Now it's burning fucking hot."

She screeched down the phone. "I bloody knew it," she said, laughing. "Did you have sexy times?"

"Phone foreplay, yes."

We both screeched down the phone to each other.

"Listen to us, like bloody kids," she said.

"It feels so good, Pam. So right."

"Did he tell you what was wrong with him?"

"No, he said he didn't want to talk about that, just about us. Oh, Pam, honestly, we laughed so much. It was like the best times we'd had all over again."

"I'm pleased, I really am."

"But?"

"I don't want you to get hurt."

"That's going to happen. I can't stop that, but I'll handle it. I called Toby, he offered to come and visit."

"He's a good man. How was the honeymoon?"

"Good, so he said. Sally's going to send over some pictures later. I'll share them with you. I think they'll come over one day in the week if you want to join us."

"You are doing nothing, going nowhere, until those edits are done. In fact, give me Sam's number."

"Nope. I'll get them done. What's the worst they can do?"

She laughed. My publishers were used to my erratic schedules. Even though they would give me deadlines, we all knew they would have been made up and way in advance of when they needed the book back. I tried really hard to keep to a schedule, but it never worked.

"I'll text Sam this morning and tell him I'm working all day. I'll have them back to you tonight."

We said goodbye and I held the phone in my hand. It was coming up to half eight and I wondered if he'd be up. He had always been an early riser; I was the lazy one.

Good morning, I don't know if you're up, but I wanted to thank you for last night ha ha I slept well, for sure! I have to work all day but wondered if you wanted to meet for dinner tomorrow? H xxx

He didn't reply immediately.

I was sitting at my desk with a cup of tea when my phone flashed up his message some twenty minutes later.

Good morning to you, as well. I was in the shower, thinking about last night. I'm at Kings College tomorrow, usually finish about four so we could meet about seven, if that suits? I'm happy to cook, I'm even better at that than before.

He added a wink and I laughed. I typed out my reply.

Seven is fine. How about halfway? I know of a nice pub with a restaurant. We could meet there? Save you cooking.

Sounds good, text me the details. I can collect you.

I'd like that, I thought. So I went online to find the pub details and booked a table. I gave him my address and some basic directions and told him I'd booked a table for half seven and he could get to me anytime.

He replied with a thumbs up. I assumed he'd be at Kings College, the hospital, because of his illness and knew it had to be serious to be there. Kings was one of *the* country's top neurological hospitals. Toby had surgery there to remove a disk that had blown, and the consultant had told him only a neurosurgeon should deal with that because of the risk to the spinal cord.

I turned off my phone, shut down all apps open on my laptop, and turned off the Wi-Fi. I opened my manuscript and worked.

I broke for lunch and to sit in the garden with Ursa for some fresh air, and then returned to it.

By five, I had it all done. I sent the document to Pam. She'd check through it, then forward it to the publisher. For once, I might be ahead of schedule.

The following day I worked on a new book. I couldn't get into it, however. My mind kept wandering. I wasn't in the mood for my detective that day, despite him being in my head and chatting away. I wanted love and soppy, not anger and bloodshed. I opened a new document.

Something popped into my head, and I started to type up notes. I created a character and a rough story arc. It wasn't my genre at all, but I was just going with the flow.

I needed to pop into town to grab some dry-cleaning and I wanted to visit Dad. I hoped I might bump into

Alison there, now I knew her name and the fact she worked there.

I got to the home and signed in. I had a bag of toiletries for Dad, and some new pyjamas.

His eyes lit up when he saw me. "There she is, come on in, Dani," he said, calling me by my mother's name. I never corrected him, of course.

"Hello, Dad," I said, kissing him.

He started to tell me about his day, none of which actually happened, and I listened. If I closed my eyes, I could be transported back years, to when he'd come home from work and tell us about his day.

"Dad, do you remember Sam?" He looked blankly at me. I often forgot not to use the word 'remember' as it highlighted their diminished memory. "He was my boyfriend for years."

"Broke your heart, didn't he?" he said, and I nodded, not entirely sure he wasn't just guessing at that.

"His daughter got in touch. She works here, Dad," I said.

He looked around. "Where? What, her?" he said, pointing to his nurse.

"No, on another floor. I met up with him," I said.

He stared at me. "Did you get on that bloody bike? Your mum told you he had to drive you in his car."

I bit down hard on my lower lip to stop the tears, only that pain caused my eyes to water. I shook my head.

"No, Dad, I got in his car."

He nodded then. "That's good. Your mum will be here shortly, she'll be pleased."

"Anyway, what happened to my cat?"

Dad had never had a cat, he hated them. Only wanted them at his lorry yard to kill the mice.

"Oh, she's around somewhere."

"Bloody useless thing, get rid of it," he said. I said I would.

"See that bloke?" he pointed to someone in a wheelchair. "Can't walk, he can't."

"That's a shame."

"Anyway, I better be off. Dani will be here soon." He stood and walked away, usually that was back to his room, and I smiled after him.

"Good day?" I heard and looked up at one of his nurses.

I nodded. "Good day."

Dad could be very difficult and many times I'd left in tears. He couldn't help it, of course. It was the fucking worst illness in the world.

"Do you happen to know if Alison Weston is on today?"

"I can find out. Do you know her?"

"I know her dad, I just wanted to say hi."

She called down to reception while I labelled up all of Dad's new toiletries.

"She's not, sadly. I can say that you asked after her."

"Thanks, please do, but I might speak to her before she comes back on shift anyway."

I said goodbye and left.

I was back home and working for the rest of the afternoon. I wanted to text Sam to wish him well, but I wasn't sure why he was in the hospital. I wasn't going to ask; he'd tell me when he wanted to. I also understood his need to keep it separate. Whatever it was, he had to live with it. I was the respite, perhaps, he needed.

I took a leisurely bath and shaved my legs and armpits. I hadn't done that in a while! I slathered on moisturiser and agonised over what to wear. Should I go ultra-casual or smart casual? I opted for wide-legged trousers, a shirt, and wedges. Nice autumn wear. Since it was still fairly warm, we might want to sit in the garden, so I grabbed a wrap as well.

I opened a bottle of wine and hoped that Sam came early. I poured myself a glass and waited.

At half six, I heard a car on the gravel drive. I looked out the window to see his car. When he stepped from it, I smiled. He wore chinos, a polo shirt, and deck shoes. Other than the chinos, it was about the same attire as I remember him wearing when 'smart' was called for. I also noticed how muscular his arms were, still.

I opened the door before he got to it.

"Hey, you look stunning," he said, coming to a halt in front of me. He leaned down and kissed me gently.

"As do you." I stepped back and he followed me in.

"This is nice, have you lived here long?" he asked.

We walked into the open plan kitchen/diner, and I held up the wine. He nodded.

"About five years, I think. Funny how I craved the city, and now look at me? I couldn't live without those views."

Sam had stepped to the window to look at the farmland behind me.

"Reminds me of our house," he said.

I stepped beside him, handing him the glass. "It does a bit. So, how was your day?" I asked.

He wrapped his arm around me. "Same as ever. How was yours?"

"I went to visit my dad, and guess what he said?"

I recounted what Dad had said to me and Sam laughed. "Bloody hell. You didn't tell him we went for a ride, did you?"

"I doubt he would understand. Want to sit?"

I walked to the end of the room where there was a sofa looking out the bi-fold doors. They were open and Ursa was lying just outside on the patio.

"Meet Ursa," I said.

Hearing his name, he looked up and his lips twitched. "Be nice," I said. He rose and walked in. At first, he sniffed at Sam's outstretched hand, then his tongue lolled out and he went in for a cuddle.

"Bloody charmer still, aren't you?" I said, laughing.

Ursa wasn't a man's dog, and I thought that might have been because he was a rescue. Perhaps he'd been abused.

He laughed and winked at me. I told him about the pub, and that I'd visited once before but a while ago. It looked good online and I'd booked us a table. He told me how long Alison had grilled him for the night when he got home.

"Honestly, Hals, I had to fucking lock her out of the house. She was driving me nuts."

I wondered if Alison lived with him, or him with her, for that matter.

"She wants to be my personal carer, except, I can actually care for myself, and do so quite successfully when she's at work or in her own house. She lives above the garages, by the way, not sure if you noticed. Kicked out the prick of a husband some time ago, thankfully. Otherwise, you might have been visiting me in prison after all."

Well, that answered who lived where. "Do you still go into work?"

"Rarely. Karl has the reins now, no need for me to. He knows he gets the business when..." He didn't finish and I didn't push. I just picked up his hand in mine.

"I think we ought to leave soon. Who's driving? Me or you?"

"I'll drive. Not sure I want to be a passenger with you behind the wheel," he said.

"I'll have you know I have never had a crash."

"Bet you've never been more than twenty miles and over fifty either," he joked. I slapped his chest and he winced, genuinely.

"Shit, sorry," I said.

He laughed and then lifted his polo shirt. He had a huge bruise on his chest. He still had my name on his skin as well.

"Got this baby yesterday."

"How?" I touched it gently. "Reminds me when the police did a number on you." I also ran my fingers over what had been my name and was still very visible. Flowers wove around the letters, swirls and other 'art.' He covered my hand with his and squeezed.

"You'll laugh. Fell off the fucking MRI table. I hate those things, claustrophobic now, can you believe that? Anyway, panicked, fell off, hit a trolley, shit went everywhere, and I ended up with this."

I shook my head. "Say that again," I said, laughing.

"Seriously. Sometimes I lose my balance a little. Sometimes I play on that to delay being shoved into that mechanical torture chamber."

I stared at him. "I have a brain tumour, Hals. But that's not a conversation for tonight, is that okay?"

"It's a massive thing to tell me then expect me to not want to ask about it."

"I know, just tonight? I fully intend to tell you everything, but I'm having fun, Hals. I haven't had fun in a while."

I smiled and nodded. "As long as you don't die on me any day soon." I wondered if I'd gone too far.

"I promise," he said, chuckling. "I might die of hunger before that, though."

He slapped my backside and we headed to the front door.

He opened the car door for me, and I slid into the car. It was all dark leather, chrome, and ebony.

"Nice car," I said when he joined me.

"Bought it last year. I had an earlier model and loved it."

He put the car into reverse and with his arm over the back of my seat, he turned to look through the rear window, despite having a reversing camera. He glanced at me, kissed my cheek, before turning back to drive forwards.

I directed him, getting my left and right wrong a couple of

times, and then we arrived. We sat in the garden, him with a soft drink and me with another wine, until our table was ready.

We scanned the menu and ordered. When the waiter had left, he took hold of both my hands across the table. He stared at me and then smiled. He closed his eyes and shook his head.

"I went mad when Alison told me she'd contacted you. But I was also so glad as well. I should have done it myself. I had your email address."

"How?" I asked.

He chuckled. "It's in your books. I have them all. Haven't read them all, but I bought them."

"How did you know I wrote?"

"It's a funny story. I was at Kings and there's a bookshelf. I was bored, so I had a look, thinking I might find something easy. I picked up a book and didn't recognise the author, to be honest. Read it, liked it, so Alison downloaded some on to my iPad for me. It was your book."

"My book was in Kings?"

"Yeah, and one of the nurses' favourites. I've added all your books to their collection."

"So you're the reader," I said, laughing. If it hadn't been for Sam buying me out of our house, and some shrewd investments Toby managed for me, I'd have not been able to afford the house I lived in. I could pay the bills with book earnings, but I was no Patricia Cornwell.

"As for how I knew it was you. Alison was reading or something and at the end there's a website that comes up? She wanted to show me what the author looked like, and it was you."

"Blimey, so those do work then?" I asked, feeling a little embarrassed.

"I said, I used to date that woman. And she put two and two together."

I used my first name on my books and a made-up surname, which was why Sam wouldn't have connected the dots, I guessed.

"She said that you talked about me."

"I did. As I said, I was always honest about you. I have your name across my chest, so they were always going to ask. I had some decoration added to it, to soften it for my wife. Then we decorated the flat and Alison saw all that writing on the wall, remember that?"

Before our first tenant we'd redecorated. I'd drawn a large heart and put our names in it. We'd joked that a hundred years on someone might be curious about our relationship. We toyed with the idea of leaving a love letter in the wall as well.

I nodded. "She was curious about you. She lost her mum when she was little, she doesn't really remember her. So, I think she sort of fixated on you."

I sat wide-eyed. "In a nice way," he added.

Plates of food were placed in front of us, and we ate. While we did, we chatted some more. I told him about my travels for my books, and he told me he'd been back to Greece on his own, but with two small children, most of their holidays were in a caravan park or theme park.

"Did you ever want to meet someone new after your wife?" I asked.

He shook his head. "I was too busy with the kids and work. You know where we should go next, that Italian bistro, remember it?"

I was happy to learn there would be a next one. "I doubt it's still there, is it?"

He shrugged his shoulders. "No idea, but might be fun to find out."

"What else is on your list, Sam?"

He smiled. "That would be telling, and I might not achieve that. We'll see."

"If I can help you with that, I'd like to."

He nodded.

Once we got back to mine, I told him I needed to take Ursa for a walk and maybe he'd like to join me. I swapped my wedges for Converse, and we walked the perimeter of the field.

"I don't like that you're out at night on your own," he said, as I waved my flashlight around.

"I'm not, I'm with the dog."

"I still don't like it."

I laughed. "Well, for tonight I have my king, don't I?"

There had been a time when I was still a teenager, he'd called me his queen. I'd upgraded from princess after I lost my virginity to him, if I recalled. I reminded him of that.

"I still remember my first time," I said, holding his hand. "You were so gentle with me. We had sex twice that night."

253

"Yeah, I had to wait until you were fucking sixteen, and then when you were—"

"If you say it, I'm going to punch your bruise," I said, laughing.

He covered his chest, just in case.

We made it back home and I offered him coffee. I saw him look at his watch.

"Unless you need to go," I said gently.

"No, I need to take my meds, they're in the car."

While he grabbed a small pouch of medication, I made coffee. We sat in the living room that time, I curled my legs under me and leaned into his side. He had one arm around my shoulders.

"Wanna make out?" I said, laughing at the term we'd used as kids.

"I thought you'd never ask." He put his cup down and stood, causing me to fall to the side.

"Thanks," I said, taking the outstretched hand.

"Bedroom or sofa?"

"Oh, let me think. What kind of a make out is this going to be?"

He rubbed his hand over his stubble and pursed his lips. He breathed in deep and exhaled slowly. His eyes darkened and he stared at me. My stomach was doing somersaults.

"You're getting me hot with that stare," I said quietly.

"I wanna play."

"I don't have anything here," I said.

"We'll improvise."

He took my hand and led me to the hall and up the stairs. I only had a two-bedroomed cottage, three rooms on the upper floor and it wasn't hard to know which was my bedroom, it being the largest.

He stood in front of me and said nothing to start with. "Might be a bit rusty, haven't done this in a while," he said.

"Stop talking and start doing, if you don't mind?" I replied.

He chuckled and stepped forward. He pulled my shirt loose of my trousers and started to unbutton it. I was conscious I wasn't as skinny as I had been in the past, I sucked in my stomach as he parted the shirt. He stared down at my breasts. He placed his hands on my chest, sliding them down over my bra. My nipples immediately stood to attention.

Sam slid my shirt off my shoulders and then stepped behind me. He pulled it off and then took each wrist in his hands and held them at my back. He kissed the back of my neck; I bowed my head. He moved my hair to the side, kissing and nipping at my skin.

The feelings that coursed through my body, the emotion that ran through my mind stripped away the past twenty-five years.

He unclipped my bra and I shrugged it down. When Sam stepped away, I moaned. His chuckle was throaty and just that sound caused my clitoris to throb.

When he stepped back, he tied something soft around my wrist.

"Scarf, I told you we'd improvise."

He moved to stand in front of me and pulled his polo shirt

over his head. He kicked off his shoes and undid his trousers. I could see the bulge of his cock.

Sam ran his fingers around the waistband of my trousers, undoing them. They fell to my feet, and I stepped out of them. He ran his hands down my sides and my skin goosebumped. When he got to the rim of my knickers, he looked at me and held my gaze as he lowered to his knees. I swallowed hard, more so when he buried his face in my pussy. I wanted to grip his head, to push him into me, but I couldn't. I could only stand still. He licked, he sucked, and he nipped.

Whatever had happened in our interim years, he was way better than before.

I came within minutes. He chuckled. When he rose, his face glistened and I leaned forwards. I wanted to taste. I licked over his chin and lips. He raised his face and closed his eyes. I kissed his throat and felt him swallow hard.

When he stepped back, I immediately missed the heat that radiated from him.

He walked around me, kissing across my shoulders and down my spine. He cupped my arse cheeks and squeezed while he nipped at my shoulder. He reached around and ran his hand over my opening. I was able to lean into him and cup his erection with my hands. He groaned as I kneaded. His breath ghosted my skin, his moan floated over me. I leaned my head back and looked up at him. His eyes were closed, and he bit down on his lower lip.

"Tell me what you want," he said, his voice no more than a growl.

"Spank me," I whispered, and my voice hitched.

Before I could take a breath in, he had slapped my arse. I hissed, gritting my teeth together.

"Again?" he asked, and I nodded.

While he teased my clitoris, he spanked me. I whimpered; my legs began to shake.

"I need you, Sam," I said, my voice hitching. I needed him, not just sexually. He had been, and still was, my soulmate.

He pushed me face down on my bed. I was bent in half with my arse in the air. I heard the rustle as he slid off his trousers and then he held my hips. He gently kissed down my spine. I felt his cock nudge at my opening and pushed back against him, impatient. He laughed and then slammed into me so hard my legs buckled, and I slid up the bed. He held me while he fucked me.

I rocked back against him, wanting him deeper and harder. He wrapped his hand in my hair, pulling my head up. He leaned down a little.

"This good for you, baby?" he asked.

I tried to nod. I whimpered as his fingers dug into my skin. He slid his free hand around my chest, cupping a breast and rolling my nipple with his fingers. I struggled to catch my breath, panting hard. I could feel his sweat drip to my back and taste my own on my upper lip.

When I was about to come, he pulled out.

"No, Sam!" I cried. He chuckled.

By the hair, he pulled me upright and my pussy pulsed with want. He turned me and kissed me hard. He held his cock and stroked. He breathed heavily through his nose.

"I need to watch you," he said.

I sat and used my legs to push me up the bed, he crawled on. When he got close, he pushed me down. I shuffled to get comfortable lying on my tied hands. He slid between my legs, using his own to spread mine. He nipped at my stomach, kissing up until he took one nipple in his mouth. He sucked.

I closed my eyes against the building orgasm. I wanted to squeeze my thighs together, but he held them apart.

"Please, Sam," I whispered.

"Look at me, Hals," he said, and I opened my eyes.

His pupils were dilated, his nose flared with each breath he took. Once again, he held his cock at my opening, teasing me, rubbing against me. He smiled, the lopsided one, and then pushed in me. As hard as he'd fucked me from behind, he did the same while on top. I was shunted up the bed. I wanted to wrap my legs around him. I arched my back off the bed, calling out his name. His stomach was taut, the muscles across his shoulders tense. Sweat rolled down his chest.

"I fucking love you," he said through gritted teeth. I wasn't sure if he meant it for real or just in that moment.

I came. My stomach tightened and heat flooded my body. My cheeks flushed, my mouth was dry, and tears sprang to my eyes. I wanted to curl up but couldn't move.

"Oh God," I said, over and over as my orgasm rolled on.

Before it had finished, Sam pulled out and sank lower. He lapped at my arousal, inhaling my scent, and holding my clitoris between his teeth. I felt his hard breathing on my pussy and when he closed his teeth, I screamed out and arched myself off the bed.

His chuckle reverberated against me.

He looked up, he was on all fours and his cock still rigid. He crawled up my body until his face was above mine and his legs outside of mine. I was able to finally close my thighs to ease the ache.

"I'm not done with you yet," he whispered.

"Good," I panted out the word.

"Turn over."

I twisted under him. Once I was settled, he untied my wrists. "You need a better bed," he said.

"Or you could just put some rings on the corners," I replied as he massaged my shoulders.

"I'm going to bring a whole shitload of things here next time."

I smiled. "Glad to know you still have them."

He trailed his fingers down my spine, up and down, and I could feel him also stroking his cock.

"You know what I want?"

My stomach lurched, I nodded.

He pushed one finger inside me, then dragged that finger to my arse. He was using my own orgasm to lubricate. He was gentle, giving me time to breathe, as he inserted a finger into my arse. He paused, then twisted. Before I could settle, he pushed two fingers from his other hand into my opening and hooked them. I gripped the bedding, dragging it to me. He stroked, and I could feel the pressure from both sides.

"Come again for me, Hals."

I could never come on command, but I very nearly did that day. His touch, his voice, and when he leaned down and sank his teeth into my arse he had me crying out his name.

I did come and I was grateful for it because it meant he stopped; he gave me some respite.

I wasn't aware of time, only the moon was high. It cast a glow over the room. One of the windows was open and a gentle breeze flowed into the room, ruffling the curtains as it did. When Sam thought I'd rested enough, I rolled to my back, and he made love to me. He was gentle to start. I wrapped my arms around him, hooked my legs over his, and I held him so tight. We'd become one, moved together totally in sync.

Sam kissed my neck, nipped at my ear, and whispered my name. His voice played over my skin, causing it to tingle.

He rested his forehead on mine, and he came. I didn't think I had anything left in me.

I held him against me for a while, his face in my neck as his heart rate slowed. I didn't want to move. I didn't want him to move.

"I think my back's gone," he said.

"Are you serious?" I pushed at him so I could see his face.

He chuckled. "No, but I sure ain't as fit as I used to be."

He laughed as he rolled to the side. I wanted to slap him. I sighed contentedly. He was lying on his stomach, looking at me. I was on my back looking back at him.

"I ache," I said. He reached over with his hand and smoothed my fringe away from my eyes.

"Next time, you'll ache more."

"There'll be a next time?" I asked, raising my eyebrows.

"You can bet that nice arse of yours there will be."

I chuckled. "I need to shower."

I slid from the bed and walked to the bathroom. I took a quick shower, yelping as the cold water hit me before it warmed. By the time I had a wash and wrapped a towel around me, Sam was sitting on the side of the bed. He held his trousers in his hand.

"Do you have to go?" I asked.

"No."

"Stay with me?"

He stood and kissed my forehead. He grabbed the towel and smiled. "Let me shower as well."

When he returned, he slipped under the duvet beside me. We fell asleep in each other's arms. It was just like old times.

CHAPTER 19

Present Day

I didn't see Sam for a couple of days, both of us were busy. We had arranged for him, Alison, and Karl to visit for lunch and I was nervous. Alison was dying to meet me, of course. I wanted them to like me.

We spoke each evening, though. Always at half ten and after I'd gone to bed. I loved FaceTiming him. He'd sometimes be in bed himself and other times he'd be sitting on the sofa. One time, he had his grandson with him.

The young lad had been poorly, so he'd said, and was asleep across his lap. I loved the way the boy held on to Sam's shirt.

"He looks just like you," I said.

He kissed his head, and then called for Alison. While still talking to me, she took him from Sam, said hi to me as she did so, and told me she was looking forward to lunch.

"I miss not seeing you," I confessed.

To me, there wasn't the usual getting to know you, it wasn't necessary. What I did need to know was about his illness.

"This is so fucked up really, isn't it?" He smiled as he spoke. "We missed out on so many years."

"Yes, and no. I know it's only been a few days, but would we be here now if we hadn't gone down the path we did? We could have ended up hating each other for the rest of our lives."

"I did hate you for a while. I regret that so much now."

"That's okay."

"That's one of the things I wanted to apologise for. I had no reason to hate you."

"Then you've done that, so we don't need to worry about it."

"The kids are looking forward to meeting you," he said. "Alison has photos she found. She made an album for me."

"I can't wait to see those. Am I hideous in them?"

"Yeah, all frizzy hair and fucking shoulder pads," he said, shaking his head in jest.

"Oh, sod off, you." I laughed. "I hated my hair. I guess I had to thank Tammy for sorting that out."

We said goodbye and I headed to bed.

* * *

The morning of the lunch I headed to the local farm shop for some fresh veg. I walked Ursa up there and he sat patiently waiting for me. He'd never been introduced to children so I was hoping he and Sam's grandchildren would be okay. I thought, as long as they don't run up to him, or roll all over him, we should be fine.

I had the beef in the oven, the potatoes ready to go in, and all I needed was to prep the veg once I had it. I spent ten minutes chatting to the girls in the farm shop and then wandered back. I started to feel a little nervous. It was important the kids liked me, I felt. I distracted myself by getting the rest of the meal ready.

I heard two cars pull onto the drive, and I walked to the front door. Sam was in his Jag, and he had the two grandchildren, Alison and Karl were in another car.

I stared at Karl and smiled. "Oh my God. You are the absolute spit of your dad," I said, then wondered if I shouldn't have mentioned that.

He smiled and walked over to hug me. I was thrilled. He was so tall that he had to lean down. "Thank you. And it's so good to meet you, finally," he said.

Alison ran over, flung herself at me, causing us both to stumble, and I laughed. She kissed my cheek, thanking me over and over, then dabbing her eyes of tears.

Sam stood back with a huge smile, holding the hands of two shy children.

"Come on in," I said.

Alison babbled away about how this had been a dream come true, and she couldn't believe how happy her dad had been the past couple of weeks. I poured wine and Sam and Karl had beers.

"And what would you like?" I asked the kids. At first, they clung on to Sam's leg.

"I'd like squash, please," the girl said.

"Got any Coke?" the boy asked.

"No Coke." I heard from Alison. "He'll be bouncing off the walls. Now, introduce yourselves properly, please."

The boy held out his hand. "My name is Sam Charles Weston, after my granddad," he said proudly. "I'm six, and I'm gonna fix up cars and race motorbikes."

The girl pushed him out of the way. "I'm Hayley and I'm named after you. He ain't gonna fix up cars. I have a motorbike, do you? Granddad bought it for me, and I like...."

I didn't hear what she said, I was too stunned by her introduction. I looked up at Sam.

"It wasn't my idea," he said.

"It was in honour of you," Alison added.

"Wow, and I am honoured. I don't quite know what to say."

I think I was more stunned that it was the first obvious display I'd been part of their lives without being there.

"No, I don't have a motorbike, I wish I did, though," I said, finally answering her.

"My mum said you love my granddad," young Sam said.

I opened my mouth to speak and widened my eyes. I bloody loved that kid already! I didn't look up at Sam, Alison, or Karl.

"Do you?" Hayley asked. "He's good looking. Oh, I'm four and I have three boyfriends. Granddad isn't happy about that."

"I bet he's not. And yes, I love your granddad very much. I

have loved him for a very long time," I replied. It was my first public confession of how I felt.

I looked up at him. Alison had tears, yet again. Sam stepped forward and cupped my cheeks, he kissed me gently.

"Eww, that's gross. Can I have a Coke?"

"No," Karl and Alison said at the same time.

I made them both a squash and we headed out to the garden. It was nice enough to sit for a while in the sun.

"Can I stroke your dog?" young Sam asked, and I nodded. I called Ursa over and he stood patiently while Sam played with his fur.

Then Ursa ran off for his ball. The kids played with him.

"That is a first!"

Ursa had a ball and would sometimes toss it around himself, but he didn't do fetch normally. However, he and the kids were running around all over the place. So much so that one of my fears came true. He ran straight into the back of Hayley and knocked her over. I stood, ready to get her, and Sam laughed. She picked herself up, dusted off her knees, and laughed herself.

"You know, this is amazing," Karl said. "I know you knew me when I was a baby, but when Alison told me she was looking for you, I was like, that ain't gonna happen."

"And here we are, told you so, didn't I?" Alison said smugly.

We talked about my writing career, the garage, and Alison running the admin side of the business. She'd said she'd often find notes from me to Sam that had ended up in old files. She'd always collected them.

It was then she grabbed her bag and pulled out two books. "I made these for Dad a while ago. I've made copies for you."

"Oh, wow. I'm not sure what to say," I said, reaching forwards to take them.

Sam came and sat on the arm of the chair as I flicked open the first page.

"Oh my God, look at us!"

Sam was sitting on his dirt bike; his overalls were pulled down and tied around his waist. He had a vest T-shirt on. He had splodges of dirt all over his face. He had one arm around my hips as I stood beside him, and I was carrying a trophy. He'd obviously won that day.

"How old were you there?" Karl asked.

"Sixteen, I think. Not sure," I replied.

I flicked through some photographs, and I laughed and dabbed at tears myself. There was one of me and Sam, Karl senior, but no Tammy, and a few old friends sitting on the bank of the pub with the river. I imagined Tammy was taking the photograph.

"That was just before you had a fight," I said, slapping his leg. "My mum had to get him out of the police station, I was terrified."

"And what did you have to do before you left to collect me?" Sam said, raising one eyebrow at me.

I blushed, deeply. "Not sure we want to know," Alison said.

"You don't," I replied.

We continued to laugh about the images, and I thanked her profusely for the gifts. I'd treasure them, I knew.

While they sat, Sam and I headed to the kitchen to finish up the dinner.

"You have an amazing family, Sam."

He kissed my temple. "I do. Couldn't live without them, that's for sure."

"And the kids! I can't believe Alison called her Hayley."

"Hals, for short, as well," he said.

"Why didn't you tell me?"

"Because Alison decided, when she met you, she wanted it to be a surprise. Bossy little bitch, she is." He laughed.

Sam helped dish up dinner and we carried it through to the dining area. I'd added some cushions to the kids' chairs and young Sam took great delight in having Ursa slobbering and begging beside him. I had to lock him out in the end, the poor kid was going to look like an army of snails had marched all over him.

We ate and talked. They didn't stop, and I loved the banter and arguing among them all. It was chaotic and a perfect Sunday lunch. It reminded me of my own family meals.

"You have a brother?" Alison asked.

"Yeah, he lives in Canada. I try to get out there every year to see him."

"What's he doing now?" Sam asked. "I used to like him."

"Dan idolised your dad," I said to Alison. "He's high up in a bank, travels the world, to be honest."

Sam told them some stories about my parents, our family trip to Greece, and how my dad was his greatest supporter on the race circuit.

"I've got some photos of your dad, I think," Karl said.

I nodded. "Probably. He towed the trailer," I said.

"Were you there when..." He didn't finish his sentence.

I nodded gently. "I was. It was awful."

We chatted a little more about Karl and we all purposely avoided talk of his mother. Once dinner was over, the kids moved to the sitting area. Alison and I cleared up, and Karl and Sam went for a cigarette.

"I wish he wouldn't smoke," she said, tutting.

I wondered if she knew exactly what he smoked.

We boxed up leftovers and put them in the fridge, and I filled Ursa's bowl with meat and gravy for his dinner later. Once we'd stacked the dishwasher. I poured us both another glass of wine.

"What happens now?" she asked.

"I don't know, Alison. He hasn't told me about his illness, other than he has a brain tumour. So that's a conversation I need to have with him. I'm guessing we just take it one day at a time."

She nodded and then started to cry. I wrapped my arms around her, and she sobbed into my shoulder. Sam came into the kitchen and frowned. I shook my head at him, he left us alone.

"Come on, now," I said, pushing her away a little. "Dry your tears, your dad won't want to see those."

"I'm so sorry. I don't know what came over me there," she said, blowing her nose on a tissue.

"Emotion, and it's okay to let it out."

She took a deep breath in and exhaled sharply. "Right, back in the room," she said, fanning her face.

We joined the others in the garden. "Oh, I have something you might want," I said.

I rushed upstairs and grabbed the box. When I returned, I sat and opened it.

"I think Alison should have these," I said.

Sam just stared at the bracelet and matching ring. They had been his mother's and really ought to go to his daughter.

"I don't want them, Hals. They're yours. Dad gave them to you," Alison said.

Sam picked up the ring and twirled it around in his fingers. I had meant to give it back when we first separated, then I'd gotten ill and just didn't. After, they sat in a box in my house. Sometimes, I'd look at them and even place the ring back on my wedding band finger. It was a spectacular ring.

He held it up and stared at me. The room went deadly silent. I held my breath.

He extended his hand. Still, no one spoke.

I extended mine, and he slipped the ring back on the finger where it belonged.

"Does that mean...?" Karl asked.

Sam just looked at me. "Yes, it does," I said.

The screams and cheers startled Ursa, who barked, causing Hayley to cry. But then, everyone cried anyway. I stood, Sam stood, and while I admired my ring for the second time, he asked me to marry him.

"Absolutely, and no waiting this time." I flung my arms

around his neck. He lifted me and while he kissed me he swung me around.

I nearly knocked young Sam flying!

When he finally put me down, I picked up the bracelet. I placed it around Alison's wrist and clasped it.

"It was your grandmother's, it's yours, and then Hayley's," I said.

"But it's yours."

"In the absence of my own birth daughter, I give this to my bonus daughter."

I let her sob then.

* * *

Sam and I stood on the doorstep and waved them all off. The kids were asleep and had to be carried into the car. Alison was drunk, I was tipsy, and we were all happy.

"What a day," I said, closing the door and leaning against it.

"What a day," Sam said, echoing my words. "How about a coffee?"

I nodded. We sat at the dining table, and I admired the ring.

"That was my grandmother's, I think," he said, and I was sure he would have told me, but I hadn't remembered.

"It's beautiful. I loved it then; I love it more now."

"So, when are we getting married?"

"Soon as. No pomp, no crap. Just us and family."

"Deal. But we have to have a serious conversation first."

I smiled gently at him. "I know. Tomorrow maybe?"

He took my hand and kissed my knuckles. "I can't believe we are back here."

"Wait until I tell Pam and Toby!"

He chuckled, and I yawned.

"I'll clear up," he said, standing.

"Are you going home?" I asked.

"Am I fuck? Alison can have the house; she needs the space more than me. I'll move in here. You have a garage, I can keep my bikes in there, can't I?"

I laughed. "That sounds perfect to me."

"Only thing," he said, looking at me as I headed for the stairs. "Gonna need a better bed."

I laughed as I climbed them and headed for the bathroom.

I was in bed when Sam finally came up. He'd smoked in the garden, I could smell it, and played with Ursa. He'd locked up and then I'd heard him kick off his shoes across the hall.

We didn't fuck or make love that night, we just lay in the dark and we talked.

"So, about two years ago, I had a seizure. Never had one before, haven't had one since, but I had to have loads of tests. I lost my driver's licence for a while. At first, it was thought I'd developed epilepsy. That got ruled out when I had an MRI. I had a small tumour."

"Is it still a small tumour?" I asked.

"No, it's not massive, but it did grow. It can't be cut out because the *root* is too far in, or something like that."

"How does it affect you?"

"It didn't for a long time. You know, I got to a point where

I forgot about it. I have regular scans and it was at the last one they said it had grown more. I get headaches now, sometimes I forget certain words, and I get clumsy. Fell off the table, remember?"

He laughed. I couldn't. He was used to hearing those words, I guessed. I wasn't. My heart stopped and I closed my eyes to stop any tears.

"I don't want sadness, okay?"

I nodded. "You'll need to give me time to process though."

We fell silent for a little while. Sam turned on his side to face me, I did the same. He stroked my hair, pushing it back from my face.

"Hals, you know I'm going to leave you again, don't you? I want you to know that before we go any further. I also want you to know it won't be because I want to or think it's for the best. This time, I have no choice."

I let the tears fall and I nodded, not trusting myself to speak at first.

"How long?" I asked, not being able to form the full sentence.

He shrugged his shoulders. "No idea. Months, years. Right now, I'm good. Well, as good as I can be."

He kissed the tip of my nose. "No tears," he whispered.

"Did you do all the things on your list?" I asked.

"All bar one."

"Shall we make a new list? All the things we should have done?"

He chuckled. "That sounds a great idea."

"How about that road trip? We could camp, drive around the UK."

"Absolutely. You let me know when you can, and we'll plan that."

"Sam, I'm going to step away from my writing. I want to spend all my time, whatever time it is, with you now."

"I don't want you to do that, Hals."

"I want to do that."

He slid his arm under my neck and pulled me closer. My face was nuzzled into his neck, his head rested on mine.

"I wish we'd found each other that day, on my birthday," he whispered.

"No looking back, only forwards now," I replied.

CHAPTER 20

Present Day

S am had to pop home to get some clothes and discuss the house with Alison. He was sure she'd be sad not to be living with him, but she knew how close he was. Karl could move into the flat above the garages, bringing him back closer to work, and Sam thought he might sell the old flat. He'd give the money to the grandkids.

There were some things he'd want from the house, and we decided we'd spend a week reorganising, maybe redecorate. He liked his big telly; I never watched it. He liked his recliner chair, I preferred to curl on the sofa. When he returned later that day, we'd made some plans. Not just for the house, but for our trip as well.

Before I called Pam, I climbed up into the loft. I fished out my camera and dusted it off. It had been superseded fifty times, I imagined, but it worked, I knew how to develop my own film

—assuming I could still buy film—and I wanted to capture every single moment I could.

I walked around the garden. It was a large plot and at the very end, under all the trees that lined the boundary, it was just dead grass. It would be perfect for his man-cave. *We could put a summer house there,* I thought.

"Guess what?" I said, when Pam answered.

"You found Elvis?"

"Nope."

"You won the lottery?"

"Nope, again," I said, laughing.

"Then I give up, I'd only be interested in those two things."

"I got engaged."

"What? Who to?"

"Sam, you idiot. We're going to get married as quick as we can. Oh, he has a brain tumour, hence the rush."

"Whoa, hold on. Hals, are you sure about this?"

"I've never been surer about anything. Also, we need to meet. I want to take a break from writing when this one is done. I'm not stopping, just not necessarily going to write anything new for a while."

"I can understand. Blimey, Hals. I can't quite believe that. Yes, we need to meet, get some plans underway. We have a lot of translations that need sorting, and audiobooks. And the movie rights. So, we'll still be busy... Or, I'll be busy," she said, laughing. "Getting married!"

"Want to come over tomorrow?" I asked.

"Erm, is the Pope Catholic? I'll be there about ten. Be up!"

She put the phone down and I laughed some more. Pam worked from her home office, and I worked from mine, but we generally met up once a week. We hadn't met the past couple of weeks because I'd been busy. It would be nice to catch up and for her to meet up with Sam again.

The next call I made was a little trickier.

"Hey, Hals. You didn't call me last week," Toby said.

"I know, I'm sorry. I have news."

"Good or bad?"

"Good, I think so, anyway."

"Well?"

"Sam and I are getting married."

He paused. "No way? Seriously?"

I looked out the window to see Sam pull on the driveway.

"He's moving in with me and we're going to do this as soon as possible," I said.

I'd given Sam a key and he let himself in. I smiled as he walked over, and he kissed my forehead.

"He's here now, just got back from picking up clothes."

"I'm stunned and elated, Hals. You tell him from me though, no mucking around this time."

I chuckled. "Toby said, no mucking around this time," I told Sam.

"Absolutely not, sir," Sam said.

"Did you hear that?" I asked Toby.

"Loud and clear. Sally and I are thrilled. Come over and have dinner with us. Or we'll come to you if you keep the mutt out," he said.

Toby wasn't a dog person, or any animal person, actually.

"I'll get something in the diary, for sure. Also, I need your legal brain. I'm going to stop writing for a little while and Pam has some offers on the table for a TV serial and foreign rights. Can I leave that with you and her?"

Usually Toby and I dealt with selling any rights I retained.

"Of course you can. Hals, I'm so happy for you both."

I was pleased he was happy. He was still important to me and it sure would make life easier, as he was my lawyer, if everyone got on.

"Toby is really happy for us both," I said. Sam was making himself a coffee. He looked like he belonged, even though he opened several cupboards to find the one he wanted.

"That's good. You should invite them over."

"I did, although he invited us to theirs as well."

Sam sat in front of me. He had a couple of document wallets that he placed down. "This is all my medical stuff, if you want to read it. I need it with me, obviously. And this is all my finances and funeral planning."

"Okay, I don't need to see either of those. We have a road trip to plan. Also, I thought we could have a summer house installed at the bottom of the garden. Your man cave," I laughed, although I'd had to force the laughter a little.

He chuckled. "You will need to know this stuff, but fine, not today. And yes, a summer house sounds great."

We chatted about the house, and then walked from room to room. He loved the house and there were only a few modifications to make to ensure he was comfortable. I didn't want him to just move in with me and forget all about his own comforts.

"I do want to paint this room," I said.

We were in the living room. The walls were brick, two of which had been painted over. There was an open fire, which I loved, and I knew I'd need to replace the windows. It was a listed building, so I'd need permission to do so from English Heritage and the local council.

Sam stood running his hand over the wall. "Shame to cover up all that brick really, but it would be way too messy to clean that paint off. I bet it's been there for hundreds of years."

I nodded. He then walked over to the coffee table and picked up a Sharpie. I had been doing the crossword the previous day.

He drew a large heart on the wall and infilled with our initials.

"There's one in my house as well. Alison will discover that when she redecorates.

"Oh, Sam," I said. It was fucking tragic we'd lost so much time when we'd still been so much in love.

"I don't think we should paint over that," I said, looking at it. "It's art."

"It's life."

"Our life," I said, snuggling into his side.

It was too cold to sit outside that evening, so we snuggled in the living room. Sam asked me about my writing, and I told him I had two books with editors and one I was finishing writing. Those three books would be published over the coming two years. I also had a streaming channel discussing the screen-play for my most successful series.

"One day, I'll write our story," I said.

"No one would believe it."

"Readers will complain," I said, and then chuckled.

"About what?"

"Underage sex, cannabis use, skipping school. They can be rather judgmental at times. I'll lie and up the age we first *did it*." I replied, chuckling.

"I hope I'm still alive for that one," he said. My heart stuttered in my chest.

"You will be. We have too much to do now."

I had a thought if he had something to live for, he would.

"Now, this road trip. Where have we never been to?"

We talked about Scotland and worried it might be too cold to camp, so opted for small boutique hotels or pubs with rooms. I had a vision of a chilly autumn evening, sitting in the bar of an old pub with a roaring fire. We also decided we'd like to visit some of the islands, the Hebrides. Sam was keen to visit some of the whiskey distilleries.

"What about Ursa?" he asked.

"Pam comes to stay when I'm away, if she's not with me."

"We could buy a campervan and take him with us?"

"And that defeats the objective. We were meant to take a road trip on a bike, and we didn't do it. You could teach me to ride, and we'll share the driving."

He snorted. "Like fuck I will. It's too dangerous. You could kill yourself."

"What? You could kill yourself."

"I'm already dying."

We paused. And then laughed until tears streamed down our cheeks.

"Okay, you could kill me," I said.

"Nah, you'd land on me. I'd cushion the blow."

When we'd calmed down, I sighed. "Oh, Sam. I don't want you to die," I whispered.

"Neither do I, to be honest. Can't do much about it though. All I can hope is the longer I go on, the more medicine advances, and the chance comes for a place on some experiment or another and they can cut it out."

"The part the root is at, where is that?"

"It's attached to the back of my brain. It's like a flat mush-room, wide, with a root that grows into the brainstem. That's why it's not possible to remove it. There would be too much damage to the brain, and I'd likely die anyway."

"But there is a chance you might not?"

"There's always a chance, but it's way too slim to consider. But, as I said, modern surgery, the longer I go on, who knows what could happen. At the moment, we have a 'watch and wait' thing going on. They can't operate, treatment may cause side effects way worse than I have now."

"So they do nothing?" I asked, sort of stunned by that.

"So they do nothing. It was my choice as well. Road trip?" he said, bringing us back to something nice.

"When do you want to do it?" I asked.

"I'm free all day, every day now." He smiled at me.

"Okay, I'll get this book finished and then that's it. So, if I give myself a deadline of a month, we can plan in the meantime."

It was settled. One month from that day we were heading to Scotland and driving around.

Sam redecorated and even started building the summer house. I had no idea how good he was at those things. In addition to fixing cars and bike, he seemed to be able to turn his hand to anything. He did paint over the heart, but not before I'd made him draw another on a canvas we could hang. He and Karl were loving the build project and I often sat in my office and just stared out the window at them. They argued, laughed, banged fingers, dropped hammers on toes, and thoroughly enjoyed themselves. They were father and son.

We ordered a new bed, one with a head and foot board. One that had rings attached! I'd about died of embarrassment when Sam suggested I lie on the bed to see the dimensions were right. He also ordered a huge box of toys. I made sure I wasn't in when they were delivered.

He had all his clothes over and we'd need to arrange some more wardrobes in the spare bedroom for all of them. He had way more than I did. And way more shoes. I'd laughed when he picked up a pair of my high heels. He reminded me of *playdates* in the garage. I highly doubted I'd get into them, but I'd have a go.

He'd been on his laptop on a Zoom call to an old customer, who was desperate for Sam to take on his restoration project. Sam passed all work over to Karl, but this one was probably a little out of his league. It was a vintage Aston Martin. I wanted Sam to take on the work, but he was adamant, no more. While on that call, I walked into the room wearing nothing but one of his shirts, and the shoes. I sat on the chair opposite him with my legs apart. He'd slammed the lid of the laptop shut and picked me up. He threw me on the sofa, and I laughed. I chuckled as I thought about it. I remember also not laughing for too long when, without any foreplay, he fucked me.

I worked; Sam built. By the end of the month, we had a functioning summer house, and I had a new book to send for editing.

I had one last thing to do. I opened up social media.

My dearest readers,

I've just finished a new book I think you'll love. You'll have to wait a year or so, however. Sorry!

In the meantime, I have news. I'm taking a break from writing any new material. Pam and I will still be involved in the foreign translations, audiobooks, and the TV series, which, I am assured is definitely going ahead.

For now, I need to concentrate on the love of my life, and what time we have together.

One day, I'll tell you this story. But for now, I need to live the last chapter to its fullest.

Hayley

I shut down my laptop, knowing I wouldn't open it again. I had a tablet for social media and emails.

I sat back in my chair and looked out. Sam was playing with Ursa. A lone tear ran down my cheek. I brushed it away, determined no more would fall. Not until it was necessary. I slid the chair back and left the room. I joined Sam in the garden, and he proudly showed me every join and every corner of the summer house.

It was perfect for him. A space for him to chill out, relax, watch whatever he wanted on the movie screen he'd installed, drink his beers, and smoke. There were two cuddle chairs, a popcorn machine, and a record player.

He pulled out an album, and with his back to me, he played it. 'Wish You Were Here' by Pink Floyd floated around the room. We sat and cuddled, listened, and remembered.

Alison came over the following day, and she and Sam made lunch for me and Pam. We had our meeting with Toby on Zoom and planned out the rest of the year. I was ahead of schedule in some respects. My publisher had delayed a project as it clashed with another of their big authors. I would have two books the following year and the latest, the first half of the year after. Toby had been on to the foreign publishers to renew some contracts, renegotiate others. And he and Pam would deal with the streaming service. I wasn't going abroad so, of course, I could be contacted if needed. I just didn't want deadlines to work to. I wanted the freedom for me and Sam to take off whenever we wanted.

Pam and Sam reminisced, and Pam told Alison all about the

fight at her wedding. Alison had been horrified, of course. More so when we told her Toby, the man I married, had been the one to defend Sam and get him off.

"By the skin of my teeth, I might add. If that was today, I'd have gone to prison for at least five years," Sam added.

"And you were prepared to wait for him?" Alison asked me.

I nodded. "Of course."

"Your dad was the bad boy of the estate. Every girl wanted his attention. When he chose me, I got a ton of stick from the other girls because I wasn't the prettiest of them. They couldn't understand why it was me and not them." I told her about the day we'd met, she knew it from Sam's side, of course, but not mine.

"Oh my God, that is so romantic!" She sighed.

"Your old man knew how to charm the ladies back then," Sam added.

"Still do, I bet," I replied.

It was nice for Pam and me to fill in the blanks for Alison.

"I don't remember my mum, but I remember you. You were always *around*. I feel like I've known you all my life," she said gently.

It was heartbreaking to hear. "I never wanted your mum to know about Hals. I didn't want it to affect her. But I had her name on my body, and... Well, I guess, as you know, I never got over her."

He took my hand in his.

"I'd have hated for your mum to have been upset by me. I'm

so sorry, and I wish she were alive for me to apologise to in person," I said.

"It is what it is," Alison said.

We chatted about the kids, her partner, who was the last person Sam had fought with, and I wasn't keen to learn it wasn't that long ago. She talked about the house, and how she wanted her dad's permission to change some things. She wanted to put in a pool for the kids.

"It's your house. I'll have the paperwork back next week. You do what you want with it," Sam had said.

It was the first time he'd mentioned he'd officially signed it over to her. It cemented his commitment to me, I thought.

"Tell me about this trip?" Pam asked.

Sam and I detailed the route we'd planned; we argued about some changes he'd made I wasn't aware of, and we laughed.

"Like an old married couple," he said.

"All we have to decide on is which bike?" I added.

Sam had his dirt bikes and road bikes. One road bike was a sleek black speed machine, so he'd called it. The kind where the passenger sits on a higher seat, and everyone has to lean forwards. I wasn't sure about that bike. I still struggled to do the leaning thing. I wasn't sure I wouldn't unbalance Sam on that.

"I prefer the Ducati thing," I said, not remembering the name.

"Desert. Ducati Desert," Sam corrected.

It was the most comfortable and for such a lot of driving, comfort had to be key. I did have a fleeting thought, should his tumour get worse, or something happen, I couldn't ride the bike. I pushed that thought aside, convincing myself nothing was going to happen because we had things to do, and he'd got through his list okay.

We made a list of things we'd need. A tent for starters, sleeping bags. I really wanted us to do a couple of days of wild camping, even if we found a pub to eat at and just slept in the tent. I didn't expect Sam to go hunting and skinning rabbits. I also had to be mindful Sam had to take a fair amount of medication and we'd have to take all that with us. I'd ordered a large backpack and Sam could put side boxes on the bike, he had told me what they were called but I'd glossed over, and we could pack some things in there. Otherwise, it was going to be what we could carry.

We'd selected some pubs to stay in, a couple of hotels, and two campsites. My idea of wild camping not really suitable for Sam.

Pam thought it the most hideous thing I'd done, Alison loved the idea. She even offered to drive up to meet us.

"No, this is our time," Sam had said, and I kept my mouth closed.

Pam and Alison left later that day and Sam and I took Ursa for a walk.

"Can I say something?" I asked.

"Sure, what?"

"Earlier, Alison offered to meet us, yes?"

"Yes," he replied.

"I think you might need to consider she wants to do all the

things with you as well. You know, make as many memories as she can with you?"

"I get that. I do, I understand. She's had me for twenty-three years. I'm just asking for me to make some memories for us. Just a little time for us."

I smiled at him. "I think we should sit with her and explain that. I don't want to jump into your life and take you away from her. Not now," I said.

He wrapped his arm around my shoulders and pulled me close.

"I get they all want my last days, but we don't know how long that will be! I think I deserve some time to do what I want, don't I? And what I want is you. We have wasted twenty-five years; I just want to catch up on some of them. Is that selfish?"

"No, not at all."

We headed back to the cottage.

Sam and I packed, and then repacked. I had to remove most of the clothes I'd packed so we could fit some essentials, like a tent, in and on top of the backpack. He'd lifted it onto my back, and I'd nearly toppled over. We'd bought a serious hikers backpack, the kind someone would have to climb a mountain. I got a new jacket and helmet, gloves and proper biker's trousers and boots.

Sam in his leathers was a sight to see, for sure. It took us much longer to get out of the house than anticipated.

Once we were settled on the bike, we set off.

"You okay?" I heard. Our helmets had mouthpieces and we could talk to each other. It had freaked me out to start with.

I nodded, then remembered to speak. "Yep. This is so strange," I said, laughing. "Don't know about these leathers, I can't feel the engine."

"Huh?"

"The engine. Was a nice feeling between my thighs," I replied.

Sam laughed. "Any more of that and I'll have to turn around."

We continued in silence for a little while. I hummed and sang, apparently we had a radio we could listen to but couldn't agree on a station. Mostly, Sam liked the music of our past, Pink Floyd and the like. I was more into modern music, the kind he called utter trash. I chuckled as he offered me singing lessons as a gift.

Our first stop was Birmingham and that was at the services. We grabbed a coffee and stretched our legs.

The second stop was because I needed to pee after the coffee, and we found a layby and a bush.

The third stop was because Sam needed to pee, and we found another layby and bush.

By the time we got to our first overnight destination, ten hours had passed.

For the first night we'd opted for a small boutique hotel. We thought we might need something extremely comfortable to get over the journey. Our room was lovely, with a large bed facing the windows and the view was to die for. We looked out on a forest of pine trees with a mountain in the background.

"We should go for a walk in the morning," Sam said, standing by the window. "I feel so content," he added, and I nodded.

"Yes, being with you is like coming home after a long journey away," I said.

"Was the journey worth it?"

I paused. "I think so. I think we needed a break to really know what we both wanted. Whether that break should have been as long, I don't know, but we can't go back. You wouldn't have Alison or Karl."

"I still can't help but feel like I wasted time."

For Sam, *time* was important, I guessed. "Then we need to make every second count."

We ate in the restaurant and Sam ordered a bottle of wine. What we didn't drink, we had sent up to the room and we decided on a walk after. Opposite the hotel was a loch, then more forest and mountains. We sat on a bench by the water's edge. I noticed a small urn.

"Someone had their ashes scattered here," I said.

"Nice place to end up, I guess."

"Did you ever find your dad's memorial stone?" I asked.

I'd remembered one time only Sam had said he wanted to see where his dad's ashes had been scattered. We'd headed to the cemetery and had someone check the records. They gave us a location, but of course, there was no headstone, so we never actually found it. Nor did we ever find a tree.

"No, never bothered. I scattered my mum in ten different places. She liked to travel around so I didn't think she'd want to be in one place."

"That's a nice thing to do."

We headed back to our room, and I ran the bath. It was large enough for us both to climb in.

"You know, I've been an orphan way longer than I ever had parents," he said. I stared at him. "Does that get me a blow job?"

I laughed. "A sympathy blow job?"

"Yeah, I'm not beyond begging if you want me to."

I stood, letting the soapy water run down my body. "You're going to have to get out, I can't hold my breath for any length of time, and you'd have some explaining to do if I die while... Well, you know!"

It was Sam's turn to laugh. He stood, grabbed a towel, and dried off his cock. I knelt in the warm water and gave him what he wanted.

Sam held my head, his fingers curling in my hair, and I ran my tongue up and down his shaft. I looked up at him, knowing he liked that stance. I opened my mouth and sucked him in.

I rolled his balls in one hand and cupped his arse with the other. He started to rock against me. He threw his head back and moaned, I sucked harder. When I saw his stomach tremble, I opened my mouth wider and took him deeper.

"Shit, Hals," he said through gritted teeth.

He pulled at my hair, but I wasn't budging. He came and I

swallowed down all he could give me. His legs shook and he breathed in deep.

"Jesus," he muttered when I gently released him from my mouth.

I looked up at him and smiled. He sank to his knees and held my head. He didn't speak, just looked at me. Then he kissed me. I was sure he'd be able to taste himself in my mouth and he didn't care. He kissed me hard. When he pulled back, we were both struggling for breath.

"Hey, you look sad. Was it that bad?" I asked, laughing but also concerned.

"Not sad. Overwhelmed, maybe?" He shrugged his shoulders.

We climbed from the bath and both sat in the bedroom wrapped in towels. I saw him squint a couple of times and he pinched the bridge of his nose.

"Sam, are you okay?"

"Just a little headache."

"Should I be worried?"

He shook his head and smiled. "No, this is just a regular headache. Probably from keeping that helmet on for so long."

"How about you get in bed, and I'll call down for a cup of tea?" I said.

He nodded. Before he did, however, he took a handful of tablets.

He was sound asleep when the tea was brought up. I sat and read and then snuggled under the duvet next to him. He was in his usual sleeping position and, looking at him, it was like there was nothing wrong. I wanted to text Alison to ask if headaches were normal for him, but then I didn't want to worry her, either. I'd already googled brain tumours and it had fucking terrified me. I hadn't been able to read too much and all I focussed on were the words that you can live with it. I didn't continue to know for how long.

The next day, we walked around the area. It was nice to wander and talk. Sam felt a lot better, so he said. He did keep his sunglasses on, and it wasn't particularly sunny.

We set off to our second destination in the afternoon. Although we'd booked a pub for dinner, we'd decided to camp in their field. It was close enough should we decide we hated it.

And we did decide that.

It was cold and not even cuddling up close eased the chill.

"Whose idea was this?" Sam said, laughing.

"Remind me of this should I ever suggest camping again, won't you?"

"Wait here."

Sam climbed from the tent, grumbling about his back, and walked towards the pub. He was back in five minutes.

"Come on, they have a room."

Like most of the pubs on our route, they had rooms to rent. We left the tent, grabbed the backpack, and headed in.

A hot shower, a large mug of tea, and we were happily settled in a comfortable bed, listening to the rain outside.

We ditched the tent the following morning, it made the backpack so much lighter.

"I'm too fucking old for camping," Sam said with a laugh. "But we can officially say we did it. Tick that off the list."

We continued with our journey, taking lots of photographs and videos and making amazing memories.

When our ten days were up, we sat for one last time looking out over a pristine white sand beach, one we'd walked up and down a few times and vowed to come back.

We started the long drive home, and that time, we did it over two days.

CHAPTER 21

Present Day

"I want us to get married soon, Hals," Sam said. We'd been home just a couple of days. "I've been online, we can get a licence at the local registry office."

"Okay. What do we need to do?" I asked.

He had a list of paperwork we needed to file.

"Is there a reason for the rush, Sam?"

"Nope. I just want it done." He smiled at me. Sam was pretty impulsive.

He also had a couple of hospital appointments coming up he wanted me to attend with him. He felt, as he had never explained his condition that well, I could learn from the consultants. In truth, Alison had told me he didn't want to know the full facts.

We asked Alison, Karl, Pam, Gregg, Toby, and Sally to come to our wedding. Alison and Pam were to be witnesses.

It took just under a month to get the licence sorted and the registry office to check our paperwork.

Sam wore a suit, and I wore a dress I'd bought especially. It wasn't a wedding dress, but a beautiful floaty blue that flattered my figure.

After, we headed to a lovely restaurant. Sam had organised that and I'd laughed as we were presented with ham and crisp sandwiches, had champagne and hot chocolate. In fact, I'd laughed so hard, tears had run down my face. Of course, there was a proper meal to follow.

"He still loves that," Alison said, waving a sandwich around, causing the crisps to fly everywhere.

"I could get used to this," Toby said.

When Toby had arrived at the registry office, not that I was there, Sam had hugged him for a long time. Alison had previously asked me what the connection was and frowned when she met him finally. I'd already told her Toby was my ex and the one who got her dad off his most serious of charges. I think the age gap had shocked her. Toby was a lot older than me.

It was nice to just sit back and watch everyone interact. Gregg and Karl laughed and talked cars. Sally knew Pam anyway and they, with Alison, talked fashion and books. Sam held my hand.

"I've missed this so much," I whispered to him. "Having friends all sit together, and now family."

We left the restaurant before everyone else. I had no idea what was happening, but Sam had arranged for Pam and Gregg to dog sit. We were off for a couple of nights somewhere.

Sam drove and I badgered to know where we were going. As we got close, I frowned. I knew where we were, and it was somewhere I hadn't visited since I was a teen.

"Remember coming here?" Sam said, pulling into a separate gate to the main one.

"Yeah. But..." It was three in the afternoon, and we were visiting a safari park!

He chuckled. We then came to a parking area with reception. Sam parked and I exited the car, aware of how my heels would end up scratched on the gravel drive. A golf buggy stood nearby.

"Mr. and Mrs. Weston, welcome," the driver said.

Sam opened the boot and pulled out a small case. I laughed as we sat inside the golf buggy. We were then driven to a wonderful looking lodge.

I'd read about the lodges and was over the moon to find out we were in the Lion Lodge. Part of the lodge extended into the lion's area. Floor-to-ceiling glass allowed the occupants to get up close with them. It was one of those places I'd always wanted to visit but knew I probably wouldn't. It was super expensive, for starters.

I walked around the lodge. There was an open fire already roaring, and a log fed hot tub that was bubbling away.

"Oh my God, this is amazing!"

"I thought you might like it. Something different, isn't it?"

Sam left the case in the lounge and took my hand. "Let's get wet," he said.

We stripped off, grabbed a bottle of champagne, and settled

in the hot tub. It sat beside a glass window and a lioness was patrolling no more than a foot away. She glanced our way once, then ignored us.

Sex with Sam had always been good. I only had one other man to compare against, of course. Toby was a little less passionate than Sam, and I always had the higher sex drive. I'd assumed that was because I was younger. Sex with Sam now was better than before.

He knew my body so well, having been the one to *discover* what turned me on. He'd encouraged me to explore my body and to tell him what I wanted.

I raised my glass in a silent toast to him.

"What are you thinking about?" he asked.

"Us. How good we are together sexually."

"Remember, I taught you everything you know," he said, crawling towards me. It had been a joke comment, of course, but the truth as well.

He kissed me, taking my glass from my hand and placing it to the side. "We can't, not in here," I said, laughing.

"We can, anywhere we want. I'll leave a cleaning fee," he said.

* * *

That night Sam had another headache. I'd woken to an empty bed and found him sitting on the sofa looking out the window.

"Are you okay?" I asked. He had an ice pack held to his forehead.

"Yeah, headache. Come and sit, they're out and about. I took some videos of them," he said, pointing to the window. I snuggled up beside him.

We watched a lion and his mate patrol the grounds, they walked past the window a few times, and once, he stopped and stared straight in. It gave me goosebumps and I was extremely grateful for the plate glass between us.

I wasn't a lover of zoos, but this safari park spent more time rehoming animals back into the wild than anyone. Their foundation was one worthy of support.

The lion didn't flinch, blink, or move. "Fuck, that's scary," Sam whispered. I nodded beside him.

"Do cats blink?" I asked.

"No idea, google it," he replied and chuckled.

Eventually, the lion moved off and we both let out a large breath.

"Phew!" I said. "Are the headaches getting worse?"

"No, not worse. More frequent, though."

"Do we need to see your consultant soon?"

"Yeah, I have an appointment coming up anyway. We'll worry about it then, not now. Now is for making memories, good ones."

He kissed my temple, and we headed back to bed.

The following day, we dressed up warm and headed for our *safari*. We were driven around the park in a buggy, which was a little worrying when we got into the big cat enclosures. Lunch was on our terrace prepared by a chef, and we sat around a lit fire pit watching the lions without the protection of glass. I just hoped they had no desire to climb up.

The afternoon was spent wandering hand in hand around the park. It was good to see it from both the buggy and the ground.

"I bet no one else can say they honeymooned in a safari park, can they?" Sam asked.

"Nope, and it's amazing."

Sam wasn't necessarily able to travel abroad, so Alison had told me. First, he'd never get the required insurance, and second, he really needed to be near his consultant. No one knew how long he had, or whether he'd get on to any programmes that might help. I'd been researching on the side. There was a clinic in Switzerland working on removing brain tumours with the least amount of residual damage. I'd requested some information.

Our last evening at the lodge was spent making love on the rug in front of the fire. With just the flicker of flames to light the room, it was probably the best night I'd spent with him. He kissed every inch of my body, nipping skin, and tasting. I did the same. We made love twice, taking our time and appreciating each other.

We sat wrapped in a blanket and just watched the fire.

"I have something to do," Sam said, standing.

He walked naked to the bedroom and then returned with a piece of paper.

"I did it all," he said, holding the paper to me.

There was a list of things that had been crossed. Diving in

the ocean, sailing, climbing a mountain, some of the things I'd seen him do in the photographs on Alison's Facebook page.

At the bottom were two things, one had been crossed off.

The first: *Find Hayley and apologise.*

The second: *Marry her, finally.*

Tears streamed down my cheeks as he screwed that paper up and threw it in the fire. We watched it burn.

When he fell asleep in my arms, I continued to weep.

CHAPTER 22

Present Day

To say I was nervous when we took the train to London was an understatement. Sam was cool as a cucumber, of course.

"What will be, will be," he kept saying.

I had gotten into this relationship knowing full well Sam was ill. He'd made a point of telling me that, but my stomach was in absolute knots knowing I was going to hear the full extent from the consultant.

I didn't like hospitals at the best of times, and that time was worse. Sam had to have an MRI before he saw the consultant, so we headed there. It wasn't a fixed appointment as such, he had to wait his turn. Thankfully, it wasn't too long, he didn't do waiting very well. There were other patients sitting in the waiting room, one or two of whom Sam knew. No one spoke about their tumour, but the sight of some with shaved heads and scars, and others looking as if nothing was wrong, was distressing. I kept that in check, of course. When we were called in, we walked into a room, I imagined, specifically designed for giving bad news. It was comfortable with sofas and a desk.

"Sam, it's good to see you," Mr. Hargraves said. He walked towards us holding out his hand.

Sam took hold of his hand and shook it. "This is my wife, Hayley," he said, introducing me.

"So you did it then?" Mr. Hargraves said, laughing.

Sam beamed. "I did."

He turned to me. "I feel like I already know you, Hayley. Sam has spoken of you so much."

"Wow, I didn't know."

"Now, shall we sit?"

Mr. Hargraves turned a computer screen around so we could see. "It's grown, Sam, but I think you knew that."

He pointed to a grey mass. To me, it wasn't that large.

"Can you see, Hayley?" he asked. He drew around the edges with his finger on the screen. "It's a flattish tumour, which is fairly rare for this type, there is a root that heads inwards and that's getting close to the brainstem."

"What happens if it gets there?" I asked.

Sam drew his fingers across his throat, theatrically. I shook my head.

"That part of the brain controls breathing, heartbeat, and other critical functions."

It was said so matter of fact.

"Can it be treated?" I asked, knowing Sam would have asked all the same questions.

"Yes, and no. The risk of damage to the brainstem is high, high enough for us to take a decision not to operate."

"But you could?"

He looked at Sam. It was then Sam who spoke.

"I made a decision not to go down that route."

"Why?" I felt bile rising to my throat.

"The chances are, I'd end at best, paralysed and being kept alive by machines. At worst, paralysed from the neck down."

"What are those chances?" I asked the consultant.

"Eighty percent," he replied.

"So there is a slim chance you might not?"

Sam reached out and placed his palm on the side of my face. I hadn't realised tears were falling until he used his other hand to wipe under my eyes.

"I'm not willing to take that slim chance," he said gently.

I nodded. I understood. I didn't like it.

"What happens now?" I asked.

"We monitor, we manage the pain, and at some point, Sam may elect to move into a hospice for his final days."

The pain I felt in my chest was real. I clasped it and struggled to breathe. Sam wrapped his arms around me, and Mr. Hargraves pushed a box of tissues towards me.

"I'm sorry," I said. "It's... It's the first time that's been said. I know it's coming, but we hadn't said the words."

"It's a shock, for sure," the consultant said.

"How long?" I asked, my voice was very small. It was a question I wanted to ask, but not necessarily wanting to know the answer.

He looked at Sam before me and Sam nodded.

"A year at most."

A year.

We had one year.

That was enough to make as many memories as I needed to carry me on until we met again.

It was hard leaving the hospital and walking to the station. I wished I'd offered to drive, and I would next time. Sam would have monthly check-ups unless he felt the need to see anyone sooner.

"I'm sorry for breaking down like that," I said as we waited on the platform.

"I expected it. It's hard to hear it for the first time. I wanted you to know what you're getting into, although maybe we should have married after, in case you want to cut and run."

I looked up at him. "I'd marry you tomorrow if I hadn't already." He wrapped an arm around my shoulders. "We have a year, Sam. We need to do all the things."

He smiled. "We will. We'll do it all."

When we got home, we started to make a list of all the things he'd never done but wanted to.

I heard Sam on the phone to Alison, filling her in on what happened at the hospital. She didn't cry, in fact she was pleased. She thought the length of time left would be shorter. It reminded me they had lived with the news for the past year or so already.

Alison invited us to dinner and insisted we brought Ursa, since her kids loved him so much. It was nice to sit and chat, and to have Karl pop in to see us. He brought his new girl-friend, and I was thrilled to be introduced as his stepmum. He'd been calling Sam, Dad, since he was little.

"So, are you our nan?" young Sam asked cheekily.

"Yes, if you want me to be."

"Will you give me pocket money? Freddie's nan gives him pocket money," he said.

I laughed and nodded. "Well, if Freddie's nan does, then so should I."

I reached into my bag and gave him a five-pound note. Alison took it from him and tried to give it back.

"Mum! Nan gave that to me, not you." He tried to snatch it from her hand.

A row ensued and I couldn't help but laugh as young Sam rolled his eyes and pocked his tongue out when his mum wasn't looking. We agreed the five pounds was to go into his piggy bank. Of course, I also gave one to Hayley.

"Be careful, he'll have you twisted around his little finger," Sam said.

"Good," I replied, wanting to be.

We spent the rest of the day playing with the kids. Sam sat out a lot, he was tired, he napped on the sofa.

"Is he really okay?" Alison asked.

"I don't know. He says the tiredness is all part of it, but lately he's been getting more headaches. He says there not worse, just more frequent."

I saw her close her eyes. "So, we're on the down slope now?"

I wasn't sure what to say. Were we?

"The consultant said a year, tops. That could be twelve months," I offered.

"Or one," she replied.

I took hold of her hand. "Whatever it is, let's make it the best."

She nodded. I told her we were making a list and if there was anything she wanted to add to it, she had to tell me.

"I want you and Dad to make the list. I've had way more years with him than you have," she said.

I hugged her. "He's your dad, their granddad," I replied.

"And you are the love of his life, always have been. I have enough memories to keep me going, you need to make yours."

Sam had called her selfless once, I hadn't realised just how much she was. She was willingly giving up time with her dad for me.

I drove us home, Sam didn't think he could see well enough, and once home he headed to bed early.

I walked Ursa and then settled down in front of my laptop. I booked tickets to Kew Gardens; I found a cottage in Dorset on the Jurassic Coast for us to stay for a long weekend and fossil hunt. I googled one hundred and one things to do before you die and added some to the list. Sam wasn't into things like skydiving, thank God, and I also didn't want to do so much that it tired him out.

I had upgraded my camera to a digital one and I downloaded images. I selected some I wanted to print out and frame. There was one I had taken of Sam. He was sitting in the hot tub looking out into the lion enclosure. His short hair was wet, and the moonlight reflected off the droplets of water on his toned body. It was a side-on view of him, capturing his broken nose and scarred eyebrow. He was handsome to me. Rough and raw, full of emotion and love. A second shot showed him looking at me and laughing. The third, which I would definitely print out was one of him rising. His cock was out of shot, just, and his stomach was muscled. It was the way he was moving that showed off his physique. I put those three in a separate file with one of us getting married, and another, a selfie, of us on the white beach in Scotland.

I got online and ordered some gorgeous frames and then thought about where I wanted them. The one of Sam climbing from the tub, I wanted beside the bed. I wanted to wake up and see him next to me when he wasn't.

I shut down the laptop and just sat in the dark. Ursa snuffled beside me, occasionally nudging my hand with his nose. I think he must have picked up on my sadness.

One year, and I was going to make the best of it I could. Yet again, I thanked my decision to stop writing.

When I got to bed, Sam was sleeping. He was in his usual position on his back but as I climbed in, he turned to me. He'd called me his gravitational pull, he could be in the deepest sleep but once I slipped under the covers beside him, he turned to me. I kissed his lips softly and wrapped my arm around him. We stayed that way until the morning.

"I need to go through this with you," Sam said one morning. He had one of the blasted folders on the kitchen table. I'd avoided them until then.

I handed him a coffee and sat. The folder contained all his funeral arrangements. He'd prepaid for it and wanted me to know where and with whom. He didn't want a fanfare, no flowers other than one on top of the coffin. He wanted to be cremated and it would be my choice as to where his ashes went. He was a firm believer funerals were a rip-off, and he didn't want mourning. What I noticed the most was he wanted to avoid anything that would cause more upset. No family carrying the coffin. He did, however, want a cracking wake, he said.

Drink lots, have fun, remember him, talk about him, and dance. Those were his words. I wasn't sure *having fun* would be on the cards, but I promised him everything else.

I was determined not to cry, Sam was being so brave himself, being so *professional*.

"I sent a copy of my will to Toby, as well," he said.

"Okay."

"I've had it redone to include you," he added.

"Sam, leave it all to the kids and grandkids, I don't need anything," I replied.

"I know you don't *need* anything, but there are some things I'd like you to have."

"Okay," I said, again. "I'll keep all this safe."

We were off to Kew that day and I'd opted to drive. I was

concerned with his reoccurring headaches he'd struggle. We took his car, and I loved driving it.

"You know, I wish I'd learned to drive a bike," I said.

"You still can."

I laughed. "You can teach me, just around the fields. I don't want to go on the road."

He agreed to take me out on one of his old dirt bikes, like the old days. He and Karl often rode around the farmland at his old house, but he'd never raced again after losing Karl.

We had a lovely day walking around. We had lunch, bought some plants, and marvelled at things we'd never see in their natural environment.

"That's one off the list," Sam said, as we started to head for home.

When he put his sunglasses on, I knew he had another headache coming. They were daily now, and I worried myself sick.

More so, when later that night he asked me to bring forwards the Dorset trip.

I didn't answer him verbally, I couldn't. I just nodded and got online, rebooking for the first available slot.

When Sam took a bath, I called Alison.

"Okay, I'm worried. His headaches are daily now."

"How long has it been since his last check-up?" Alison asked.

"Two months. Should I call the consultant?"

"I would."

"He asked me to bring forward our Dorset trip, Alison."

She fell silent but I heard the tiniest sob.

"I've done that, but I think you and the kids should come."

"No, Hals. The last thing he needs is the kids around him if he's declining. You go, just the two of you."

"What if... What..." I couldn't finish.

"Then he has you by his side."

It was probably the next to worst phone call I could make.

Two days later we took off for Dorset.

Like our honeymoon, we chilled out, walked, and fossil hunted. I took as many photographs as I could. I was over the moon when I found a small fossil, it was an ammonite, one of the most common fossils in the area, but to me, it might as well have been a dinosaur leg.

We ate in the cottage and sat wrapped in blankets in the garden drinking wine. Ursa loved all the walks along the beach and would sit on the back seat of the Jag with his head resting on Sam's shoulder. Every now and again, he'd lick Sam on the cheek. He knew something was happening. He wouldn't leave his side.

"I think my dog loves you more than me," I said, laughing.

Sam reached back to stroke his face. "Well, I love you more than your dog loves you, so I guess that makes up for things."

"No way, my dog loves me so much," I said, also trying to pet him. He moved his head away and back to Sam's shoulder.

We laughed.

That level of adoration continued at home. Ursa was firmly stuck to Sam's side. I was happy about that, of course. Despite how tired Sam was becoming, he still insisted on walking Ursa with me. It got Sam out, which was good. Even when it was raining, we donned our wet weather gear and wellies and sloshed through the fields.

We got into a good routine. We walked the dog, either went out or watched movies, all the ones we'd seen as kids and then all the ones on the list we had wanted to see. We carried on with our list, visiting some stately homes, having another week away in Cornwall—which we both loved—and then spending days doing nothing but lounging around the cottage or having family over.

It was noticeable the kids were a little too much for Sam. A couple of times he'd had to retire to the bedroom, the noise was too much. Sam didn't want the children to know anything, I disagreed, as did Alison. She wanted them to know something so it wasn't such a shock and as the parent, she overruled.

While Sam was sleeping the perfect opportunity came up.

"Where's Granddad?" Hayley asked.

"Come and sit down, both of you," Alison said.

Hayley had a look that suggested she thought she was about to get told off. She sat with her hands in her lap and her eyes wide. Young Sam sat and grinned, showing brown chocolate-coloured teeth.

"Granddad isn't well, so he's gone to bed now. But here's the thing. He's going to be poorly for a while, so we have to be careful and quiet around him," Alison said.

Both kids nodded, but I highly doubted they understood what it meant though.

"Is he gonna die?" Sam said.

Alison looked at me. "We're all going to die, darling. Sometimes people die before we want them to, but you're going to outlive us, for sure."

He didn't answer but did nod. "So we have to look after Granddad, don't we?" Alison added.

Neither child said anything. "Do you want to ask anything?" I said.

"You're not going to die, are you?" Hayley asked.

"No, darling, I'm not."

"I might lose my name," she said quietly.

"Even when I'm not here, you get to keep your name," I said.

She smiled then, but I think it more out of confusion.

"Who want's ice cream?" I asked.

Both kids jumped off their chairs at that and we were back to normal. They had a bowl each and I poured some chocolate on the top.

"I have your dad's funeral plan here, do you want it?" I asked, when the kids had headed back into the garden with the dog.

"You're his wife, Hals. I'll have whatever you want me to, but not because you think I should rather than you."

I squeezed her hand. "I'm dreading that day," she whispered.

"So am I. But let's concentrate on what time we have left."

It had to be the headaches that had Alison worrying and talking as if Sam was on his way out. I looked at it as just a blip.

Sam was still asleep when Alison and the kids left. They'd

drawn him a get-well picture I had to stick on the fridge for when he got up, they'd told me. I waved them off and then made a coffee for Sam. I took it and the drawing up the stairs.

I crept into the room and placed both on the bedside cabinet. Sam lay on top of the covers, still in his clothes. He looked so peaceful. I leaned down and kissed his lips, his eyes fluttered open.

"Morning," I said.

"What? What time is it?" he asked sitting up.

I laughed. "It's only five. Alison and the kids have gone, they drew you a picture. Alison told them you were poorly, Sam."

He sighed. "I didn't want them to know."

"Would you rather they have the shock of losing you? This way, we can prepare them," I replied gently.

He picked up his mug and sipped. "Sit with me," he said. I climbed on the bed beside him.

He held my hand, running his thumb over my knuckles. "I love you so much," he said.

"Not as much as I love you," I replied, smiling at him.

"Do you know what's happening?" he asked.

I swallowed hard. "Yes, and if you want to talk about it, then fine. Otherwise, I'm happy just to live each day as much as we can."

"Sometimes I want to talk about it, sometimes not."

"I'm here, Sam."

We fell silent for a little while. "I'm scared," he whispered.

"Of what?"

"Of leaving you. Of it being painful. Of not knowing exactly what is going to happen."

"Don't be scared about leaving me, Sam. We found each other again and the love we have is enough to see me through, for sure."

I didn't know the answers to his other questions. I knew he would have a dedicated nurse to help him and there was the opportunity of a hospice.

"Did you read the stuff I sent you about that clinic in Switzerland?"

I'd gotten myself up to date on progress there.

"Yeah. I think I'm too late for that."

"Would you mind if I contacted them? Just ask the question?"

"If it makes you feel better," he said, smiling gently at me.

Present Day

When Sam had a seizure, I was in a mass panic. I had no idea what to do. I'd been dealing with some laundry and walked back into the kitchen. He was sitting on the sofa and his eyes were open. I spoke to him, he didn't reply. At first, I thought he hadn't heard, and it wasn't until I stepped closer, I saw that his body was rigid. He then started to shake violently. I rushed to him as he slid from the sofa and held him. I didn't want to let him go for fear of him banging his head. I cursed I'd taken the cushions off to clean the covers that morning. I couldn't reach my phone so searched his pockets for his.

When I couldn't find his phone, I whipped off my sweat-shirt and laid it under his head. I rushed into the kitchen and grabbed my phone. It had a dead battery. I cursed.

I didn't have a physical home phone; I'd never needed one. That was my first mistake.

I ran upstairs to see if Sam had left his by the bed. It wasn't there. By the time I got back down, he had settled. I sat beside him. His body relaxed and he gently opened his eyes.

"Hey," I said.

He didn't speak initially. It was as if he was still coming to.

"I'm here, Sam," I said. "You're okay."

Adrenalin had flooded my body and that was starting to wear off. I felt tears prick at my eyes.

"Did I have a fit?" he asked. His voice was strangulated.

"You did, but it's all okay now," I replied.

We stayed where we were for a little while until he felt ready to move. He took a deep breath in and exhaled loudly. Then he pushed himself back up on the sofa.

"Fuck," he said quietly.

"I couldn't find your phone to call an ambulance," I said.

He gently shook his head. "No need for an ambulance, baby," he said, then reached out for me.

I sat beside him and held his hand.

"Did I scare you?" he asked.

"Yes, but that's okay. I didn't know what to do."

"You did good. I need to sleep," he said.

I helped him lie on the sofa and he closed his eyes. I was too frightened to leave him, but I needed to get my phone on charge. My hands shook and it took forever to get the blasted charger in the phone. Once it had, I returned to Sam. I sat on the floor holding his hand while he slept.

He did that for about an hour. When he woke, it was as if nothing had happened and he'd just woken from a nap.

"You're back with me," I said, smiling gently at him.

"I am. Thirsty, though."

I jumped up and filled a glass of water for him. He drank it straight down and handed it back. While I refilled it, he straightened himself up.

"I'm sorry, baby," he said.

"What on earth for? Don't apologise for that, Sam."

He smiled at me, and I knelt between his thighs. "I need to learn what to do in these situations," I said.

"All you can do is make sure I don't bash my head, I guess. Don't try to hold me still, when I relax, just get me on my side."

I nodded. "What about any medication?"

"There's nothing I can take in that moment. That's only the second one I've had, so I could be talking utter bollocks," he said, chuckling.

"Should we call the nurse?" I asked.

"I'll do that later."

Sam rested for a couple more hours before declaring himself fit. He wanted to carry on fixing a bike he'd bought for young Sam. I was unsure. I didn't want him out of my sight, but he kept insisting he was fine.

While he was in the garage, I googled seizures. It seemed my instinct had been spot on. I debated whether to let Alison know but decided that should be Sam's call. I might be over or under reacting. I did push him to let his nurse know, however.

For the next couple of months Sam seemed to rally. The headaches lessened, or he didn't tell me about every one. He wasn't as tired, or he was just pushing through, and he didn't have another fit that I was aware of. I stuck to him like glue, to the point he had to tell me to leave him alone one day. He did it in a jokey way, of course, but I got the message. I was smothering him.

He had informed the nurse, who had asked him to make notes of dates and time and if he could remember what he had done prior. I bought a diary for him. He wrote on the back of an envelope.

As the winter set in, so his days in the garage lessened. He was determined to get the bike done for Christmas. He'd promised Sam his own bike, a *big boy's* bike as he called. Both kids had all sorts of motorised vehicles, Hayley had a mini quad that she roared around on, but Sam wanted a bike like his granddad, and my Sam had promised they'd go for a ride together on Christmas Day.

I was looking forward to Christmas. On the day we would be at Alison's, her house was much larger and could accommodate us all easier. On Boxing Day, Toby, Sally, Pam, and Gregg, were coming to us. Alison found it strange I still had a friendship with Toby. We all thought that hilarious. Especially when young Sam had asked him once if he was my dad.

I was still visiting my dad once a month, but it was getting tougher to do so. He had become so withdrawn and he had no clue who I was, but my presence was upsetting him. I knew that conversation was coming, the one where I was told it might be better not to visit, and I was dreading that. I had taken Sam to visit with me one time, and there had been a glimmer of light in Dad's eyes. I knew he recognised Sam, but his speech was going so he didn't communicate well. In one way, I hoped he just fell asleep and didn't wake up. I knew that was what he would have wanted.

I was in the kitchen when Sam came up behind me. He wrapped his arms around my waist and rested his chin on my shoulder.

"Hey," I said. "I hope your hands are not all greasy."

"Yep. What are you doing?"

"Playing tennis, what does it look like I'm doing?"

"Looks like you're butchering that piece of meat," he said, and then laughed. "Let me do it."

He washed his hands, which weren't greasy, and took over. He was a good cook when it was basic meals, and he preferred straight up basic, *good old-fashioned* meals, as he called them. I was preparing a leg of lamb. I'd scored the top and was stuffing it with rosemary and garlic. He smeared some salted butter over the top before he wrapped it in tinfoil. It was ready for the oven then.

Sam loved a roast dinner and not just on a weekend. I was making a point of feeding him all his favourites.

"While that's cooking, I know of something else that could be eaten," he whispered.

I raised my eyebrows at him. "Do you now? And what might that be?"

He stepped towards me with his smirk and raised eyebrow. I stepped back. He smirked some more.

"You think you can run from me?" he asked, his voice a growl.

"Right now, probably, not like you're twenty anymore, is it?" I replied.

He cocked his head. "Mmm, you might have a point." Before he had finished the sentence, he rushed me, threw me over his shoulder, and carried me up to bed.

I laughed all the way, more so when he dropped me on the bed and then complained about his back.

"I could never get enough of you," he said, pulling his T-shirt over his head and undoing his jeans.

I lifted my arse as he pulled down my jeans and panties at the same time. He then knelt between my thighs and placed his hands on my hips.

"You still have too many clothes on," he said. I wriggled out of my T-shirt and bra.

He stared at my body, his eyes roaming over my skin. He leant down and kissed my stomach, trailing down to my pussy. His tongue lapped and probed, tasted, and sucked. When he added two fingers, I came.

Sam crawled up the bed beside me. I pushed him to his back and straddled him. I just stared at him for a little while, he still looked like the boy I fell in love with, with just a little grey over his ears. I leaned down to kiss him. I started to feel emotion well up inside, I pushed that down.

I needed to take as much of him as I could, while I could.

I positioned his cock at my entrance and teased myself with it. He raised his hips, wanting to be inside. I denied him that. He chuckled, and it was a throaty sound. He didn't like to be teased.

When I thought I'd pushed it far enough, I lowered. The sigh that left his lips was enough to satisfy me. He held my hips and I rocked against him.

I rode him harder and faster as my desire rose. His breathlessness matched mine, his moans echoed mine. When he called out my name as he came, my emotions flowed out. I came again and I cried. I slumped against his chest, and he held me.

"Hey, don't cry, please," he whispered.

I sniffed and gently nodded. "I'm sorry," I replied. I slid to the side and faced him.

He reached over and stroked my cheek. "No tears," he said gently.

"Can't promise that."

He kissed my eyelids.

Sam could come and stay hard. That was one thing I loved the most about sex with him.

He gently rolled me to my back and slid over me. I wrapped my legs around his and he made love to me. He was gentle and tender, cupping my face with his hands and kissing my face and lips, my throat and neck.

When he held my hands over my head, gripping my wrists, I knew the gentle was gone and I desperately needed his rough.

He fucked me hard, jolting me up the bed with every thrust. He bit my shoulders and sucked on my skin to mark me.

When he stopped, I shouted out his name. He pulled out and told me to turn over. I'd only just done that when he grabbed my hips and raised them. He slammed into me again. I gripped the bedding, dragging it towards me as the most delicious feelings coursed through me. My skin felt on fire, and ice ran through my veins. When he pinched my clitoris, holding the swollen and sensitive nub between his fingers, I exploded around him.

I came so hard I could feel it run down my thighs. My stomach cramped and sweat beaded on my forehead.

I moaned, called out his name, and he still slammed into me. He finally came, I felt his fingers tighten against my hips. His nails dug into my skin. He held himself inside and I felt him shudder and his cock pulse. Finally, when he was done, he slumped on the bed beside me.

I slid down, lying on my front and looking at him.

"Fuck," he said, and then laughed.

I shuffled over and kissed his shoulder.

"You are amazing, do you know that?" he said.

"So you say. How many girls have you fucked like that?"

"One, you."

"Liar," I said, chuckling.

"I'm serious. I've fucked many, but not with any shred of emotion or meaning. That has just been you, always you."

"What about...?" I was afraid to ask about his wife.

"It's always been you. I wasn't fair to her; I should never have married her. It was a total rebound and she knew that. But,

I guess, she loved me more than I could have loved her back, and I thank her for that."

I smiled at him. "And for giving you Alison. I thank her for that," I said.

* * *

We trundled along, Christmas came and went, and we had a wonderful time. I didn't think I'd taken many photographs until I had to download them all. I selected the ones I loved the most to print off and add to the memory wall that was growing in the kitchen. The back wall above the sofa already had ten photographs of Sam and all the kids, Sam and the dog, Sam on his own, Sam and me.

It was a month later Sam went downhill again.

The headaches returned, coupled with nausea. The nursing team had visited at home and that conversation started. The one I didn't want, but knew I needed.

"What can be offered in a hospice that can't be offered at home?" I asked.

Sam hadn't spoken. He knew the tumour had grown before he'd even seen the MRI. He also knew he was on borrowed time.

"Nothing, we can arrange for nurses to come in."

"I need to think about this," Sam said.

"What worries you?" the nurse asked.

"I don't want to be a burden on you," he said, turning to me.

I shook my head. "You could *never* be a burden, Sam. My preference is to have you at home. But it's your decision. Don't put yourself in a hospice if the only reason is so you're not a burden, please," I begged him. "Please."

The lump in my throat was huge, causing my voice to become high pitched.

"We can easily set up here," the nurse said.

Finally, Sam nodded.

It was agreed my study would become our new bedroom. We had a small shower and toilet in the utility room, should Sam get to the point where he couldn't navigate the stairs.

It was the end of the month that Sam started to use that room.

He lost weight, having no appetite and I started to make protein shakes for him. His vision was getting impaired. He found he couldn't see long distance. That upset him. All I could do was comfort as best I could.

He was fitted with a morphine pump to keep the headaches under control and, when I was taken aside, I was also told it would keep any agitation in check. It was likely Sam would get confused, possibly hallucinate. The morphine could act as a sedative if needed.

I slept beside him every night, we wrapped our arms around each other and held on tight. I cried a lot.

"You know this is it, don't you?" he asked.

It was early hours of the morning and he'd had a restless night. Often, in the dead of night, he *came back* to me, he was his normal self without the pain and anxiety. This was one of those times.

"I do. What can I do for you, Sam? What's the one thing you need from me that I haven't done yet?"

"Anal?" he said and laughed. He then coughed.

"If that's what you want, I'll gladly do it," I replied.

He chuckled some more. "I highly doubt I could get a hard-on right now. I was kidding."

He sighed and smoothed my hair from my face.

"There isn't anything you haven't already done for me. You love me, that's all I need."

"More than life itself, Sam. I don't know what I'm going to do without you."

"You'll survive, I need you to. You have to look after my kids." I nodded. "And they'll look after you."

I watched him swallow back the tears and I let mine flow.

"I've loved you for over thirty-five years. That's more than half my life. I hope I've loved you enough," he said.

I noticed he had become breathless. I was on alert.

"More than enough. Are you hurting?"

He gently shook his head. "Only in my heart."

My tears dripped to the pillow, his rolled down the side of his face.

He closed his eyes. I reached for my phone and sent a quick text to Alison. I didn't want to disturb him by speaking.

I gently slid from the bed and dressed.

"Hals?" he called.

"I'm here, Sam, right beside you." I climbed back on the bed. I held his hand to my chest. "Can you feel me?"

He nodded. "I love you," he said.

Those were his last words.

I wasn't sure what I expected, watching him die. It wasn't as traumatic as I'd thought. His breathing slowed, became shallow. He stayed that way for a while. I called the palliative team to let them know.

Alison and Karl came rushing through the front door and I shushed them. Alison nodded and looked stricken. She pulled a chair beside the bed and took his other hand. Karl stood at the end of the bed; his knuckles white as he clasped his hands tightly in front of him. His jaw was rigid, and tears rolled down his cheeks.

"I'm here, Dad," she said. She said she felt the smallest squeeze of her hand.

We sat for a little while, just watching, and not talking.

I leant down and kissed his lips, then moved to his ear. "You can go now, baby. Let go. We're all okay here. We'll look after each other."

He took his last breath.

CHAPTER 24
Present Day

Sam's funeral was as he wanted it. No pomp, just a simple service and I made sure to have Pink Floyd's 'Wish You Were Here' playing. It had been his favourite song all those years ago and totally befitting. It was how I felt.

My heart was cracked, and it would never heal. I didn't want it to.

I lay at night with his sweatshirt that was so faded and threadbare and I sprayed it with his aftershave.

Alison had wanted me to stay with her after Sam had died, but I needed to be in my own home surrounded by his memory. I sat in his chair, I slept on his side of the bed. I stared at the memory wall for hours.

I cried and sobbed and screamed at God for the injustice of it all, and then I semi-healed.

I'd never heal fully, that was for sure. I didn't want to. I'd loved him so much, ever since I had been fifteen years old, and I'd continue to love him until the day I died.

I started to write our story.

I wrote and wrote and got lost in the memories and the words, wondering if I'd ever release it.

It was cathartic, and when I got Sam's ashes, I printed off the first draft version, set fire to it, and added them so he had a copy as well.

* * *

"Nan, look," I heard. Young Sam came rushing through the door.

It had been five months since his granddad had died and although he still looked for him every time he came over, he'd grown used to not finding him. I wished I could get to that point myself.

"What, darling?" I said, drying my hands on the tea towel. I was preparing dinner for us all.

He grinned at me, and it took a moment.

"Oh my God," I said, leaning down and looking in his mouth.

"Yep, chipped my tooth, Nan," he said.

He had chipped one of his front teeth in the same place Sam had done so many years prior.

"Fell off my bike. Went right over, Nan. You should have seen me."

"And he cried, Nan," Hayley added, coming into the room.

"No, I never, I didn't, Nan. Did I, Mum?" he said, looking at Alison as he entered.

"No, you were a brave boy," she said.

She stared at me, I stared at her, and we both laughed.

"Sam would have been bloody pleased," I said.

I watched young Sam, the spit of his granddad, run around the garden. He had his blond hair cut short, a little spiky on top, and he was pretending to ride his bike then re-enact his accident.

Alison hugged me. "Is it getting any easier?" she asked.

"A little."

She smiled at me. "At least you have us," she said.

"And you have me, forever."

The End

If you enjoyed this story, you might like A Virtual Affair or
Letters to Lincoln

Acknowledgments

Thank you to Francessca Wingfield from Francessca Wingfield PR & Design for yet another wonderful cover.

A special thank you to Riley Wingfield for the background photography.

I'd also like to give a huge thank you to my editor, Karen Hrdlicka, and proofreader, Joanne Thompson.

A big hug goes to the ladies in my team. These ladies give up their time to support and promote my books. Alison 'Awesome' Parkins, Karen Atkinson-Lingham, Ann Batty, Elaine Turner, Kerry-Ann Bell – otherwise known as the Twisted Angels.

My amazing PA, Alison Parkins keeps me on the straight and narrow, she's the boss! So amazing, I call her Awesome Alison. You can contact her on AlisonParkinsPA@gmail.com

To all the wonderful bloggers that have been involved in promoting my books and joining tours, thank you and I appre-

ciate your support. There are too many to name individually –
you know who you are.

About the Author

Tracie Podger currently lives in Kent, UK with her husband and a rather obnoxious cat called George. She's a Padi Scuba Diving Instructor with a passion for writing. Tracie has been fortunate to have dived some of the wonderful oceans of the world where she can indulge in another hobby, underwater photography. She likes getting up close and personal with sharks.

Tracie likes to write in different genres. Her Fallen Angel series and its accompanying books are mafia romance and full of suspense. A Virtual Affair, Letters to Lincoln and Jackson are angsty, contemporary romance, and Gabriel, A Deadly Sin and Harlot are thriller/suspense. The Facilitator books are erotic romance. Just for a change, Tracie also decided to write a couple of romcoms and a paranormal suspense! All can be found at: author.to/TraciePodger

Stalker Links

https://www.facebook.com/TraciePodgerAuthor/

http://www.TraciePodger.com

https://www.instagram.com/traciepodger/

Also by Tracie Podger

Books by Tracie Podger

Fallen Angel, Part 1

Fallen Angel, Part 2

Fallen Angel, Part 3

Fallen Angel, Part 4

Fallen Angel, Part 5

Fallen Angel, Part 6

Fallen Angel, Part 7

The Fallen Angel Box Set

Evelyn - A novella to accompany the Fallen Angel Series

Rocco – A novella to accompany the Fallen Angel Series

Robert – To accompany the Fallen Angel Series

Travis – To accompany the Fallen Angel Series

Taylor & Mack – To accompany the Fallen Angel Series

Angelica – To accompany the Fallen Angel Series

A Virtual Affair – A standalone

The Facilitator

What's the time, Mr. Wolfe? – A Standalone.

Written under the name T J Stone

Gabriel

A Deadly Sin

Harlot

Written under the name T J Podger

The Second Witch of North Berwick House

The Last Witch of North Berwick House

Printed in Great Britain
by Amazon

20420873R00197